GW00536110

Stella *and* Margie

By the same author

Blueberry

Stella *and* Margie

GLENNA THOMSON

BANTAM
SYDNEY AUCKLAND TORONTO NEW YORK LONDON

This is a work of fiction. Names, characters, places and incidents either are the product of the author's imagination or are used fictitiously. Any resemblance to actual persons, living or dead, events, or locales is entirely coincidental.

A Bantam book
Published by Penguin Random House Australia Pty Ltd
Level 3, 100 Pacific Highway, North Sydney NSW 2060
www.penguin.com.au

First published by Bantam in 2018

Copyright © Glenna Thomson 2018

The moral right of the author has been asserted.

All rights reserved. No part of this book may be reproduced or transmitted by any person or entity, including internet search engines or retailers, in any form or by any means, electronic or mechanical, including photocopying (except under the statutory exceptions provisions of the Australian *Copyright Act 1968*), recording, scanning or by any information storage and retrieval system without the prior written permission of Penguin Random House Australia.

Addresses for the Penguin Random House group of companies can be found at global.penguinrandomhouse.com/offices.

A catalogue record for this book is available from the National Library of Australia

ISBN 9780143782056

Cover images courtesy of CSA Images/Getty Images
Cover design by Nikki Townsend Design
Printed in Australia by Griffin Press, an accredited ISO AS/NZS 14001:2004 Environmental Management System printer

Penguin Random House Australia uses papers that are natural, renewable and recyclable products and made from wood grown in sustainable forests. The logging and manufacturing processes are expected to conform to the environmental regulations of the country of origin.

For Betty, my mother

Stella

THEIR high-pitched squealy calls come first. Approaching from the north, behind the fig tree, black cockatoos fly slowly and settle into the silver wattle. They're a sign rain is coming, and I want that to be true. Someone told me that each bird represents a day of rain. So, sitting on those thin branches is a week's worth. Maybe a hundred millimetres. I hope so, yet it's hard to imagine wet ground, rivulets, cows having their backs washed.

I drag the hose across the parched lawn, thinking that this is a waste of my time. Standing, waiting, counting to fifty, sometimes a hundred. Even so, there's something satisfying about a wet garden on a hot day. The shade trees and roses manage best; it's the shrubs that struggle. I've spoken to Ross about putting in an irrigation system – underground pipes, sprinklers and a button to press so I can walk away. He says that's a complicated thing to do in an old garden like this. That means it's too hard for him to work out, he's got enough on his mind, and I suppose that's fair enough.

It just needs to rain. I look up into the glare of a flat white sky.

When I'm standing at the wilting hydrangeas, the cockatoos take flight. They have a secret language; the way they uplift together and head in one direction. It's in this vacancy, the birds gone, that my mind delivers its list of tasks. Take the cream cheese out of the fridge. Search for birthday candles. Go online and check out the *New York Times* review of *The Moment*. It's a production about life and the choices people make, and shares similar themes to the play I've written. And there it is, as I straighten up and move along to an azalea – the notion of a possible other life where I wouldn't be holding this hose.

From an open window comes the faint strike of Isobel's finger on a piano key. A rapid scale follows.

And my phone rings. Felicity.

She launches into telling me about an email she's just opened. 'Three nights in late April. Thursday the twenty-eighth. Friday the twenty-ninth. And Saturday the thirtieth. What do you think?'

I stare into the azalea. 'That's only six weeks away.'

'They want nine hundred and forty-five dollars for the three nights. Extra for rehearsals. Plus, costs for insurance and cleaning. And there's a bond.'

This is when I feel fully alive.

I twist the nozzle off.

'Let's do it,' I say. 'It's our chance.'

Before I go inside, I pull a lemon from the tree.

*

My study is the high-ceilinged dining room with three bronze chandeliers. Heavy furniture sits against the walls. There are two fireplaces with identical slate mantels. The morning sun shows that I only occasionally dust my desk, the twenty-seater mahogany dining table. It's covered with hundreds of play scripts, which I collect and read like some people do books.

Around the table are twenty high-backed dining chairs, and the one I'm sitting on has a red-tasselled cushion on the seat.

I log on and attempt to download a Victorian Rural Arts funding application to see if our theatre group, the Yellow Box Players, is eligible – and if I can make the deadline. The internet is so slow. Sunday morning and everyone on the tableland is online.

I open my hands, resigned. While I watch the bytes tick over, I give my nails a quick file. Then sit back and keep waiting.

My view across the room is into the faces of Ross's male ancestors. The women are nowhere to be seen; only the Ballantine men have their portraits displayed – five generations of father and eldest son. Each wears a dark suit and a self-important expression. They've all got that creamy Scottish skin. Four of the five have brown curly hair. Two have beards.

The portrait closest to the light switch is a colour-tinted photograph in an oval-shaped, polished maple frame. It's of Ross's late father, Norman. There's a striking resemblance between them; handsome in an urbane sort of way, they look as if they belong in a city somewhere, not here in the north-east. What I mean is, they don't look like farmers. Although I will say Ross has grown into himself, and these days mostly looks the part.

On the other side of the swing door is our wedding photo. We have happily-ever-after grins. I'm wearing a knee-length dress of ivory lace with a petticoat of coffee-coloured silk – an inspired choice, because after fourteen years I still love it.

The funding application opens and I start reading. Its criteria are more detailed than I expected. I jot down notes, already doubting I can do this. The question about my artistic concept puzzles me. Do they want to know that my play is about an angry mother trying to explain her life to her kids? Or are they looking for the subtext of one woman's guilt and regret? I need to think about it, so I get up and push through the swing door to the kitchen.

Cream cheese, butter, icing sugar, and lemon juice in a bowl. And by the time I'm spreading the frosting on the carrot cake, I've decided I'll do whatever it takes to meet the deadline in five days. The door flaps as I return to the dining room.

The question about my arts background will go in my favour. I was a founding member of the Robinson Street Community Theatre and have worked on about twenty plays.

I start filling in the template. Page after page of required fields. Yes, we're an unincorporated community group. Yes, we have an ABN. No, we don't require an auspicing organisation. I follow the navigation.

When I'm trying to find the right words to summarise the project, I look up. Norman's portrait is directly opposite me; the border between the maple frame and his staring face is a lovely apple green.

The drone of a motor is far away, a doubting thought, then growing certainty that Ross's ute is approaching. He's back earlier than expected. In between his jobs around the property it's difficult to know when he'll turn up, so I'm always half-alert, waiting to be interrupted.

They want to know my qualifications. As far as I'm concerned, that's a nuanced question. It'd be so much easier if I could just eyeball someone and not fill out this thesis of an application. I keep four-finger tapping, testing different ways of explaining why I didn't get the piece of paper from uni.

Beside me is an antique ceramic vase filled with long-stem roses, a mix of every colour and still gorgeous. They're the third bloom after a long summer. An aphid crawls along a yellow petal, and I realise I'm overdue to spray the rosebushes. Actually, I'm overdue to do a lot of things.

I hear the ute pull up. Ross will want coffee. But will he come inside, or will he want to avoid taking off his dirty workboots? And there he is, a single knuckle-tap on the window behind me. He points to the side door and I know what he wants.

*

We sit in the courtyard outside the dining room's double doors. Ross slowly scoops the froth on his latte with a teaspoon. His unhurried manner annoys me; I'm impatient to get back to my desk. I sip my herbal tea, a liquorice taste, trying to visualise where the video of *Bed-alter* is. Perhaps the buffet. And I'll need to get it transferred to a CD so it can be uploaded as part of my portfolio. I want to tell Ross about all of this, but he's saying that he needs to sell the last of the weaners. Prices are good; there's been rain up north. 'And there's no feed in the cocksfoot paddocks.'

'Ross,' I say.

He licks the spoon.

'I'm going for the maximum for a solo project.'

'How much?'

'Fifteen thousand.'

'How do you think you'll go?'

I shrug. 'Just trying. There's a lot involved.'

He sips his coffee while I tell him how detailed the application is, that it'll take me every spare moment between now and the deadline on Thursday to complete it. I know by his slow moves that he's ready to get going, back to the shorting electric fence in the Tullys paddocks.

The faraway sound of the gas gun.

'I've made your mum's birthday cake. Carrot with lemon frosting.'

He rubs his forehead as if easing pain.

'No getting out of it,' I say. 'It's her eightieth.'

'What time?'

'Visiting hours are at two.'

'Kids coming?'

'They should,' I say.

There's black mould on the concrete bench where he's sitting. Underneath there's a sprout of deadly nightshade and dry tufty grass. And cow shit on his boot. I toss my tea across to the garden bed. A fairy-wren flits onto a branch of the Japanese maple, then another joins it, and I wonder what it's like to be a bird.

'Can you give me a few minutes?' Ross asks.

'I told you I'm busy.'

'Won't take long.'

'I've just started on the application.'

'Fifteen minutes.'

I'm trapped. 'Doing what?'

'One of the Angus bulls has broken down. Need to get it to the yards.'

'I don't want to.'

He drops the teaspoon into the mug; it jangles. 'Can't do it on my own,' he says quietly.

'Get Eddie to help you.'

'It's Sunday. And I'm not getting him here for a small job.'

'What's involved?'

'The usual. Drive him to the gate and try to block the others from getting there first.'

'What will you be doing?'

'Quad bike, working in with you.'

'I hate the bulls.'

He stood up. 'Just stay in the ute.'

'All right. But it's crap.'

'Fifteen minutes, less if we get on with it.'

I go to the back porch and pull on my workboots. Of all the outside jobs, this is the worst. I feel afraid because I've seen the power of a bull intent on getting its way. But Ross and I work in together; it's a responsibility.

Being married to a Ballantine carries a number of obligations. The primary one was to have a son, the next heir. We've got two daughters. Isobel is fourteen. Jemima is ten. Harry, our son, arrived at twenty-one weeks. He breathed for a short time before dying in my arms. That's Ross's and my private business: we didn't tell anyone that he breathed or that we gave him a name. Ross wanted to try again, but I turned my back on him, saying I didn't want another child if the prerequisite was a boy. What if we had another girl? And another? And what's wrong with girls, anyway? It was all too hard, the devastation of Harry, those silent rosebud gasps.

I hear the quad bike ticking over. Ross is waiting for me at the shed.

Hurrying down the back path, my mind is full of the application. I'll need to email the theatre group for their CVs. And who exactly are our primary and secondary audiences? I've never considered this before. Why the distinction? They want photos of previous work and I don't know what I've got.

There are weeds in the veggie boxes. The zucchinis have finally finished. Green tomatoes droop withered from the wire trellis. I need to chase up the girls to get ready to visit Margie.

Through the avenue of silver birches, I head to the ute. Ross sees me and raises the revs. We don't speak. I've got my instructions and have done this before. There's a cobweb on the side mirror. The cabin is thick with dust. The passenger seat is cluttered with stuff that never gets put where it belongs: a thermos, a tangle of bungee ropes, a power drill, a mallet.

Ross is riding out in front, his shirt puffing in the wind; his shoulders are wide and open. The ute rattles down the lane and I pull up behind him. About twelve bulls are grazing in the paddock, white Charolais and black Angus. Ross lopes off on the bike, opens the gate and points to a black bull forty metres away, the one closest to the gate. I drive in and go wide around the beast, its neck as thick as a 44-gallon drum. Its green eartag says M41: M for Maryhill, our property name. It's written in large cursive letters on a board at the entry to our driveway. The first Ballantines came from Maryhill, Scotland, in the 1850s, and somehow found their way here. Alice Ballantine's sideboard still sits in the family room, beside the sixty-inch plasma.

The black bull slowly turns and studies the ute. Then it looks at Ross, who comes in fast and whacks its rump with a metre-length of poly pipe. It doesn't move or seem to care.

In first gear, I edge closer, three metres from its shitty bum.

Ross whacks it again, and M41 is suddenly interested. The bull lowers its head and scrapes its front foot on the ground. A bad sign. Ross sets about reversing. The bastard bucks up, trying for the front of the bike. Ross retreats, but the bull is going for him. It's on.

My heart races. I accelerate and manoeuvre between them, and the bull abruptly turns away, outdone by the bigger force, and heads to the gate. I steer carefully, edging left and right to keep the bull moving. When it sees the open gate, it hesitates before sauntering through. Ross grins and gives me the thumbs up.

Another bull, a Charolais, is hurrying along the fence. The gate needs to be shut and I'm closest. It's instinctive, a dumb impulse. I'm out of the ute. Running. Breathing hard.

The metal gate is in my hand and I hard-swing it to Ross. He's waving at me to do something as he catches it and steps outside to safety. The white bull is fast trotting towards me, towards the closed gate. I'm trapped. Shit. My way back to the ute is blocked.

Ross's voice is urgent, but I don't understand what he wants me to do. The bull's nose is wet and pink; its green tag number is M28 and dangles like an earring. It shakes its monster head as if disbelieving the gate is shut. But it still comes.

I close my eyes and cover my face with my hands. I'm stupid, stupid.

This is how I die. Isobel. Jemima.

It's Ross who shoves me into the gate. His hands on my backside and leg, lifting. Dead grass and dry hard dirt as I drop onto the other side.

I can't breathe and gasp up at Ross. Sweat on his face, he's breathing hard as he pulls me up.

'Don't touch me!' I scream, stepping away.

'You okay?'

'I told you I hate those fucking bulls!'

Already I'm on my feet, running up the lane towards the house. I don't look back.

Margie

I am eighty today and my birthday lunch is a bland poached-chicken salad. Someone has counted out three asparagus spears, two cherry tomatoes, one quarter of an egg, one lettuce cup. The bread is white and not particularly fresh. Red jelly and diced peaches are in a small plastic bowl at the back of the tray. The uniformed young man who delivered this meal is a new migrant. I know because he is dark – skin, hair, eyes – and he walked fast and smiled at the same time, showing very white teeth. He's the most cheerful person in this place.

I pull myself higher in the bed – dragging my right leg along the thick hospital sheet – and stare into the tray, deciding if I'm hungry enough to eat. At home I've got four waist-high vegetable boxes and, before I ended up here, I attended to them every day. If I was there now, my lunch would be a handful of sweet cherry tomatoes, slices of salted cucumber, a few cos lettuce leaves and some blanched beans, with a drizzle of syrupy balsamic over the top. Perhaps a cup of tea. And because it's Sunday and my birthday, I'd have two chocolate-and-candied-ginger sweets. To finish it off, a small, sweet sherry.

After ten days, this sterile room is closing in – it's too familiar and has always been boring. The roses on the shelf in the blue glass vase are from Ross and Stella. No one has topped up the water, so they're almost dead. I know exactly where Stella picked them, all from her home garden – that was once my garden. Buff Beauty is from the bush outside the main bedroom window; the others are Peace, Queen Elizabeth and Admiral Rodney, from the courtyard outside the dining room. I say the dining room, but last time I pushed the swing door and looked in, the room wasn't fit for formal eating. The long mahogany table was covered with folders, newspapers, CDs and empty mugs. Even a television.

I press the buzzer. I want the roses removed before the next bunch arrives this afternoon with my visitors. No one comes, but I hear nurses moving around in the hallway. I'm jaw-tight angry with the incompetence around the place. If only I could toss back the bedcovers and sort it out myself. I waggle my foot, a private test to make sure my leg still works. I keep glancing at the door, still hopeful for a nurse. And it's still an hour before the family will arrive.

I eat everything on the tray and am disgusted with myself. There is nothing else to do but fall into the self-serving hospital routine. How strange is this place of medicine and healing – you'd think they would have different mealtimes and healthier food. Here in East Ward, Room 17A, I am served three meals in nine hours, precisely at eight, twelve and five. For the rest of the time, I get nothing except cups of tea and cream biscuits, sometimes a scone with translucent apricot jam. I know the menu cycle. Tonight's dinner will be heated canned soup, a square of dry cake and a small shiny apple. Prisoners in jail would riot if they were served this food.

The bed beside mine is empty and I'm happy about that, although I wish Dot was here. She was my neighbour for fourteen years in Bishop Street, but she died five months ago on the coldest-recorded day in north-east Victoria. It wasn't that specific weather event that took her away; she had a chesty cough that developed into pneumonia. I imagine her being in the other bed, just three metres away. It's a ridiculous thing to do, but I give her a little wave. The bed is flat, its pillows crisp, waiting for someone else.

Dot and I always did our grocery shopping together, and once a week we'd go to Tamarind Thai for dinner. Three months before her illness, we started Thursday morning yoga, but I didn't continue after she passed away. Most days we had morning tea in her glassed-in back porch so we could feel the warmth of the sun. Her cat, Diva, was always on her lap or around her ankles, though I never felt comfortable about having a cat so close. Dot made me promise to care for it 'if anything happens to me'. So I fed it for those days she was in hospital. But I detest cats and certainly had no feelings for that one, with those all-knowing, staring eyes. Stella caught it for me and put it in a box. I asked her to take it to the vet. 'A good home,' I said, although I didn't hold out much hope for it.

I'm so bored.

I stare into my hands, looking to see if anything has changed. My wedding ring is loose as if my fingers have become smaller, yet my knuckles are large, swollen. I glance at the side table, hoping for a nail file even though I know there isn't one and I don't know who to ask. The nurses said to get someone from the family to bring one in. I mentioned it to Caroline, my daughter, but she won't remember. My nails aren't very strong; they tear easily and need regular tidying up. Overall, I appraise my hands as ugly. But I'm not ashamed of them. They remind me of the good things in my life: gardening, knitting, fruit bottling, preparing meals, writing in my bird books. Holding my babies. My hands caressing a man's body, holding tight – and I can hardly believe that was me. I'm in awe. More like shocked disbelief. When I remember those years, it's a relief to be an old woman.

I turn my wedding ring around and remember the day in 1961 when Norman and I were married at the Holy Trinity Anglican Church in Benalla. It's as though I'm viewing the home movie my cousin filmed – there I am, walking up the aisle. The organist is playing Wagner's bridal march. All the guests are standing, staring at me. A tulle veil covers my face, the gown flows and I am beautiful. The bodice of Alençon lace is firm – my waist measures twenty-two inches – and the full-length skirt hides my satin shoes. And there's Norman, stiff-backed with nerves, waiting for me at the altar. He turns. There are two large vases of white lilies, and I try to remember who would've arranged them. My father releases my arm and sits down. I wish he'd never let me go.

It is now two o'clock, visiting hours, and no one is here. I've had enough of myself; this rumination gets tiring. I flick back the bedcovers and twist around, thinking I might go to the toilet. Apart from wanting to empty my bladder, I'd like to tidy my hair, but it's a long way from here to the floor. My right foot tingles, and suddenly I'm not brave enough to make the leap for my crutches. If I fall, then what? My hip has been replaced with a metal and plastic one that was made in England. 'A nasty fall,' the surgeon said. 'Tendons were torn and had to be repaired too.' Those back steps at Bishop Street were always waiting for me, I knew it. But the surprise was falling on a dry sunny day. I'm sure I was looking down, watching. A split second, and the terrible feeling of knowing. I heard the bone snap.

To the left, towards the window, I hear the call of a rufous whistler. I close my eyes and see its small tan body, white bib, black mask and breast band. But I'm unsure if I really hear it, or if the sound and image are inside me, a random memory. I don't like this strange reality or the confusion that comes with ageing.

And now, for some reason, my thoughts switch back to Dot. She was my only real friend and she wanted me to go on a cruise with her. We'd even been to the local travel agent to see about a ship that was leaving in January for lots of places including England, where my hip prosthesis comes from. In 1954, when I was eighteen, Queen Elizabeth and Prince Philip visited Benalla. I was front row in the crowd at the railway station and saw her close up: her pink silk dress with a pleated skirt, white pillbox hat, long gloves and white slingback shoes. For years after I thought of nothing else except going to London, to see Buckingham Palace, Windsor Castle and the real Monopoly board – Mayfair, Piccadilly Circus, Oxford Street, Old Kent Road, Trafalgar Square. Susan Kissock, a friend from school, went to England in 1959; I don't know what happened to her, because after a couple of years she stopped replying to my letters. Anyway, my dream of travelling to England never came true and my only chance was going on the cruise with Dot. The ship would've set sail a couple of weeks ago and god knows where it is right now. Dot's buried in the local cemetery. Perhaps when I leave here, I'll visit her and take some flowers. She used to jolly me along and I miss her terribly. If she'd survived that bout of pneumonia, she'd be visiting me here and saying, 'We'll be back at Tamarind Thai for dinner in no time.' But then if she'd lived we'd be on the ship, maybe even in England by now.

'Mum.'

I open my eyes and see Norman at the end of the bed. No, it's Ross, my youngest son. But it's Stella, his wife, who comes and kisses my cheek. She always wears nice perfume.

The girls are already backed against the wall, staring as if they've never seen me before and glancing around as if to find an escape route other than the door they just walked through.

I wave for them to come to me, but I'm suddenly unsure of their names. Then I remember that Isobel is the older one, today wearing brown-framed glasses that don't suit her. Her fingernails are painted dark green. She has the Ballantine face: pale skin, slightly hooded eyes, and light, curly brown hair. I quite like the little ginger-haired one; she's got something about her that I'm attracted to. I'll wait till I hear someone else say her name. It starts with . . . and I fly through the alphabet, waiting for my youngest grandchild's name to find its way from wherever it's hidden in my brain. I'm at the letter J when she smiles into my face and I remember she's Jemima. 'Thank you for coming to visit me, Jemima,' I say. She feather-kisses my cheek. Lovely child.

My daughter, Caroline, strides into the room. 'Happy birthday, Mum.' Her lipstick is too thick and dark, and she avoids smearing any on my face by only pretending to kiss me. She's put on weight, or perhaps it's the black dress – you'd think she was attending a funeral.

I push back into the pillows and smile across the room. As I'm doing this, I realise they will think my cheerfulness is because I love them dearly and am glad they are visiting. That is partly true. I would much prefer to be on the cruise with Dot, not bothered with this charade of happy families. Caroline hates Stella. Ross doesn't have time for Caroline. Caroline's boys haven't bothered to come. But we pretend none of that is happening.

There is only one chair and Caroline sits in it. Ross leans against the wall, folds his arms and crosses one leg over the other. It is Stella who's talking to me, wearing her typical garb of tight jeans and a silky blue shirt with too many buttons undone. I've always considered her look cheap – the untidy way she wears her hair, the high-heeled boots – over-the-top and inappropriate. But she's got a nice figure, I'll give her that.

'I could only find five candles,' Stella says. She lights them and holds the cake near my mouth. I do my best and blow three out. She waits for me to do the other two.

When I turned fifty, I didn't think I would be in hospital on my eightieth. I try to remember what we did to celebrate my fiftieth. If it was observed, I would've made my own cake. It was the year that Mark, my eldest son, died and everyone's life changed after that.

They've only been in the room a few minutes and they're already singing 'Happy Birthday'. Ross has his hands in his pockets and Stella's are raised; she's acting like a conductor, always the show-off. I have never really taken to her. She's not a farmer's wife, I know that much. It is a mess, really. I'm glad the other Ballantine wives can't see from their graves the woman who is now running the family home – it would reflect poorly on me, as if somehow it is my fault. I wanted Ross to marry Alison Clarke, a pretty girl from the Wagyu beef property over on Barry Mill Road. He seemed keen on her for a good while. But it was Stella he brought home, with her bottle-blonde hair and jeans low so we all got a good look at her pierced navel.

'Hip hip . . . hooray!'

Stella hasn't brought a knife and runs from the room to find one.

I ask Ross about rain.

'Nothing coming. Only one hundred and thirty mils this year.'

There's nothing that I can say. It's the ongoing worry of a farmer.

Then I ask Caroline about the nail file. She looks at me blankly, then shakes her head.

Stella is hacking into the cake with a breadknife, cutting large slices as if we are all starving. She pulls paper plates from a cane basket and asks the little one to hand them around with plastic forks. Someone says her name. Jemima. I try to rhyme it so I won't forget, but I can't think of anything. *Jem-ima. Jem-ima.* I press my fingers into my arm as if that might help me remember.

I position my smile to appear grateful for this birthday celebration. The cake is quite nice, especially the icing. There are no gifts, and I forgive my family because they think I have everything I need. A birthday card with a big gold 80 sits on the cabinet beside my bed. Inside is Stella's large handwriting, and a row of kisses and smiling faces that strike me as juvenile. Caroline's card is from her gallery and so abstract I can't make sense of it.

'When are you going home?' Caroline asks.

I stare at my children, Ross and Caroline, exasperated because they already know this. I'm sure of it.

'There's rehab first,' I say.

'But the rehab place is full,' Stella says, looking at me as if I might disagree.

'It is,' I say.

'How is it here?' she asks.

I wonder what she means. 'It's a hospital,' I tell her.

She glances at Ross. 'Do you want to come home to us?'

Ross shrugs and doesn't look at me, which is not enough for me to consider the offer.

'Absolutely not.'

I know the house where they live. It was my home for forty-one years. I am the longest-serving Ballantine wife: from when Norman and I returned from our honeymoon in Portland until 2002 when I left so that Ross and Stella could move in. Norman died in 1988, so it was just Ross and me for about fourteen years – although I didn't see much of him. He was either out on the farm or flying aeroplanes. And when he took up with Stella he spent all his time driving up and down the Hume Freeway, to and from her place in Brunswick. In the end, it was a relief when they married and moved to Maryhill because he'd finally settled down. Plus, I think she was pregnant; the first girl came along pretty quickly.

'It'd be easier, Margie,' Stella says. 'It'd save us having to travel up here to visit.'

'You're all too busy to be looking after me.'

Caroline is staring into her phone. She's divorced and lives in Eltham with her sons, Timothy and Adam, dull-eyed from staring into their computers. I am relieved she's not making a show of wanting me.

'Trust me,' Stella says. 'Having you in the house with us would be a hell of a lot easier than driving an hour up here to check how you're going.'

It's not been put like that before, what a burden I am. I shake my head, no. 'You don't need to check on me. The nurses do that.'

'Think about it,' she says, smiling, and I can't help but think she's quite striking-looking in a fashion-magazine sort of way.

I turn to Ross, wanting some acknowledgement or enthusiasm from him. But he's talking to his daughters. And there before me is another problem. Ross doesn't have a son. I don't know why they didn't try again after the second little girl. It took Norman's parents five goes to have a boy. I think it's too late for Stella now: she's forty-two. I can't put my mind to what that means for Maryhill with only girls. It feels like a tragedy.

'When are we going?' Isobel whispers to her father. She's been having piano lessons since she started school, and remembering that gives me something to ask her.

'Are you still playing the piano?'

'Yes,' she says.

'So you're having lessons?'

'Yes.'

I'm really not interested in her one-word answers, so I turn to Caroline, letting the child know she's dismissed.

My daughter is on her feet, saying she needs to go. 'The boys are on their own,' she tells me, as if I haven't worked that out.

'But they're fifteen and seventeen,' I say.

'All the more reason.' Caroline swoops on me and blocks my view of the room. She gives me a sort of hug, barely touching me. 'Bye,' she says. 'Take care.'

She leaves with hardly a backward glance and suddenly there's more space in the room, more air. I take a breath.

'I'll look after you, Nan,' the little one says. Lovely red hair. Freckles on her nose. Already I've forgotten her name. She's a beautiful, innocent child with her whole life ahead of her. I can't imagine what the future holds for her – all the talk about climate change and terrorism. Hostages and haphazard bombings and refugees storming country borders. By the time she's old enough to really wonder about me, I'll just be a name in the family tree. Margaret Jean Ballantine.

'Thank you, sweetheart,' I say. 'But I'll stay here until a place becomes available in rehab.'

'Think about it, Margie, it'd be no trouble,' Stella says, gathering up the dirty paper plates and dropping them in the basket. The way she does things bewilders me. Why not put them in my bin?

When the four of them leave, the room is very quiet. There is some upset further along the corridor; I hear the fast pacing of people in the distance. The old roses are still in the blue vase – Ross and Stella didn't bring me a fresh bunch, and I feel let down. I close my eyes and put myself in their garden, my old garden. The padded lawn under my feet. I breathe in the fresh air, lemon, dust, the hint of distant cows. I wander under the oak and claret ash where hundreds of daffodil bulbs are buried in the cold ground, dormant until early spring. Then across to the pergola, where the grapevine is lush and shady. Past the clothesline to the south side of the house to the rhododendrons, each bush as big as this hospital room. There's daphne, gardenias, camellias, azaleas. It's my favourite place in the garden, so I pause and put myself on the concrete bench. I see the wisteria and know it needs pruning at this time of year. Then I'm at the roses. My head against the pillow, I wince, knowing Stella hasn't tended them, no pruning or spraying, and there will be black spot and aphids, and the hybrid tea bushes will be covered in powdery mildew. Fourteen years ago I willingly divorced myself from this house and garden, but it's suddenly a fresh insult that all my hard work has been let go by her. I imagine turning to the house and admiring the row of hydrangeas – that I propagated and planted – along the base of the veranda with its fluted posts. The red Japanese maple, the snowball tree, the mauve crepe myrtle. I hear an eastern rosella call – its song and habits are recorded in the books I once kept.

I open my eyes and am dazed by the sudden sterile white of the room. I wish for Dot, so I can tell her how I feel: that I'm lonely and my children don't like me.

And then the nurse is beside me, checking my blood pressure and temperature. She pumps the velcro sleeve up twice. 'A bit high,' she says.

I'm waiting for the rattle of the dinner trolley when one of those happy refugees pushes in a bed carrying a white-haired woman on her back, eyes closed. She seems very thin; her skin has the translucence of white crepe paper. A nurse swipes the curtains closed around her bed, and I listen to their murmurs, but can't make out what is being said. When the curtain is pulled open, I glance across at my new neighbour. She's asleep.

Soon she stirs and, with one limp hand, tries to lift herself by pulling on the suspended bar in front of her. She is stiff in her back; perhaps she's in pain. She reaches down the side of the bed for the buzzer but cannot locate it. I can see it, a little further back. Her fingers tickle the air.

'I'll ring for you,' I say, reaching down to my buzzer. I press the button repeatedly, giving them the message that someone must come immediately.

She looks across at me, watery blue eyes and a weak smile.

Then she slowly blinks.

We both look away.

My heart skips out of rhythm.

Silence.

And we're breathing upwards into the room, our chests rising and falling. We had been dead to each other for more than thirty years, since the twenty-eighth of October, 1985.

Laura Sullivan, who crosses the street when she sees me coming, who walks out of shops when I enter, and who turns her back to me at public events, is in the next bed.

Our boys caught the school bus together every day, swam in the dams, camped up the back in the bush at Tullys. They played in the same footy team. Mark and Justin were best mates. It was my son Mark who was behind the wheel that night.

Justin was her only child.

The nurse arrives and I signal for her to go to Laura. She swipes the curtain around the bed and I hear them talk quietly. My face is hot, as if I have done something wrong. When the nurse leaves she glances at me, flat-faced. Laura and I are alone again.

Our boys had separate funerals.

My hands are fists pressed into the sheet. I feel agitated and my hip aches, or perhaps it is my stomach. I don't want this intrusion – not by anyone, but least of all her. Never her. Suddenly everything in my life seems overwhelmingly unjust and intolerable. And as the handsome faces of our boys appear before me, her television comes on.

It's too loud. Is she trying to block me out? Or is she deaf?

I want to tell her to turn it down – I clear my throat and know the words. I will say 'please'. But when I prop myself up and inhale, I lose my courage. I put my hands over my ears to block the noise and rising panic.

Dinner arrives. It is what I expected: thin tomato soup, a square of fruitcake and a small apple. She eats behind the cotton wall; at least, I assume she does. The television is still on. I push my tray away, the food untouched.

Chester, her husband, walks in. I am shocked by this, yet why wouldn't he visit his wife? He sees me and we both look away, then back to each other. I feel clammy and self-conscious. He makes an awkward bow and hesitates, as if he's going to come to me. The last time I saw Chester was about three years ago in the ANZ bank in town. We walked past each other, a confusing moment.

I see he's narrower across the shoulders and slightly stooped – a weathered old farmer. But before he disappears behind the curtain, he smiles at me; he's still got that thing, the easy charm of a cheeky lad. His hair is short and almost all grey, his forehead is high, but he's grown a grey-speckled moustache that I'm not sure suits him.

Her television goes quiet, but not off, and they whisper together. I'm outnumbered. No one visits me.

It's profoundly awkward, me lying there with them so close. I close my eyes and try to be somewhere else. Over the years, especially during my marriage, I became quite good at transporting myself away. Usually I thought of birds: mostly black cockatoos because they're my favourite, and it always feels special to see them. But right now this doesn't help because, with Chester and Laura so close, I can't help but think of my husband and marriage – a tangle of moving images, more felt than seen. You would think at my age I'd have dealt with past hurts, worked some things out and said a peaceful goodbye to unfulfilled dreams. I'm afraid it's not the case. All I know is there's no time left. I live with regret.

When Chester steps from the curtain to leave, he stops at the end of my bed and stares at my birthday cards.

The volume on Laura's television goes up to a ridiculous level. That's it, then – she must be deaf.

Chester comes to me and asks, 'When was your birthday?'

I'm too shaken to speak and only manage to mouth, 'Today.'

He reaches for my hand, a little squeeze, and my breathing goes strange. Then he moves forward and I think I'm going to be kissed. I don't know what to do, so I sink into the pillows and close my eyes. Chester's dry lips touch my forehead; there's the slight brush of his moustache. He smells of laundry soap. 'Happy birthday,' he whispers.

I open my eyes and am startled to see he is still bending down. He is so close I inhale his warm breath. We stare at each other; his brown eyes are deeper in the sockets than I remember. We are all ancient now. He puts his hand on his lower back, slowly stands and turns to the door.

I lie still; my hands tremble. I breathe deeply and feel the spot where his lips were. I am tired, confused, happy. I don't want to remember his tenderness, so I keep my eyes wide open and look around the room. The dying roses in the blue vase. I would like to die, too.

The volume that Laura has the television on is a joke. Yet I'm chastened by Chester's affection and will let her be. I glance around for something to read, knowing nothing is there. My library books are finished and I've read the local paper; the obituaries twice in case I missed someone. Ten minutes of Laura's television noise is enough. I cannot think or relax, and I feel that her inconsideration is a taunt.

'Laura,' I say. 'Can you please turn it down?'

Nothing happens and I call out louder.

She is ignoring me and I feel a rising agitation.

I press the buzzer, a good long hold. The nurse is slow to come. It's Penny Lyons on the night shift. I knew her mother, a zealous fundraiser and gossiper at the local school when my children were small. But Penny was a few years behind and probably doesn't know me. Even so, the Ballantine name used to have some currency – people took notice – and I want to believe they still do.

'I'm Margaret Ballantine,' I say, looking her in the eye. Then I point to the curtain and, in a loud whisper, tell her the volume needs to be lowered.

'It's okay for her to have the TV on until ten.'

'But I want to sleep now and it's too loud.'

She looks exasperated, like an adult sorting out a baffling squabble between children. She enters Laura's curtain den. The volume reduces.

But I still can't rest.

I try to see through the curtain. I stare at it with laser eyes, but there's only the gathering of the heavy white cotton.

Laura was never the friendliest of women. But when our babies were small, we did lean on each other from time to time. I used to babysit Justin. Sometimes she had Mark. Often the boys had sleepovers. He was a nice boy, Justin. I quite liked their boy being Mark's friend because they would be farmers together, both taking on their birthright as property heirs. When the boys left school they worked hard, both tall and strong enough to lift a sixty-kilo calf. They loved their footy and beer. And all the girls loved them.

That fateful Saturday is embedded in my mind, both long scenes and snippets, some in slow motion, and all in a faded, sad colour.

Mark is playing for the Saints in the local grand final. He leaps and climbs for a mark and takes the ball. But he's winded and bends over, putting his hands on his knees, waiting, stalling for breath. He kicks an easy goal. At half-time it is drizzling so I stay in the car. I unwrap the date scones I've baked; they're still warm, and the butter melts when I spread it on. I pour hot water from a thermos into a mug; a tea bag string hangs down the side. I add milk. Third-quarter, and the boys play in the mud. I'll be soaking his gear when he drops his footy bag inside the back porch.

The Saints lose by sixteen points. Mark doesn't come to the car to see me. I wait, but leave after a few minutes. By then, I know he's gone straight to the clubroom.

I'm in the woodshed throwing pinecones into the black coal bucket as the sirens fly up Maryhill Road – wailing for our soon-to-be broken hearts. The air is cold, but the sky is clear. The moon is a gold globe surrounded by twinkling stars. We had homemade minestrone soup for dinner; the dishes are done. I fold laundry, waiting, feeling anxious. I place everyone. Caroline's in Melbourne; she goes to university. Norman is watching television. Ross is in his room making a model aeroplane. Mark is expected home.

Norman drives off in the Holden to see what the trouble is. He's gone half an hour and is white when he returns; his hands shake. I meet him on the path and tell him to sit on the bench. He kneels on the grass and vomits and cries into his hands. Justin was dead when the police and ambulance arrived. Mark's car is wedged into a tree, halfway down the embankment near Gall Bridge. 'That corner is too sharp,' Norman says.

Although, I never had a problem there.

Mark died the next day. We turned him off. That's what they say, 'turn him off'. He was too brain damaged, nothing there. Norman spoke very seriously to someone in intensive care to be certain.

'Sit with him and say goodbye,' a doctor with kind eyes said.

I held Mark's warm hand. The tubes and wires inserted into and attached to my child looked complicated and uncomfortable. A nurse pressed some buttons on the machine then stood back. It didn't take long. Norman was on the other side of the bed. We were separate in our experience. I had run out of tissues and was gripping a wet, useless thing.

So Mark never came home. And even though I watched the monitor flatten to a single line, for years I waited to hear him walk through the back door, with the slap of the flywire, stride into the kitchen and open the fridge. He used to wink at me as he drank milk straight from the carton.

The stone that grew in Laura's heart is understandable. I'm sorry for her loss. I'm sorry on Mark's behalf because he was driving. I turn back to the curtain, wanting to speak to her. There's a heavy weight on my chest, and my tears are hot and useless as they roll down the side of my face onto the pillow.

I can still feel Chester's kiss, or I imagine I can.

The television is off and I'd not noticed. Her light is on, a pearly glow through the curtain.

I don't know why, but I speak as if I'm someone else. My voice trembles when I call her name. 'Please forgive Mark.'

Her light goes off.

Then it's clear to me what she wants. She would like me punished for something my son did and a strange justice will be done.

'It wasn't my fault,' I say into the dark.

Yellow light filters in from the corridor. The hospital is settling for the night. I know I won't sleep. I twist my hip to feel the pain, to be reminded of why I'm here. My situation feels intolerable and I'm tired of coping.

I press the buzzer and count to ten. Then wait.

Penny Lyons enters the darkened room, pointing a pen-torch out in front.

'I want to be moved to another room,' I say.

'Why?'

I turn towards Laura. 'There is ongoing conflict between us and I refuse to be stuck in this room with her.'

'What's happened?' Penny asks. The torchlight warps her face.

'It's a long story.'

She stares at me, thinking. 'But Mrs Ballantine, it's past nine o'clock. We'll see what can be done in the morning.'

I will not be patronised by the daughter of a gossipy overbearing school fundraiser. And what is Laura making of all this behind her cotton shield? Perhaps it satisfies her, witnessing my discomfort. She might very well be smiling.

'That won't be necessary,' I say. 'In the morning I'm discharging myself.'

Stella

I'M in bed, waiting for Ross. I pick up *Soulmates*, a David Williamson play, from the bedside table. Ross and I saw it performed by the Sydney Theatre Company back in 2002. I loved it, and occasionally I study the script for inspiration. It's my touchstone for rhythm and pitch; the wit is so perfectly timed. Sometimes I lack confidence about the depth and insightfulness of my writing – even though I've dedicated years to scripting my play, I'm still not satisfied. But in a way the self-doubt forces me to try harder and keep improving, and that can only be good.

At Act One, Scene Four, my hand slowly drops. The script falls on the bed and I jolt awake. Where is Ross? I think about turning the light off or going to find him. He'll be in his office monitoring the weather: satellite, radar, various sites. Or paying bills, doing our BAS, maybe shopping. His internet shopping is different to mine – he buys rubber bands for bull-calf castrations, eartags, irrigation fittings, fencing insulators. Or maybe he's writing a letter to the local paper or council; he does that sometimes when he gets fired up. Our local rates just arrived and we're the eighth highest payers in the country, which seems extreme when our shire is definitely not affluent.

I stare ahead into the Aboriginal dot painting on our bedroom wall, pinks and browns boxed in a white frame. Below it is a scalloped oak mantel. The plaster edges around the ornamental fireplace expose the original brown ceramic brickwork. It reminds me of my old place in Brunswick; that things don't have to be perfect to look and feel good.

When I moved here fourteen years ago, I could only find three fireplaces, yet four chimneys level with the trees that surround this old house. It was Margie who had the fireplace in this room plastered over and a heater installed. An easy decision to pull it out. Ross complained about the lack of insulation in the walls and tried to scare me with stories of how cold it gets here in winter. But I said I'd rather freeze than look at a false wall and ugly heater. It's true the winters are so bracing that I race from the ensuite to the bed on tiptoes, but then the electric blanket is warm, and so is Ross.

Margie was the last Ballantine wife to decorate this room. She chose pale olive-green walls with a wallpaper stripe of pink roses below the oak picture rail. It would've been all right thirty years ago; much too pretty for me, but I don't mind its subdued, faded tones. The bay windows are bordered by heavy lace curtains – another Ballantine wife's choice, probably Norman's mother.

Five wives have slept here. The heirs would've been conceived in this space: not in this bed but right where it stands. And the second and third sons and all the girls, too. It's a weird thought, if I dwell on it, sharing a bedroom with the Ballantine ghosts, who for generations slept, dreamt, made love, lay ill, gave birth and died right here.

Margie holds the record for the wife longest in residence. Twenty-seven years with Norman, followed by 'too many' with Ross, according to him.

Apart from recovering the bedroom fireplace, my contribution to this room is the annexation of the nursery where all the Ballantine kids slept before they were scattered to their own rooms throughout the house. The nursery is now our built-in robe and ensuite with a claw-foot bath big enough for two.

I feel a deep slowness in my body and give up on Ross coming to bed. I turn off the lamp. And just as the room falls into darkness, he opens the door. Thinking I'm asleep, he walks silently in the moonlit shadows, trying not to disturb me. He quietly closes the ensuite door behind him. Then the toilet flushes. He's in the shower. He's drying himself. He's brushing his teeth. I turn on the lamp and start back on the play, the bit where Greg and Fiona are in New York visiting Gordon and Katie.

Ross comes to bed and lies on his side, a hand under his head, watching me.

'I can't concentrate if you watch,' I say.

'What is it?'

'*Soulmates*.'

'We saw that in Sydney.'

I look at him. 'You remember?'

He smiles and I move close, our bodies together. Nothing is said; we feel warm skin.

'Sorry about this morning,' he says softly.

'I'm not helping you with the bulls ever again.'

'You should've stayed in the ute.'

'I don't want to talk about it.'

'Neither do I.'

He pulls me close, we kiss, and I know where this is going. I love this man, but I'm exhausted and want to sleep.

He hears me sigh. 'Come on, Stell.'

Sometimes sex is like relationship maintenance, the thing that keeps us close and in harmony with each other. Right now it's something he needs, and I know if I go with it, it'll be satisfying and totally worth it. He's beautiful, and most of all it's me he wants.

Ross is looking down at me, and I relax. I've decided to participate and want the closeness it'll bring. There's enough shadow to see his face, and I try to ignore that he's overdue for a haircut. It's only significant because I'm the one who cuts his hair. He won't commit to an appointment in town and he tells me I do a good job.

We kiss again. He smells clean.

The summit ringtone. My phone is radiating on the bedside table.

We tense.

I'm conflicted between Ross's erection and the rare event of my phone ringing after ten. I reach across and pick it up, looking at the screen. 'It's your mum,' I say.

'Shit.'

I answer on speaker. 'Margie, what's wrong?'

'Why is Ross's phone off? I need to speak to him. I want him to come and get me.'

He shakes his head.

I try to make sense of the situation, taking a few seconds to realise she can't speak because she's crying.

'What's wrong?' I ask.

'I can't . . .'

'Are you in pain?'

'No,' she says.

'Should I call the hospital?'

'Tell Ross to come now.'

Ross is waving his hands and mouthing that he's not going anywhere.

'Margie, you need to tell me what's wrong.'

She sniffs.

'I'm sorry you're so upset. But he'll come and get you in the morning, first thing.'

'I want to leave here tonight.'

I make a face at Ross, asking what we should do.

Margie hangs up.

We stare open-mouthed across the room.

'Bloody hell,' he says, sighing.

I phone the hospital and speak to the ward nurse, who tells me, 'Margie's had the room to herself for ten days. She's unhappy another woman is now sharing with her.'

'Can you move her to a private room?'

'There's no singles left, only doubles.'

I'm told Margie has just been given some medication to settle her down. That she'll be fine now.

'What the hell?' Ross says, falling into the pillows with his hands over his face. 'Why did you ask her to come here?'

'Because she's got no one else and I feel sorry for her. And she's your mum.'

Ross has no words and I can't tell what he's thinking.

'She was crying,' I say. 'And she's not the crying type.'

Ross rolls onto his side.

'You'll have to go and get her,' I say. 'I've got the deadline on the arts funding.'

'Can't. I've got to sort out the bore, probably pull the pump apart.'

'You serious?' I say.

'How long will she be here?'

'Till she can go home.'

'Jesus,' he sighs.

Ross's breathing quickly steadies as he falls asleep. I'm always envious of how easily he can do that. All I can think of is Margie crying, the shaky way she tried to control her breathing.

The moonlight through the lace curtains makes a distorted swirling pattern across the room and ceiling, and I stare up into the oval moulding and remember the first time I met her.

*

That day Ross picked me up at Benalla Railway Station and drove me around the place, showing me things: a waterhole called Polly McQuinns, kangaroos grazing along Earnshaw Track, a produce store in the middle of the bush where we had lunch and a beer. It wasn't until we were meandering along dirt roads that I realised he was stalling rather than taking me to meet his mother.

'What's wrong?' I asked.

'It's all good.'

'You're nervous.'

He reached for my hand.

'What's going on?' I said.

He shrugged.

'Should I be worried?'

Of course, I wanted his mother to like me. When I saw the big old house with the green corrugated roof and wisteria trailing along the back veranda, the manicured vegetable boxes and garden, I knew the woman who would step out and welcome me: she'd be warm, energetic, interesting. I approached her full of expectation, smiling. She didn't offer her hand or embrace me. But I was only twenty-two, needy and desperate to please, so I overlooked her rudeness, supposing it was just her way.

Ross didn't look like he belonged to her; I couldn't pair them. She was dressed nicely – I believed for the occasion of meeting me – in black pants, a white shirt with a sleeveless fitted grey vest. She wore pink lipstick. Her hair was light auburn, the colour of honey, neatly swept up in combs.

I'd dressed for my boyfriend, not her. And so her gaze fell to my naked waist, my navel and the silver barbell piercing I'd recently had done. All I could do was smile and not care, be myself. So I got on with it and followed her and Ross inside. I chatted, admired the house, still trying to please. Ross was quiet, watching.

We sat at the dinner table on stiff-backed chairs. Margie poured us tea from a silver pot into dainty china cups – a pink floral design and green scalloped edges – which sat on matching saucers. A crystal two-tier plate carried lemon curd tarts and tiny club sandwiches. If the vibe hadn't been so intense, it would've been funny that this was where Ross lived – the person I knew didn't fit here, taking high tea with a woman who didn't seem to know which facial expression to wear.

Her eyes narrowed on me. 'And what do you do?'

I wanted to please her so much that I babbled along, not stopping to catch up with myself to see what was really going on. 'If you mean what I do for money, I'm a waitress at Dudley's All Day in Carlton. But my thing is producing and directing community theatre. I'm one of the founders of the Robinson Street Theatre.' I beamed and paused, expecting another question. But she waited for me to go on. So I did. 'We're currently working on an adaptation of *Who's Happy Now?*' I gave details of the three main characters. 'One is called Horse. But ultimately it's about domestic violence and family dysfunction, told in an endearing way. If that's possible.' I laughed, then broke off and sat back, satisfied I'd done a good girlfriend interview.

Margie sat silent.

The jolt came and I knew this was all a mistake. And there I was, so quickly nervous and insecure. I glanced at Ross, who was bloody well staring into his hands.

Seconds passed.

Margie turned to her son, who was now looking out the window, and told him she had a headache. She asked if he could take care of dinner. 'I will not be eating,' she said.

I didn't see her for a long time after that because when she closed the hall door behind her, I asked Ross to take me to the train.

'I won't be judged by her, or you,' I said. 'The old bitch.'

He drove me all the way to my place in Brunswick, arms ramrod straight on the wheel. I watched the profile of his lovely worried face as he told me how he'd had different plans for his life, but when he was thirteen his brother was killed and from then on he was expected to take over the farm.

'Dad had a really good bloke working for him, Keith Sanders. When Dad checked out, he stayed on managing the place until I was old enough to take over. But I was set on getting my commercial pilot's licence. One day, down at the yards, Keith told me I was good with cattle, that I wasn't even twenty and I had a house and farm for life. Then he convinced Mum to send me to ag college in Dookie. And that's what happened.'

'What about Caroline?'

'What about her?'

'Well, I know she's *just* a girl, but didn't she get a look in?'

He turned to me with a wry smile. 'She got an education and a bus ticket to town.'

Over a crest, the road stretched far; trucks and cars in the double lanes were nudging against the limit, pushing hard going south.

'But you love the farm, right?' I asked.

'Most things.'

'Do you regret not flying?'

He answered with another sidelong smile and shrug that I supposed meant he didn't know.

By the time we arrived at my place, I'd softened. We bought Japanese takeaway and ate it in my bed. At five in the morning, he said he had to get going. A herd of cows needed to be moved to more feed, and another group were calving and had to be checked.

But before he pushed out of bed, he put his face close to mine and said, 'You're my beautiful girl, and I want to be with you all the time. Marry me, Stella.'

My answer was quick. 'Not if you expect me to live in that house with your mother.'

*

When I enter Margie's hospital room, she's sitting on the chair, dressed in baggy grey trackpants and a pink floral blouse. A white curtain has been drawn around the bed closest to the window.

Margie looks to the door, waiting for Ross to follow in behind me.

'The bore is playing up,' I explain. 'There's no water going into the troughs.'

As if she understands Ross's dilemma, she nods and tries to stand on crutches. I go to her, reaching out to help. She stiffens, either because she's in pain or because I've touched her.

'How are you this morning?' I ask.

She doesn't answer but points to a bag on the floor. 'There are things in the bottom drawer I can't reach.' It's her dirty washing. She glances at the curtain that blocks out the other bed. 'Can we go?' she says.

The discharge process takes too long. The nurse thinks this too; the way she flicks the pages, rapidly ticking boxes. She tells us that a district nurse won't get to Maryhill until next week, but Margie is marked down as a priority patient. 'It'll be either Joanne or Alicia – but not to worry, someone will call first.'

Then, as if Margie is deaf and not sitting beside me in a hospital wheelchair, the nurse shows me a diagram explaining her exercises and says she must do them twice daily. The incision site must be checked once a day for infection. 'And she has a physio appointment on Thursday at eleven in Benalla.'

Margie is clutching a plastic bag with pharmaceutical packets inside. Her neck is craned upwards like she's wanting to say something.

'Yes, Margie?' I ask.

But all she does is look around as if to see who I'm talking to.

I push her along the dim corridors to the front entry. 'I'll bring the car to the door.' It's almost ten. Carrying her bag and crutches, I run to the carpark, anxious to get back to the funding application.

As Margie pulls and eases herself up into the passenger seat, she braces and winces. The Prado is too high off the ground for an old woman recovering from hip surgery; Ross's ute won't be any better. I stand close, poised to help, watching. I know not to touch her.

Down the Hume Freeway, slowing to forty kilometres for roadworks, I talk while looking ahead through the insect-splattered and dusty windscreen. 'What happened last night, Margie? Why were you crying when you phoned?'

I glance at her. She's ignoring me. Her hands are tightly clasped.

'It was after ten, so late for something to go wrong,' I say. 'The nurse said it had something to do with the woman in the other bed.'

Margie replies, staring forward. 'She had her television up too loud.'

'Why would that make you cry?'

'It doesn't matter,' she says, putting her shoulders back, hiding behind that proud look of hers. Yet she appears pale and somehow vulnerable, as if last night's tears could return. She must be very tired.

'We'll be home soon,' I say.

There's not much of Ross in Margie's face – perhaps the shape of her nose, but for sure Ross takes after his father. I see a resemblance of her in photos of Mark, and perhaps in Caroline. Margie's hair is fine and short, no longer that lovely honey-auburn, but now silver. And when she's mobile, she's got a sort of innate ballerina grace – the fluid yet upright way her spine and limbs move, and the way her chin is almost always up, as if she's waiting for someone to bow to her. As far as I can tell, Margie is the archetypical Ballantine wife. So, I've always been on a hiding to nothing.

Today I've been up since five to put in a couple of hours on the application. The detail they want for a fifteen-thousand-dollar grant seems unreasonable. And will they really assess everything I send in? Impatience is running through my veins, through my arms, and I'm sitting on 115 because I need to get home. But it's risky – a cop in an unmarked car could be anywhere along here. An impulsive thought: a few kilometres from Violet Town, there's a short cut. It's coming up on the left. Locals sometimes use it to save time, maybe ten or fifteen minutes. Ross has taken me this way a couple of times, but I've never travelled it on my own: the road is too isolated, no mobile coverage, and the GPS doesn't know the bush tracks. It doesn't even have a sign giving it a name.

I slow down, indicate, and slip into the exit lane.

Margie grips the armrest. 'Why this way?'

'It's quicker. I've only got four days left to get the goddamn application in.'

I don't expect her to ask me about it. Since our first meeting all those years ago, she's never questioned me about anything unrelated to Ross or the farm. I know she's got her stuck-up opinions about me, but the way I see it, if it wasn't for her I wouldn't have Ross. So it's mainly out of gratitude that I make the effort to be kind to her. The other reason is that I've sometimes seen an awful fear on her face, and every so often she flinches for no obvious reason. Ross says he doesn't notice.

When we married, Margie moved to a timber house in Benalla, about the same vintage as Maryhill but smaller. It didn't take long for me to become Ross's proxy, often standing at her front door to hand something over or reassure her about a letter, things she'd phoned Ross about that he never got around to. She now seemed a sad, lonely figure to me, the way she would painstakingly rake up the plane tree leaves and was absorbed in her veggie boxes; the way she stared at birds with an ear turned like she was listening to Mozart. The inside of her house has always depressed me: it's dull, silent, and has the feeling of waiting.

Thank god for the neighbour, Dot – a tall, cheerful woman who looked at me with a steady gaze, as if saying she understood the predicament. After she died, Margie got thinner and visibly smaller, and somehow more afraid. Perhaps she was just more isolated.

A weatherboard farmhouse is close to the unsealed road. Red, blue and white horse-jumps are in a paddock. Granite outcrops, eucalypts, wattles and shrubby grass flash by. Dust trails behind the car. It's very dry here; a spark from anything would set the whole place off. At least fire season is almost over, a relief because there have been no major problems – not here in the north-east, anyway. The dirt road widens and slowly rises to a pine plantation. There are trails with small numbered signs that only mean something to the logging trucks. At a V in the road, I hesitate. Margie is staring at me, frowning. I go with the track that's had the most traffic. An echidna waddles along the edge of the road.

Already I've decided to put Margie in the small guestroom close to the kitchen. It's not ideal and needs cleaning, but the other spare room was once Mark's, and even though I've painted it, put in a double bed and shifted the furniture around, she mightn't like sleeping where he once did.

I'm relieved when I recognise a large concrete water tank. 'How do you feel about returning to Maryhill?' I ask.

She glances at me. 'I don't like going this way.'

'It's quicker. I know where I'm going.' And to change the subject, I tell her what's going on at home: that Isobel worries me because she's preparing for her Grade 8 piano exam in July and hardly leaves the front room. 'Wait till you hear her, though,' I say. 'She's bloody amazing, takes after my father.' Then I ask her, 'What's the history of the piano?'

Margie talks through the windscreen, and I think that Isobel isn't the only shy introvert in the family. 'It was Evelyn Ballantine's. She played well, I remember.'

'We had it restored. Cost a fortune, but the man said it was in good nick and had a clear tone. Did you ever play?'

She shakes her head.

Here I am, in full flight, chatting away. I can't help filling in the silence. 'Tonight the theatre group is coming over. We meet every Monday night in the dining room at seven-thirty.' Still nothing from Margie, but I stubbornly persist because the play is important to me and all this will be going on around her while she stays with us. 'It's a big deal for me because it's the first play I've ever written. I've been working on it since the girls were little. And the group has been rehearsing for the past few months.'

She looks out the passenger window, a snub.

I think of putting on some music; instead I keep talking, because I'm totally obsessed with the play. 'It's being performed at the old Town Hall in Benalla at the end of April. That's why

I'm desperate to get the funding. There are only eight members in the group and I'm hoping Ross will help out.'

At the mention of his name, she glances at me. I wait, thinking she's going to ask me something, but she remains silent.

'We've got a lovely old bloke doing the staging and lighting, but he's in his late seventies. He'll need help.'

On the left is a narrow creek and a line of blackberry bushes the size of houses. Kilometres pass, dust billows behind, and I think about the application, the budget, the emails I've got to send to chase up references, the publicity with the local paper, an update on my group's Facebook page.

We cross an angled bridge that takes us left across the creek. Redbox and peppermint gums arch the road like a eucalypt guard of honour. It's isolated up here, but I decide I'll come this way again because it's quicker and less boring than the run south down the Hume.

Up ahead, to the right, I see an animal – a cow? – and brake. We stop suddenly. Margie puts her hand to her mouth.

I inhale. A sambar deer, majestic in its stance and gaze, steps onto the road. No antlers, a doe, and we watch her turn back towards the scrubby undergrowth as if there's no hurry, and in seconds she's gone.

I slap the steering wheel and rave about how incredible it was. 'Bloody amazing.' I ask Margie if she's ever seen a wild deer.

'Yes,' she says, hugging herself even though it's not cold.

I can't tell what she's thinking when we turn into the driveway, how it must feel to return to where she lived for more than forty years. I stop and reach into the milk-can letterbox, pulling out the *Weekly Times* and *Stock & Land*, and other mail.

She holds herself tight as she limp-shuffles her way on the crutches to the back door. She won't accept my help, but agonises over how to step up inside the back porch; then again as she steps inside to the family room. This place is so familiar to her, yet she's tense and I don't know how to make it easier for her. I direct her into the room beside the kitchen and she stares at me as if I've done something wrong.

'Make yourself at home,' I say. 'Can I get you anything?'

She shakes her head but then tells me her laundry needs doing. 'I'm out of clothes.'

Inside the bag, her garments are thin and frayed: trackpants and tops, a pilled cardigan, a threadbare pink nightie, bras and undies with no elasticity. They're in such bad shape that I wouldn't even shove any of them into a garbage bag and dump them in a Vinnies bin.

The cotton quilt on the bed should be the right weight for her. I fluff the pillows. Then part the curtains, and open the window. A breeze hushes in. Magpies warble.

I'm gathering up Margie's laundry when I realise she will struggle to change from her clothes into her nightie. 'Need help?' I ask.

She shakes her head.

'When you've changed, would you like to sit in the family room to get the sun?'

'I'd like to rest in bed,' she says.

'It'll be easier if you let me help you.'

'I can manage,' she says, looking out the window as if distracted.

So I take her washing and go.

Margie

WHEN Stella comes to my bedroom door, she barely knocks before hurrying in, already onto the next thing. It's not even four in the afternoon and she's pushing my freshly laundered clothes into the set of drawers – it's not possible they've dried on the line since she took them from me. It's a warm day and she's used the dryer and I can't quite believe it.

She tells me I should get up, that she'll make me a cup of tea. 'And perhaps you can sit outside. The pergola is gorgeous in the afternoons.'

I had already thought the pergola would be nice, but I won't go now. She'll get the idea she can tell me what to do. 'A cup of tea and a biscuit,' I say, 'if you have one.'

'No worries,' she says, off again.

I'm in the room beside the kitchen. She said it will be easier for her to check on me. But she didn't think of the noise. I won't rest here.

A tap runs; a cupboard opens and closes. And the girls aren't even home from school. I can't imagine how I'll cope.

Stella doesn't know it, but this room once served as my overflow pantry. Alexander Ballantine designed and built the house in 1920 – a good job except for the small kitchen, which only has one narrow storage cupboard. Ross and Stella have redecorated the kitchen, all white and stainless steel, but it still sits inside the original cavity. They don't do what we did – the other Ballantine wives and I – eking out space that wasn't there when we bottled fruit, made jam, or baked and prepared six dozen lamingtons for the footy cake stall. Norman and I didn't entertain, so the dining room was not a problem, but I've always wondered how our ancestors managed to cater for their guests around the twenty-seater table.

My bed is along the wall where metal racks were stacked with my preserves and Fowlers bottles of cherries, peaches, apricots, pears. Stella now refers to this room as the guestroom. So I am a guest in my old pantry. Propped against the pillows, I see my ghost walk in, wearing the tweed skirt and pale-blue twin-set that I once favoured. I'm efficient, the way I pick up a size-seventeen tapered Fowlers jar of peaches. I close the door behind me, leaving the room in the cool and dark. How bizarre it is to be in this room and notice that time is unstoppable. I feel every one of my eighty years.

The room has been painted a too-bright blue, like the sky on a clear summer's day: the same colour is also above the picture rail and on the ceiling. All the ceilings in this house are twelve feet high, but the vibrant paint here creates the illusion of a perfect square and I feel as though I'm inside a large box. I know this house very well and can testify that the ceiling roses in every other room are symmetrical clusters of curly leaves and thistles; except in the main bedroom, which has an entwined pattern of roses and lilies in a large oval shape. The plaster rose in the centre of this ceiling is plain, unadorned, a statement about the room's insignificance. The light fitting is a large white paper-and-wire ball, ridiculous and modern. And, worse, the window is framed with a hessian curtain; it's unhemmed and lengths of fabric drape on the floor.

*

For half an hour now I've been listening to Ross and the girls. They've been in the kitchen and moved to the family-room table. I hear laughter, his tenor voice and the light banter of happy children. I'm curious, and recall that Norman was never inside at this time of day. But then Stella would have told Ross to pick the children up from the bus because whatever he was doing wasn't as important as this concern she has about funding her play.

I get the impression that Ross is heading out; I know the sounds: the retreating steps to the back door, the clipped tone of his words. He has not come to see me, and I decide I am unhappy here. With this bung hip, everything is a disaster.

I weigh up my options. They are few. Only one is possibly satisfactory, and that's going to any rehab place with a vacancy. Shepparton might be an option.

There's a knock on my door.

The little one comes in and smiles. Her red hair isn't tied back and I'd not realised before that it's got quite a kink to it. She won't like it when she gets older.

'Hi, Nan,' she says.

'Hello, pet.'

She stands in front of me and starts talking, long, fast sentences, and I'm confused, worrying about which of us is in the wrong. Should I be following this?

I smile. 'Did you say rabbits?'

'Yes. Dad's going to gas them. But rabbits have two holes to every burrow, so you have to fill one in so they don't escape, then put poison down the other hole and block it with newspaper.'

I tell her I know all about that. 'Your Uncle Mark,' I say, 'had a ferret.'

She smiles more widely, as if I said something funny. 'I don't have an uncle.'

She's ten years old, so I don't blame her for not knowing. But Mark is in our family, his hand was warm when I held it that last time, and we can never forget him.

'Yes, you do. He was your father's older brother. My first baby. But he died.'

She seems unconcerned by this and continues to smile. 'How did he die?'

'Never mind,' I say. I sit up and hang my feet over the side of the bed. 'Can you push my slippers on?' I ask, trying for her name – when I remember, I must write it down.

She bends over and I curl my toes so she won't see my long yellowing nails. I am ashamed to appear so ugly in front of this child. She tickles my feet, thinks it's funny and giggles. I am not amused and reach for my dressing-gown and put it on. I tie the sash. Then move forward, like a launching ship, and stand on my left foot while balancing on the wretched crutches. 'Open the door,' I command.

If she notices a shift in my mood, she doesn't show it or care. She's talking at me again. 'Dad's getting more dung beetles to live in the paddocks. They eat the cow poo. Did you know that?'

I walk out of the room slowly, gripping the handles of my crutches, and decide this child thrives on attention and should not be encouraged.

I stand hunched and scan the family room. Immediately I notice things that I would straighten up, throw out, clean, dust, make disappear.

The girls are staring into their iPads. Dot had one, and it amazed me how often I'd find her staring into it. These children seem affected in the same way. There's nothing for it, so I go to sit on the edge of the couch and look at what they're doing. But I can't describe what I am seeing because everything is moving too fast – animated people flying in space that then appear to be on land. I can't keep up and become more interested in the children, their transfixed faces. It's not normal. They should be outside in the fresh air.

'Have you got school readers?' I ask.

Isobel glances at me. 'No.'

'Why don't you have a reader?'

'Because I finished my book and get another one on library day.'

I don't like her impatient tone, as if I'm a nuisance interrupting her.

The little one tells me she's reading 'level thirty' words, as if that means something to me. She smiles, and I see she'll need braces. I glance into their iPads, but this bores me and I don't know what to do next. I feel a sadness for these children, that they're being entertained with this rubbish and not outdoors.

On the coffee table is a bird book with coloured tags that someone has used to mark identified birds. I flick through it and count thirty-five that have been spotted. My tally – after fifty years of birdwatching here and at Bishop Street – is one hundred and fifty-two.

Another book lies underneath a tissue box: Maggie Smith's biography. I recognise her face from *Downton Abbey*; she played Countess Violet. I pick it up and start reading.

I move to a window where the light is better and disrupt the sleeping cat. It reminds me of Diva, Dot's cat, and runs to the couch where it curls, as it pleases, on Isobel's lap. Having an animal in the house depresses me; I feel the disquiet of unseen germs. But the book engages me, and suddenly Stella appears, demanding the children stop what they're doing. 'Isobel, set the table,' she yells. 'Jemima, feed the cat.'

Jemima – the name reminds me of a ragdoll and I don't know why.

It's all action: kids running, Stella reaching and bending in the kitchen, getting dinner.

I always knew what the meals would be at least a day in advance – a private menu in my head that I delivered, almost without fail, every day for the years I was married to Norman. When it was just Ross and me, I hardly bothered because I never knew when he was going to show up.

Once Stella is finished in the kitchen and Ross has returned, the five of us sit around the table. I'm at the end where Norman used to sit. I wonder if Ross remembers the places where we always sat: Norman, me, Mark, Caroline and him. I decide not to ask. He seems tense; his shoulders aren't relaxed. The demands that Stella puts on him must stress him.

We eat penne from bowls. All she's done is boil the pasta up in a saucepan and tip a jar of shop-bought tomato pasta sauce on top. There's no cheese to sprinkle over it. And no meat – a working man needs his meat for strength. I watch Ross scoop up the penne; he seems hungry and this will not be enough.

'When is calving?' I ask him.

He moves his neck as if to ease pain, and before he can answer, Jemima interrupts, telling everyone I've got the longest toenails she's ever seen. 'You should see them,' she says, holding her fingers apart to exaggerate the length.

I bear my humiliation by ignoring her and repeat my question to Ross. But if he answers, I don't hear it. Stella and Ross are clearing the table.

'They'll be here any minute,' Stella says.

When my bowl is whisked away, there's still a spoon of penne left. I would like to eat it, but no one asks me.

I need a pain tablet, but the idea of hobbling along to my bedroom to get one, then to the kitchen for a glass of water – versus asking someone to bring everything to me – is too complicated. I do nothing and my hip hurts.

There's a knock at the back door and Stella is light on her feet, rushing to the porch and smiling as if she's happy. The narrow heels on her shoes will surely damage the floor. In the few minutes since the dinner table was cleared, she's changed into tight white jeans and a pink knit top. Red lipstick, and her blonde hair is clipped high on her head and somehow stays there. Gold dangly earrings make her look more dressed up than she is.

I return to the Maggie Smith biography, but I'm listening, not reading. Piano faintly drifts down the hallway from the front room – scales up and down the keyboard, then other blocks of keys, but not a real tune. I suppose that's what practice is. Ross is running the taps in the kitchen to rinse the dishes and pack the dishwasher; not Norman, he never washed a dish in our whole marriage.

A casually dressed young man, holding a violin case, enters the room. His black hair is strangely shaved on the sides but long and slick on the top, an exaggerated version of what we used to call short back and sides. I can't keep up with the fashion. When he turns to face the room, I see his eyes are large, soft and dark, like those of a sooty owl, and I think this fellow might be very handsome. He raises his hand in a half-wave to me. 'Noah,' he says, and before I think how to reply, he enters the kitchen – as though he knows his way around – and starts talking to Ross.

Stella has rushed off again. Someone else has arrived. I feel this evening might be very long, yet for me the day has ended. I decide to go to bed, and already I know I will be disturbed by all this coming and going.

I'm on my feet, gripping the crutches.

From the back porch, Stella laughs. Then I hear a familiar man's voice – and with that deep mellow sound comes the image of a face. I freeze.

In they walk, Stella and Chester. She's holding his arm as if they're going for a Sunday afternoon stroll. His smile is as it always was: charming, slightly crooked, his eyes narrowed to a squint. He looks cheeky, a handsome rascal, and I'm furious with the situation, him here in this house, and with her. He's wearing a very nice blue herringbone jacket and a white shirt with light-brown trousers – unusually dressed up for the occasion, I would've thought. These days he's slightly stooped. I don't like his moustache; it's as though he's trying to look younger and distract from the fact that there's not much left on top.

'Margie,' Stella says, 'you know Chester, don't you? He's the group's poet, and our set-and-lighting man.'

I know a lot more about Chester Sullivan than she'll ever find out. I wasn't prepared to see him yesterday at the hospital. And I'm not prepared now. I don't want the upset.

'Fancy seeing you here,' he says, smiling.

I don't know what to say. My hip aches and I shift my weight.

Stella notices. 'Margie, you look a bit uncomfortable. Why don't you sit down?'

Then I do smile. 'I'm perfectly fine. But it's been a long day. Have a good meeting.'

It is my intention to breeze out of the room with my head high, but my slipper kicks against the Persian rug. My step falters.

Chester's arm is around my back. 'Steady there.'

Other people are walking into the room, a man and two women about forty or fifty years old; I can't tell people's ages anymore – everyone looks young.

Stella goes to them. And Chester releases his hold on me.

My hair hasn't been washed in days and I feel embarrassed. I look down to see my baggy trackpants and dowdy maroon slippers. Chester is wearing modern shoes, brown leather with little holes patterned on the sides. His trousers have a pressed crease and sit exactly in the right spot on his shoelaces. I don't want to lift my face – I'm shy now and don't trust my facial muscles to remain composed – but I can't keep staring at our feet. There's nothing for it. So I glance up at Chester – as he turns to the others, a small group, strangers to me. They're all talking and there's so much noise. A woman has brought a cake. A young girl with big-framed glasses and auburn hair is holding a bottle of wine.

I hobble away on the crutches and don't look back.

It's a long, slow hassle in the bathroom. And when I lift myself into bed and finally reach for my tablets, I decide to take two of the blue ones: one for my hip and one for my heart. They're the ones that deaden pain.

I turn off the lamp. There are magpies outside and I close my eyes to their lovely sound. A pleasant breeze comes through the window. How terribly strange to be lying in the storage room while Chester is so close in the dining room, with Stella and those other people in her theatre group. I can hear the murmur of their voices, soft bursts of laughter. I feel my breath and wait for sleep.

A tap on the door; someone peeks in.

'You asleep, Nan?' Isobel whispers into the dim light. 'Mum said to bring you this.'

I don't move or speak.

She creeps in, hovers next to me and tugs the blanket a little higher over my shoulder. Something is put on the bedside table.

The door shuts quietly.

When I put the lamp back on, I find a cup of tea and a slice of apple cake on a bread-and-butter plate. I recognise the plate, green scalloped edges with a pink floral design; it's from the old Royal Doulton set that Evelyn Ballantine used when I first visited here, before Norman and I became engaged. She served slices of coconut and raspberry jam tart, and this could be the very plate I so nervously held. Both she and Freddie smiled a lot; they seemed eager, as if they themselves were nervous.

I decide not to eat the apple cake or drink the tea so I can pronounce in the morning that I was very much asleep when Isobel walked in. But I'm weary with the effort of keeping my guard up; most times I don't understand why I feel so irritable and driven to be difficult. Perhaps it's habit? Whatever the reason, it's tiring to be in this house with all the old memories.

Then through the wall floats the soft hesitant sound of a violin – mellow, almost flute-like. It's quite lovely and unexpected. I recognise the tune, but can't quite remember its name. It stops and I strain to hear. The patter of voices. The violin starts again: the same tune, but a little faster, which I think is better.

It's no use. I cannot sleep knowing Chester is in the house. I sit up and reach for the tea. It's lukewarm but quite nice. And the cake looks very moist. So I eat it.

Stella

AFTER Isobel was born, it was so quiet in the house, lovely though – and I'm not complaining – but I missed the theatre. And because I had swollen breasts and a baby sucking on me, that precious closeness, it was natural to think of my mother, Grace Adams. She died when I was seventeen, so a lot was left unsaid between us, and I'd say now that I misunderstood her. She had an executive position in a bank and spent all her time at work, on the phone or asleep in her bed. I wrote my two-act play as a way of getting to know her.

It's centred around a family gathering she held one hot Saturday afternoon in the late 1980s. She asked my brother, Tommy, and me to sit at the kitchen table. It felt formal, like a meeting she'd have in her office. A fan oscillated on the bench. The vinyl chairs were sticky on our bare legs. Our household had been unhappy for some time. Mum had recently kicked out our dad and within a fortnight introduced us to her new lover: a tall, quiet man with downcast eyes called Graham.

The family meeting didn't go well. We couldn't forgive her for discarding our wonderful red-headed, piano-playing dad.

And we had so many other complaints. I tell them in the play: some are funny, others sad. Mum was trying to explain to us she was a person, an individual, not just a mother. 'I did my best!' she cried. That's where the play's name comes from. Tommy and I were cruel; we told her that her best wasn't good enough.

In between having my three babies, working with Ross on the farm, volunteering at the school and being a part of various local theatre groups, it took me fourteen years to write *I Did My Best*, and when it was finished I realised it wasn't really about Mum anymore. To give it pace, pathos and humour, I exaggerated the characters and their grievances, compressed time and made lots of things up. And I can't say I understand the decisions she made anymore today than when I started. But if anything, I now agree with her – she did her best. Just like I'm doing with my girls. Will I do any better? I hope so. Maybe.

Two years after that meeting around the kitchen table, a brain tumour took her away. It accounted for all the headaches, why she so often closed her bedroom door on us. Even so, Graham was allowed in.

I don't care about any of that anymore. Truly. What I care about is *I Did My Best*, the production, making it a success. And I suppose I owe Mum an apology for reshaping her story and turning it into something else.

*

Noah, who I've cast as my brother, stands in front of the unlit fireplace giving a rendition of 'Lucy in the Sky with Diamonds'. There are faint traces of grease on his fingernails. He plays his violin with his beautiful dark eyes closed, moving his body, ignoring us. For the second piece, he puts his phone on the end of the table and opens a violin-playing app that prompts him with a Bach minuet. He seems awkward with this choice of music and doesn't play with the same confidence. I'll talk to him privately about maybe sticking to contemporary pieces.

When he finishes he looks at us, waiting for applause. Some actors want loads of praise even if their performance is just average.

'Brilliant,' I say. Someone claps. He takes a cheerful bow and sits.

Noah is our tractor mechanic. Maybe once every six months, Ross calls him to come to the farm to service and repair the McCormick: to change the oil and filters, grease the points, and check the belts, seals and hydraulics. Last time he repaired the clutch, a six-thousand-dollar job. Ross and I gaped at each other when he turned up at the auditions and said he was also performing as the Scarecrow in *The Wizard of Oz* with the Wangaratta Players.

I hand the funding application to Chester, who passes copies around the table. The mood is relaxed – perhaps too relaxed, or I'm just wired.

'Bloody hell,' Felicity says. 'What's all this paperwork for fifteen grand?'

Felicity, who plays my mother, is in her fifties: a little old for the role, but she's tall and her voice is strong, which gives her a good presence. I'm not convinced she empathises with the character – that she's going deep enough into the domestic tragedy. She's been married twice and I've wondered if that's the problem, that it's too real for her. Ross listened to the audio of her reading and said she was good. She's brilliant at the humour. I find it hard to be objective because I've been involved in it for so long; I need to let go and trust her. I've known her for years; we kept bumping into each other at various productions in the north-east, and when I floated the idea of starting our own theatre group, she kept hassling me until I did it. She's a retired drama teacher, loves community theatre and is as obsessed as me.

Owen is sitting beside Felicity. He's playing my father, the abandoned husband, who appears in Act Two. He's about Felicity's age, but they don't look like a couple, and his appearance is nothing like Dad's. Owen is bald, wears square tortoiseshell glasses and dresses like a male model in a farm-clothing catalogue: handsome, clean, neat and boring. He fancies himself as a better actor than the rest, but there's often a cast member like that. The negative energy between him and Felicity works perfectly; it makes sense that their characters aren't together. Owen's a radiologist and perhaps didn't have dinner before he came – he's on his third piece of apple cake and casually brushes crumbs onto the floor.

'I've got till five on Thursday,' I say, drawing attention to the budget items I need input on. I ask Chester how much he'll require for the sets and lighting.

He tugs a piece of paper from his trouser pocket and pushes it towards me. 'About a thousand for the sets, but it depends on the final design. With lighting, I've had a look on YouTube – I reckon we can get away with six spotlights.'

Amber is texting. She plays me. Her gorgeous copper hair covers her pale face and hides her black-rimmed glasses. 'Teddy's waiting out the front . . .' she tells me as if asking permission to go meet her boyfriend, but I know she's leaving now.

After she's gone, I worry this meeting has been a waste of time. I'd have done better to work on the application alone, but I thought it a good idea to have their input, to involve them – that's how community theatre works.

Next to Amber's empty chair is Holly. She plays one of Mum's girlfriends, and she's also put her hand up to help with the marketing and PR. Tonight she has a bruise on her neck, an unmistakable lovebite. It's been a long time since I had one – and I've never seen one on a woman in her forties before. She should be wearing a scarf. As I think this, I consider myself a prude: finally I have something in common with Margie.

Three others faithfully come every week. They're reserved, perhaps shy, and the man is very overweight. They're willing workers and will take care of everything back of house – setting up, ticket sales, seating; there's so much small stuff.

We work through the funding application quickly. I've nothing else for them, but it feels too soon to end the evening. I hesitate, wondering what we should do. Perhaps we could read through Act Two, Scene One – it's when Dad arrives, the tension builds and Grace breaks down, saying, *I'm entitled to have a life!*

The Ballantine portraits are in the shadows. The bulbs inside the chandeliers aren't strong enough to throw a decent light in the long room. The high-gloss polish on the table shines in spite of the dust. The lovely green and pink bread-and-butter plates are now empty, spaced around the table with silver forks on them. I decide to call an end to the meeting.

But Chester raises a hand. We all turn.

'I have a poem I'd like to read, if I may.'

I'm intrigued by this man, the flirting poet, farmer and handyman. Ross has told me he's the father of the boy who was killed in the car crash with his brother, Mark. That the boy was Chester's only child. I know he lives with his wife, Laura, behind the hedge on Black Wattle Road. Ross picks up gossip around the place – for certain men gossip more than women. He told me that Laura has a serious heart condition and has recently been in hospital. In all the years I've lived up here on the tableland, I've only seen her a couple of times. Thin and unfriendly. It's always seemed odd to me that Chester has such a stuck-up wife when he is so outgoing. All I know about Laura is she's a dedicated botanical artist; we have one of her pieces in the front room beside the piano.

Chester reaches inside his blue jacket and flaps out a sheet of paper. He takes his time to find his wire-framed reading glasses and put them on. He tells us he wrote this poem forty years ago. He smiles as if remembering something that pleases him. 'It's called "Purple Clematis",' he says.

Beyond the row of hollyhocks
Through bracken lush and green
I see
A gash of purple
A slice of skin
Your face, your wrist
A trick, a dream
I hear

He has a good voice – deep, slow and commanding. It requires our attention; we're all looking at him. If he was younger, he'd be perfect for the husband that Owen is playing.

Your laugh
The rustling leaves
The drumming of my heart
Or is that rain
Upon the eaves
It feels as though the sound will shake
The birds from watchful trees
Time will shudder to a halt
And wind forget to breathe
You're here; you've come
Purple clematis

Unravelling her hair across the
Forest floor
Lifting up her dancing skirts
Her legs uprooted from the earth
A fierce, sweet, need . . .

His voice is very quiet now, like he's hearing his own words, thinking his own thoughts, and I try to imagine his wife. This is for her. The poem is beautiful; we're all transfixed and perhaps a little embarrassed for him, that this farmer cum set-and-lighting man is sharing something so intimate. I'm confused about why he's reading this to us – his poems are usually clever observations of people, politics. Chester is a philosopher, but tonight he is also a romantic.

The apples are fresh
You hold one to my mouth
I feel the cool, crisp texture on my tongue
Sweet thirst
And then your hand retreats too sharply
And you laugh
A bull ant works its way across the sill
The damp skin
Where lips and white flesh touched
Burning still

Chester's voice trails off. He's not looking at the sheet of paper because he knows the last words.

We lie like this
Entwined and yet unwound
The purple clematis dress abandoned
Half-eaten apples on the ground

When he's finished he looks at us, taking us in. Noah and Felicity surround him. We sit in silence; no one moves until Chester sits down. He wipes his eyes, but I didn't see tears.

'Bloody awesome,' Noah says.

I kiss Chester on the cheek and pat his arm. 'Thank you,' I say. But I'm now worried for him. That his wife is ill and whatever that means for him, I can't imagine.

I'm not expecting it when he puts his arm firmly around my waist. 'So you've got Margie back in the house with you?' When I nod, he says, 'She was a beauty in her day,' and mouths a kiss.

After they've all gone, and Ross is helping me clear the plates and glasses, I try to explain Chester's poem, his voice, the feeling of it.

Ross shrugs. 'Always been on the unconventional side of things. But he's handy in a toolshed.'

'And he says your mother was nice-looking when she was younger. Why would he say that?'

Ross pauses, thinking. 'There's something, I remember.'

'What?'

'Dunno. Nothing.'

'Bullshit. Tell me. What do you mean, *there's something*?'

He smiles at me across the table. 'Nothing. Truly. Nothing.'

Margie

IT'S Thursday morning and Stella has been in the dining room for almost two hours. I've heard the kettle boil, the cutlery drawer rattle. Ross has already left the house; I think without breakfast because I didn't hear him in the kitchen.

My hip aches, so I shift onto my back. I don't like this hard mattress. Or the effort it will take to get out of bed and go to the toilet, then dress. My scalp itches and I can't remember when my hair was last washed. I've not showered in the four days I've been here and I must smell a bit off. I can't really tell, although I do feel on the sour side of things.

I'm supposed to do exercises, so I move my feet up and down a few times. It hurts to lift my right leg, so I don't. I'm uncomfortable, my bladder is full, and I hate this room and Stella for putting me in here. I turn to the hessian curtains. Not far from the claret ash and magnolias, over where the tap is, magpies start carolling. There are a few, eight or more, claiming their territory. Hearing them cheers me up.

I sit and carefully position my legs over the edge of the bed. I move slowly, gripping as hard as I can onto these perilous crutches. I'm not bothered with the dressing-gown and step-hop my way out of the storeroom-bedroom and along the hallway in my short pink nightie. My feet are bare and I see my toenails are yellow talons, but I can't bend down to clip them and don't know how to solve the problem. The cat disappears around the corner; its tail gives a little wave and is gone. It should be outside, but then it'll kill birds.

More than my hip hurts as I pass my old bedroom door. It's disorientating here at Maryhill – I feel like I'm reaching back in time and claiming this place again. Everything is indelibly familiar, but there's no doubting that this isn't my home anymore.

Stella has put a toilet chair over the bowl. I lower myself. It takes an age. Everything in my body is slow, yet my mind is impatient. My mother's raspberry liqueur trifle in the diamond-cut crystal bowl comes to mind. A family gathering in my parents' dining room. Lemon cordial. Laughter. I'm at a loss to understand the things that spring into my head. I exhale. I have no idea what I will do once I've had breakfast, how I'll fill this day. It's seven-forty-five on a school day and I wonder why the children are so quiet.

Back in my bedroom, I put my dressing-gown on and lumber out to the kitchen on the crutches. The kettle is still warm and full enough, so I press the button. While I wait for it to boil, I push open the swing door into the dining room.

Stella looks up.

'Shouldn't the children be awake?' I say.

'What time is it?'

'Quarter to eight.'

'Shit!' she roars, lunging from the dining chair, and without a thank you she's through the door, yelling at the sleeping children as she runs down the hall.

For the next short while I watch Stella empty day-old contents from lunchboxes into the bin, then refill them with roughly cling-wrapped cheese sandwiches: uncut, just two slices of bread slapped together with a square of processed cheese. And a banana.

Isobel barely ate one Weet-Bix for her breakfast and left at least a cup of milk in the bowl. She is so thin and those dark-framed glasses are too big for her pale, narrow face. And Jemima only ate half a slice of toast; the other half is in her hand as she hurries out the door to the car. 'Bye, Nan,' she says, waving. Neither child has brushed her teeth.

When I hear Stella's car speed down the driveway, I settle in a lounge chair with a cup of tea. It's not possible to count how many times I've sat in this family room. The couches, coffee table and television are different, but most is as it always was. The fireplace, the eight-seater dinner table and chairs. Alice Ballantine's sideboard is where it's been for more than a hundred years. I am alone and breathe in the quiet. It's peaceful enough. And there by the bay window is the cat, staring at me. I look away but feel its eyes on me. Another image of Diva, Dot's cat, returns: the way it smoothly curled through her legs and sprang onto her lap. They look the same, Diva and this one. But Stella said she was taking it to the vet. I will ask her.

The pulsing discomfort in my hip reminds me I have a physio appointment at eleven, and I wonder if Ross and Stella have forgotten.

Stella is back; the car stops abruptly.

My chair is too low and I struggle to stand. I don't want the pain that will come with the effort, but there is nothing for it. I edge my bottom forward and push up as I inhale, and I'm on my feet.

Stella's through the back door, half-running, in a terrible hurry, and I wonder if something is wrong.

'Margie,' she says, smiling, and I think her smile is very nice and she's got good teeth. I can't say the separate parts of her are attractive – her nose is on the big side and in profile has a slight bump at the bridge – but all put together she is quite eye-catching. 'Can I get you anything? Are you all right?'

'I'm fine,' I say.

'Why are you standing in the middle of the room?'

I look down at myself and wonder the same thing. Then I remember I have something to say. 'I've got a physio appointment at eleven.'

'Really? Crap. Where's Ross?'

I look towards the back door, but she already has her phone out, pressing his number. And as she waits for him to answer, she hooks a strand of hair into the mess at the back of her head. Wherever my son is, he doesn't answer and she leaves a message: 'Your mother's got a physio appointment at eleven. Where are you?' Then she turns to me and asks, 'Have you had breakfast, Margie? You look a bit lost standing there.'

The cat is at my feet and I lightly kick it away. 'Is this Dot's cat?'

'Oh, Margie, you're a shocker. Of course it is.' She picks it up and hugs it close. The cat stares at me, hateful eyes.

God help me. I have nothing to say.

She phones Ross again, as if for some reason he'll answer this time.

The morning sun shows the dust on the floor, and I wonder when it was last vacuumed and mopped. On the table are the children's dirty breakfast dishes, Ross's iPad and the local newspaper, which I've already read. It's got a large photo of Stella in it, with a story about her play, *I Did My Best*. The article says she's an award-winning director and producer, something I don't know anything about. I'm more suspicious than curious.

'Where is Ross?' I ask.

'How would I know? I'm buried in the bloody arts funding application.' She smiles at me as if I understand.

'I don't know anything about those things,' I say. 'But when's he coming inside?'

'God knows.'

The back door slaps. We wait for Ross to appear. He walks in wearing his socks.

'Missed your call,' he says, looking at Stella.

I must be invisible.

'Your mum has a physio appointment in Benalla at eleven. You have to take her.'

'Can't. I'm sorting in the yards. The truck's coming at midday for the weaners.'

We look at him.

'It's the Euroa sale tomorrow,' he explains.

'But the application deadline is today at five,' Stella says.

My mouth is open, and I'm trying to decide how I feel. Angry. Hurt. Yet, it's clear I'm a nuisance.

Both Ross and Stella are looking at me, my son in his filthy work clothes that he should not have on inside the house.

'I'll take you,' Stella says.

And there I am, apologising that I'm a bother.

'Weaners going to market wins,' she says.

Stella makes Ross coffee in a machine. I hear their voices in the kitchen while I hover between my thoughts and movements. If I'm going to town I need to shower, but I can't manage on my own. The state of my hair upsets me. Stella has offered to help me two or three times, but I've refused because I can't work out how I'll keep my modesty.

Then she's in front of me, staring into my face as though to see if I'm all there.

'There's nothing for it,' she says. 'We need to get you in the shower.'

'When is the home-care person coming?'

'Next week.'

She puts her hand on my shoulder and I pull away. 'I can manage.'

'Very good. Off you go. I'll check on you in a tick.'

It's as if she's talking to one of her children.

I take small steps down the hall to the bathroom. There's a film of dust all along the skirting boards, a couple of dead blowies, and I remember myself as agile, moving fast down this hall with a damp cloth and mop. I was a good housewife; the things I could get done in a day.

I close the bathroom door and sit on the shower chair, still wearing my dressing-gown. I'm tugging at the sash when the door opens and Stella walks in. 'No,' I say.

She ignores me. 'Come on, Margie, we need to get your gear off.'

Before I can protest any further, she's leaning down to undo my dressing-gown buttons. I lift my bottom so she can tug the gown free. Then she holds a towel up like a curtain and instructs me to remove my nightie. I do as I'm told. Even though she isn't looking, my nakedness shames me – the loose flesh of my body is white and a little scaly, like the underbelly of a silver perch. A towel is draped over me. Stella is bending side-on, taking off my slippers. Her jeans are so low I'm confronted with the crack between her buttocks.

'Bloody hell. Look at your toenails. I'll deal with them after the shower.'

I pull my feet away. 'No you won't.'

'Don't be ridiculous,' she says.

Feeling chastised and embarrassed, I stare into the plain white tiles, different to when I lived here – it's all white and chrome, like at the hospital.

She's got the water running, waiting for the right temperature. She hands me the shower hose and a face washer. 'I'll leave you for a bit.'

When she's gone I throw the towel away. The warm water is lovely. Stella has put some liquid soap in a bottle beside me on the chair so I don't have to bother with dropping a slippery bar. I hold the shower nozzle as high as I can, but my arm is stiff.

Stella peeks through the door and comes in.

'Go away,' I say.

She acts as if she's not heard. 'We need to wash your hair.'

And before I can speak she's taken the hose from me and is wetting me down like a horse on a hot day. Then her fingers are massaging in the shampoo, just like they do at the hairdresser. I keep my eyes shut tight and try not to cry. I go to the black cockatoos I once saw preening each other in a silver wattle: it looked as though they were kissing. With that memory, I consider the first time I was tenderly kissed, being pulled forward. And I'm overtaken with confusing emotions because Chester was in the house this week – his swagger, laughter, and the impertinence of him being involved in her little play.

The warm water abruptly stops and I sit dripping.

'That'll do,' Stella says. She wraps a towel around my shoulders and starts rubbing, helping me dry off. 'You okay?'

'I want my privacy.'

'I bet you do. I'm really sorry.' Another towel is dropped over my lap; my body is now enclosed in a tepee of white fluffy cotton. She's kneeling, nail clippers in her hand. 'Give me your foot,' she says.

*

I was forced to accept Stella. After that first meeting where she spoke of a play, something about a horse, all I could take in was the metal hook in her navel, her blonde hair falling over her face, the thick red lipstick and heavy, dark eye make-up. I hoped Ross would come to his senses and tire of her.

After a few years of him spending increasing amounts of time with her in Melbourne, and of constant arguments between us, the farm showed signs of neglect. Several times he was needed and I couldn't get hold of him.

Once he returned a call from an island somewhere off the coast of Thailand saying he wouldn't be home for a week. I reeled off the jobs that required his urgent attention. A fallen tree across a fence. The hay contractor wanted dates for a job. The bulls were still in with the heifers. The tractor was due for servicing. The lawns around the house needed mowing.

He was bad-tempered and it wasn't the first time he'd spoken rudely to me. 'I'm not rushing back to mow the bloody lawns.'

'What'll I tell the contractor?'

'What do you think? Tell him I'll call next week.'

'But he'll take on other jobs before ours.'

'I'm having a break,' Ross said. 'Don't call me again.'

I stopped arguing with him because I feared he would quit the farm completely. And then what? Mark and Norman were gone. Caroline – well, girls didn't work outside with the animals. Besides, she'd never shown any interest; although, to be fair, it was never encouraged.

While Ross was still sunning himself on the Thai island, a letter arrived with a Qantas logo in the corner of the envelope. I thought it might be important and my thumb, as if of its own accord, peeled the letter open. I read it. And sat down.

He had an interview for the pilot's cadetship program; an appointment date and time were in bold letters.

I poured a sweet sherry and wandered the house. I stood at Mark's bedroom door and stared in. A poster of a bearded Eric Clapton playing guitar was hanging on the wall. One corner was drooping; I pressed it against the Blu-Tack with my thumb. I could almost hear the guitar work that Mark loved and played too loudly in his cassette player. His footy boots were side by side on the floor near the window. I had cleaned them with polish and my tears. In my heart I asked Mark how he was, and waited. Of course, there was no reply.

In the grand old dining room, I stood in front of the Ballantine portraits. I looked into their serious faces and asked them what to do. William. Charles. Alexander. Fredrick, always known as Freddie. Norman. I considered the Ballantine heritage, the birthright of the eldest son. The house was still and silent. Through the window, the crepe myrtle was leaning against the wind. Trees all over the farm would be doing the same.

William cleared away the bush and granite, and built the stone house, sheds and fences. He named the property Maryhill and died before he was forty. Charles sunk the bore and introduced the first sheep bloodlines. Alexander bought the first Angus cattle and built the house in 1895. Freddie expanded the landholding by buying the adjoining properties, known as Kirks and Tullys; he was the second son, and by all reports a good farmer. His older brother, John, died in Amiens, France, in 1918. Freddie was a big-hearted man and I think he liked me. I liked him.

The space beside my husband's photograph had been intended for Mark.

To sell the farm and give up all those generations of work was unthinkable. It would be Ross's portrait that would hang there with his forefathers. He'd been working the property for several years, but he needed to settle down. This flying ambition and running after Stella were distractions.

It wasn't hard to do. I opened the firebox and threw the Qantas letter in. For a moment it flared bright.

When Ross arrived home, I sat him down. He looked different, tanned; his hair was sun-bleached and too long, like a surfie's – making him look less like Norman, who was always fussy with his grooming. Ross's stubble wasn't quite a beard. On his left wrist were ridiculous coloured-string bracelets. When he folded his arms in defiance, I saw the line of a Sanskrit tattoo on his right muscled bicep. And I thought, *He thinks I'm old and dull, that I know nothing, that I've never had fun or enjoyed sex, that I might have precious memories and still have dreams.*

'Why the tattoo?' I asked.

He glanced at his arm. 'Why not?'

I stared at him to let him know I disapproved. 'Do you love her?' I asked.

'Yes,' he replied.

'Then marry her and bring her here.'

He shook his head.

'Why not?' I asked.

'She likes her job.'

'She's a waitress.'

He was indignant, defiant. 'Don't put her down.'

'I stated a fact.'

'She's into theatre production.'

I couldn't help myself. 'Is she a suitable partner for you?'

'The question you need to ask is, am I a suitable son?'

'What does that mean?'

'Mark was supposed to be the farmer.'

'Maryhill is your responsibility now.'

He moved in his seat and glanced out the window, as if deciding something. Perhaps he was summoning the courage to tell me he was leaving the farm to fly aeroplanes. I held my breath. I thought of the Qantas letter and saw its brief flash in the firebox. Would there be a follow-up? Would he call them to enquire where the letter was?

I felt the pulse in my neck. 'I put you through Dookie. It's expected that you're taking on the property.'

'Stella won't live here,' he said.

'Why not?'

The hard set of his jaw, and I knew the hold she had over him was far greater than mine.

'Because she won't live here with me?' I said, sniffing. 'I wouldn't ever suggest we live under the same roof.'

I outlined my plan to Ross. We would sell Kirks because the pasture wasn't very good: waterlogged in parts, with too many granite plates. The sale would free up enough cash to buy me a place in town and provide me with a modest income. 'I've been looking,' I said. 'There's a house on Bishop Street that interests me.'

His quick, alert glance confirmed the problem. It wasn't about him not wanting to farm, but Stella refusing to share a house with me – as if I would ever entertain such an idea.

'If she agrees, you'd better treat her properly,' he said.

'Don't use that tone with me.'

'And stop treating me like a kid.'

I twisted in my seat. There was nothing for it. 'You have my word. I'll treat her properly.'

*

Stella reaches for my other foot. She is very quick, and I expect to feel pain and see blood at any second. I curl my toes to prevent the disaster.

'Relax,' she says, prising them open.

She washes the clippings down the shower plughole. Another towel appears – that's the third one used just on me and I'm anxious about all the washing. The dryer blasts and her fingers pull my short fine hair into some kind of shape.

I shake my head to have her leave me alone, but she keeps going. 'Sit still,' she says.

I slump forward. Then sit upright in case she orders me to do it.

'Margie,' she says, 'can you manage to dress yourself? We're leaving in ten minutes.'

She is always in a rush.

'Yes,' I say.

Then she's telling me she wants to be back by lunchtime, as if somehow I will prevent this. The arts funding business is all she thinks about. My appointment is at eleven and she's the one driving so I cannot see the problem.

'Yell if you need anything,' she says, leaving me and closing the door.

Clean clothes are folded on a chair. I put my underwear on and feel ashamed that Stella has seem my private garments, which are thin and frayed. Knowing she's laundered them, it's as if I'm seeing them with fresh eyes. I pull on a pair of black tracksuit pants – the elasticised waist is the attraction; I've got three pairs. The blouse buttons are fiddly, or my fingers are clumsy, but I manage. I push my feet into black slip-on shoes. When all that's done, I feel very good. There's nothing like a hot shower, clipped toenails, clean hair and clothes.

The mirror above the vanity covers half the wall. I'm practised at not looking, turning away so I don't see my tired old face. But I look now. It's almost a punishment to see myself. There I am. It's because I don't smile that the lines defining my cheeks are so deeply engraved. There are fine wrinkles around my lips and eyes. My eyelids sag. I'm past grieving for lost youth and middle age, my vanished beauty. I've been invisible for many decades. Stella's efforts have puffed up my grey hair, but there is no doubt that I am a miserable-looking woman. If my lipstick were handy I'd perhaps put some on. And earrings. I have jewellery pieces in my dressing-table drawer back at Bishop Street. I turn my head, imagining the square-shaped pink sapphires set in rose gold. They once belonged to Elizabeth, Norman's grandmother.

Stella knocks and calls out that we're going now.

It's like an experiment when I smile into the mirror. The lines stretch and tighten and almost disappear.

Stella

ON the road to Violet Town, granite plates slope along Little Clemet Creek. Willows lean gracefully to the water; some leaves are already yellow. The rising hills are tinged green from the February rain; the rusty patches are from the bushfire last year. Cows are grazing on the flats among the tussocks. I love this time of year, the turning from parched summer to the colours of autumn.

Margie is gripping the door's armrest, and I wonder if she's bracing from pain or she's a nervous passenger. Adele is singing my favourite song. Track 9 – about regrets, wanting to live a little more, missing her mother. I can't say whether I love the lyrics or her soulful voice the most, but she transports me into my play and the opening night at Benalla Town Hall.

The theatre is dark. The audience is silent, staring, anticipating. The stage is lit. And Grace tells her children she wants to discuss her 'defining choices'. A pause. I see the actors poised, waiting. Timing is key. Then Ruby says, 'You put your career and Graham first – that's what defines me.' Lifting his violin,

Jack winks dramatically at the audience. He plays the first few bars of Ellie Goulding's 'Love Me Like You Do'.

'The music is too loud,' Margie says.

I make a small show of lowering the volume because I'd already turned it way down out of consideration to her.

At the S-bend I slow, accelerate around. A white ute is coming up fast the other way and Margie puts her hand to her mouth. Along the flats my mobile signal is stronger. I press Jannon's number – a stage manager in the Robinson Street Theatre days, he's now working with the Melbourne Theatre Company. Three days ago he promised to send me a reference letter for the funding application. In the open space of the car, Margie and I hear the lovely Irish lilt of his voice ask for a message. I try to sound upbeat and undemanding when I say, with a smile, that I'm desperate for his letter, can he email it today? 'Let me know if there's a problem.'

Margie walks very slowly from the car into the physio. She's clenching the crutches and only tentatively puts weight on her right leg. My laptop is heavy in my shoulder bag as I move ahead to show her where the ramp is and open the glass door. She enters reception like the Queen of England and stands in the centre of the packed waiting room. There's a young man with a walking stick, and everyone else is geriatric or obese.

Margie is told to take a seat. But she doesn't move and demands to know how long she'll be waiting. I know this is because she wants to be considered important, not because I need to get the application off in six hours.

The receptionist looks at a screen. 'Two before you.'

Margie sniffs and shuffles away to take a seat. She says no to a magazine, but I see a copy of *Women's Weekly* with Kate Middleton's kids on the front and she takes it from me without saying thank you.

With my laptop resting on my knee, I answer the question on the timeline and my proposed touring itinerary. It's an easy question, I finish it and move to the next one.

Margie is called in, and I don't offer to go with her.

Victorian Rural Arts want to know how our theatre group will engage and collaborate with the community and what strategies I'll employ to optimise the investment. Jesus. I read it again and can think of about five ways to answer. I decide to explain who in the district supports us, the publicity we get in the local media and my vision to expand the theatre group through the success of this play.

The physio is looking for me, calling my name. I collapse my laptop and stand up.

He's around sixty, fit-looking, wearing shorts and runners like he's about to go for a jog. He's a good ad for his business. I follow him into his room and he closes the door. Margie is lying on a low bed, flat on her back. She won't be happy.

'What's wrong?' I ask.

'I've just spoken to Margie's surgeon. He wants her to have an X-ray.'

The physio tells me it's to assess how the socket is sitting, that she should have more movement. Her pain is five out of ten and by now should be much less.

There's a lag in my thinking because already we're on our way home: a plan has been unfolding, how I'm going to ask Ross to pick up the kids from the bus and organise dinner so I can finish the application. Margie will not stop me.

'When?'

'They've cleared an appointment. It's at one.'

Margie is silent, listening. Her hands are clasped over her stomach. She knows I need to get home. I hate her. Yet a small voice says, *You did this to yourself. You took her on.*

'Something wrong?' he asks.

'Can we do the X-ray tomorrow?' I say.

His eyes widen like I've asked a stupid question, then he steps back as if to separate himself from my way of thinking.

Already I know I will take her. I see myself doing it, helping her in and out of the car. Of course I will do it. But I want to drop to the floor and cry. Then my thoughts flip the other way and I see that my manic rush to get the funding application in is ludicrous. All this panic for nothing, because we'll get knocked back anyway.

'Margie, let's go,' I say. 'We'll have lunch first.'

She slowly eases herself off the bed.

'I'd like her in a wheelchair,' the physio says, 'until we know what's happening.' He must see in my expression that this is another problem to solve. 'We rent them here. Fourteen dollars a week.'

*

It is much easier getting around with Margie in a wheelchair. She grips the sides as I push her into the Harvest Café and find a table towards the back where I can tuck the wheelchair in. She looks pale and asks for a glass of water. I watch her fumble with the foil blister strip and want to help her, but she keeps it close, not looking at me. She swallows a blue tablet.

This is new for both of us. In the fourteen years I've lived at Maryhill, we've never socialised alone. If I didn't go to her place in Bishop Street when I went to shop in town, I'd never see her. For some reason she separated herself from the farm and has only visited us three times. The first was after Isobel was born; Margie brought a homemade sponge cake and a crocheted blanket with washing instructions pinned in a corner. I never used it because I was afraid I'd ruin it.

Then one year we had a family Christmas, a day that will never be repeated. After drinking a bottle or more of chardonnay,

Caroline raged that Alice Ballantine's sideboard should be hers, that Ross and I have everything 'and I have nothing'. There's some truth in this, but what can I do? Those inheritance decisions weren't made by me. And besides, I like the sideboard. Later that day, I noticed that one of the silver candelabras in the dining room was missing; Caroline's initials were written in the dust beside where it had sat.

The last time Margie came over was when Jemima was eight weeks old. She said she didn't like her name. Two granddaughters twenty-five minutes away and Margie's hardly seen them, except if they were with me when I popped in. Sometimes I think things would be different had Ross and I had a boy, if Harry had lived. The Ballantines always worshipped boys.

I order a chicken salad. Margie asks for the roast of the day and I wonder how long this is going to take. The silence while we wait for our food is killing me, so I gush about the grant application. I describe the questions I'm trying to answer, what the artistic concept is. I hear the intensity and passion in my voice, and I can tell my face is beaming. Margie seems startled. I keep going because I am obsessed and bored and frustrated, telling her and the air between us that Victorian Rural Arts want to know how we plan to capture our audiences.

Then I stop. Because I suddenly remember doing all this before, a long time ago when I met her for the first time. Her mouth is open in exactly the same way. The only question that needs to be answered is, why am I trying to please this cow of a woman?

Our meals are served.

I'm sad, wretched. Tears wet my eyes because I realise we won't get the funding. Time has run out. I need to think, to process this information so I can move on.

She cuts into the lamb.

I move a cashew around in my salad.

Then I hear my voice and am surprised at the kindness, the calm beseeching. 'Margie, do you understand that the play I've been writing for more than thirteen years requires funding? People are counting on me to get the application in. It's due today, and now I'm not going to make the deadline.'

She sighs and pushes roast potato onto her fork.

'Do you understand what I just said?' I ask.

She looks at me, her knife and fork in midair. I want her to see the tears on my face and don't wipe them away.

'I can see it's important to you,' she says. 'But it makes no sense to me. Your floors need vacuuming and a good wash with metho diluted in water. And there are cobwebs and dust in every room.'

She slays me. I lift my face and silently laugh into the café. 'Don't you care about me, Margie?' I wipe my eyes, blow my nose. The table is a small white landscape with salt, pepper, glasses of water, sprigs of flowering rosemary in a small vase. 'What do you care about?'

Margie leans forward. I get a feeling of confidentiality; her mouth is moving as if whispering something too soft for me to hear. I blink in surprise. Her lips tremble. She clasps her hands together. Something seems to terrify her, and it is her turn to cry.

'What's wrong?' I ask.

She quickly dabs her eyes with a serviette. Then pushes the plate away. 'Take me home.'

And I know she means Maryhill, not Bishop Street.

'The X-ray first,' I say.

'I can't bear it.'

'What?' I say.

'Never mind,' she says, but there's childlike pleading or sadness in her tired brown eyes. I reach out and touch her hand, and she doesn't pull away.

*

We wait thirty minutes for the X-ray. I've left my laptop in the car and sit in silence, mulling over the funding questions, still composing answers – but my thinking is perverse because I know it's not going to happen. When I get home I'll send an email to the group. Margie is beside me, asleep in the wheelchair. She looks uncomfortable, her head lolling to the side.

At three we are on our way home in time to get the girls from the bus. I phone Ross and tell him.

'No worries, my darling.' He's forgotten his mother can hear, because after he tells me the truck was on time to pick up the weaners, he says the electric fence energiser 'is completely fucked' – that he'll have to replace the whole unit. 'But I need new chainsaw blades and some fuel, so I'll go to town tomorrow.'

I tell him I've not done the grocery shopping and he'll have to do it.

Down the Hume, I set the cruise control to 110. A police car is behind me, and even though I'm on the limit I slow down. At the Violet Town turn-off, I get a brave idea and pull over; the tyres spit on the gravel and I park under a yellow box. How appropriate.

When I get out of the car, Margie doesn't ask what I'm doing. And I don't say.

I dial and walk away with my phone to my ear. I'm staring back up the freeway – cars dash by, a campervan, a B-double – when I ask the cultural partnership person at Victorian Rural Arts for an extension. We've spoken before: she understands the project, and now she knows that my mother-in-law, who is recovering from a hip operation, has moved in.

'Is it possible?' I ask.

Silence.

'Please,' I beg.

I'm put on hold.

Margie is sitting stiffly in the car, watching me with tight lips.

'We'll give you another twenty-four hours,' the cultural partnership woman says.

Fist in the air. 'Yes!'

Margie

STELLA drives too fast. I glance at the speedo and see we are on the limit, but even so the gum trees and paddocks rush by. On Black Wattle Road a swamp wallaby stares at us from the verge and I expect it to jump towards us, but it turns and disappears. Driving this stretch of winding road from Violet Town to Maryhill is hard work, although Stella's automatic car seems to make the corners easier to deal with. Norman always insisted we drive manuals, even when I had that trouble with my left knee.

The painkiller has done its job; the constant ache in my hip has gone, but the tablet has made me sleepy – or I'm just generally weary from our excursion today.

Stella is happy. Someone has just given her more time to organise the application. She's staring forward, smiling. Her pale hands on the wheel are free of blemishes, the nails short and neat with no polish; they help give her the appearance of a practical person, yet she's not like that. She doesn't have an engagement ring. Her wedding band is gold, wide and studded with rubies – it suits her and I can't explain why, except that it's unconventional.

We're listening to the same woman vocalist as this morning; her mournful voice comes from a speaker somewhere on the dash and fills the car. I hear lyrics about not becoming who she wanted to be and missing her mother. I take those words inside me. They uplift me because whoever the singer is, she understands how I feel.

You'd think at eighty I wouldn't be nostalgic for my mother. Her name was Lillian, and Dad called her 'my-Lily'. Images flit through my mind of her moving around in the Arundel Street house where I grew up. I recall the closeness of her soft body when I sat beside her on the couch. She used to scrub her strong and large hands with lemon juice. When I married and moved to Maryhill, I modelled myself on her industriousness and sometimes pretended she was standing in a corner admiring my work. Sometimes I had to block her out so she wouldn't see things, those times I went to the black cockatoos . . . *see how they're low-flying, five, six, as they land in the wattle branches.* There was that one time I needed medical attention and Mum visited me in hospital. I hoped my practised lie was convincing – that I'd been careless and got myself between a cow and new calf in the home paddock. But her face was flat, a mask, and I knew she guessed my troubles with Norman. I couldn't hold her gaze because there was nothing to be done. She didn't ask any awkward questions and I knew not to tell her. When she left, she patted my arm and I had the feeling she was disappointed in me – as though it was somehow my fault that I was in hospital with a fractured forearm and a bruise to my cheek. She didn't know that the doctor's main concern was my pink urine.

Even so, when Mum left the hospital, I apportioned a share of blame to her – for encouraging me to marry Norman in the first place, and then not rescuing me when she knew I was in trouble.

I breathe my mother away, with love. It's just the way it was.

Coming up on the right is Chester and Laura's place, concealed by an overgrown garden as if they're trying to hide. I know it's a two-bedroom granite house he built with his own hands between 1958 and 1961. And there it is, the hedged row of lilly pillies and the cluster of silver birches; hundreds of snowdrops will appear among them in early spring. I remember that day Chester and I first spoke – at his back door when I was picking up Mark from an after-school visit with Justin. The ground was matted with gold and red leaves from the liquidambar beside the water tank. Autumn and overcast. I was looking up at Chester standing on his back step. 'Why are you wearing sunglasses?' he asked.

Stella is talking to me and it's all such a tangle, and I clasp my hands together and squeeze so they don't tremble like they did in the café at lunchtime. I make a promise to myself never to be weak again.

'How are you feeling?' Stella asks.

I nod to say I'm all right. It still rankles that she knows Chester, that he's involved with her play. It makes no sense to me.

I consider the self-assured way Stella carries herself – staring ahead, thinking, listening, knowing what she's going to do next, and all the time caught up in this theatre interest. Ross loves her, I can tell. And he's made a go of the farm. Freddie would be satisfied with what he's done: rotational grazing and an increase in the stocking rate. The *Weekly Times* says the cattle price is high and I know Ross is shipping heifers to China. I'm not sure about that, but Stella told me the Chinese buyer came to the cattle yards and said the cows were going from one good home to another. I wonder what the Ballantine forefathers would make of that, Maryhill cattle going to China.

Stella pulls up at the corner of Maryhill Road and Marion Road, where the school bus will stop. There's a mat of fallen bark all around, as if the manna gums are shedding skin. When I used to pick up my children, I parked across the road in whichever model of Holden we had at the time. I liked the Premier best; it was the first car we had with air-conditioning. Mark was always off the bus first, looking up, grinning when he saw me. And here I am waiting for Ross's daughters. Time passes so fast, and yet so much has happened. Some wounds never heal, yet I'm tired of it, the regret, and now I don't even know what I'm thinking. Stella is staring into the screen of her phone, not talking but reading. I'm curious to know what, but I won't ask.

The bus arrives. The little girls hurry to the car. Isobel and – I've got her name now – Jemima. The back seat is filled with backpacks and smiling faces, a sort of jumbling, light happiness. Stella chats with them and I don't understand what they're talking about, something to do with India, then I realise it's a girl's name. I turn and smile, and they look at me as if I'm a zoo animal, something to stare at and admire. Then Stella is up the driveway at sixty, a dust storm behind.

The children grab their bags and leave us. Stella is already adept in unfolding the wheelchair and positioning it close to where I need it. She's patient as I gather myself out of the car and sit. Then we're off. She almost runs to the house. From the path I see a couple of dozen green tomatoes drooping from the trellis. It's too late for them to ripen, but they'd make up beautifully into a relish. I won't mention it; Stella's not the relish-making type. And there's washing on the line that was there yesterday and it'll be dry by now.

It's too difficult to manoeuvre the wheelchair inside the house, over the step from the back porch into the dining room, then past the narrow turn that leads to my storeroom bedroom. I return to the crutches and move slowly to a dinner-table chair. The girls quickly disappear to the back of the house with mini packets of shop-bought biscuits. Jemima is holding Dot's cat in her arms, close to her face – while eating. Stella makes us tea and then vanishes into the old dining room, carrying her mug and phone, her enormous bag over her shoulder. I watch the door sway behind her. Faint tapping of piano scales comes from the front room.

I am alone. All around are the stirred-up ghosts of my past. It's Chester who's done it. At his back door. The liquidambar's gold and red leaves at my feet. I was looking up as he carefully reached forward with both hands – his watchband was brown leather – and lifted my sunglasses away.

The way his mouth moved, as if he, himself, were in pain. 'Who did this?'

His voice was very quiet.

But I didn't tell.

The muted sound of Isobel practising piano, a faltering classical piece difficult to recognise at this end of the house. Her hands, green fingernails, flitting and pausing across the keyboard. I'd like to wander up there to watch and hear properly, but I'm distracted by my bladder. The idea of standing and finding my way to the toilet feels too difficult; nonetheless, I must act. I lift myself up, struggle with the crutches and launch myself towards the bathroom.

It is only four in the afternoon with two or more hours before dinner. After the bathroom I ease myself onto my bed and pick up the Maggie Smith biography. I open the cover. And blink. It's a month overdue for return to the library and I now can't concentrate on it. The book must be returned without delay.

A cobweb is dangling in the corner of the room and it reminds me of how useless I am. Once I would've taken a swing at it with the broom.

Then the call of a red wattlebird in the maple, and I lean back against the pillows to enjoy it.

I'm surprised to discover I've napped; a whole blessed hour has passed all by itself. There are voices in the dining room. Ross is inside. I sit up.

'How's it going?' Ross says to me when I appear at the family-room door.

It's too big a question because I have a lot to explain to him and don't know where to start. The cat. The overdue library book. The dust in the house and the cobweb in my room. The hard mattress on my bed. The unsatisfactory meals. The condition of the garden, the unmown lawns, the weeds in the vegetable boxes. The dry washing on the clothesline. He has no idea I'm a prisoner to my disability.

He turns away before I answer, announcing he's having a shower before dinner.

What dinner? Stella, I assume, is still behind the closed dining-room door. The girls are now sitting orphan-like, gaping at the television.

I sit and watch the clock. Time moves slowly and there is no movement in the kitchen. Sometimes I hear Stella on the phone, short conversations. The cat is staring at me from the couch. I look away, disturbed by its presence.

Finally, Stella slaps the swing door open and moves around the kitchen. The gas lights, the fridge door opens and closes, the toaster pops. A handful of cutlery is dumped in the middle of the table. Ross takes the newspapers and drops them on a chair. As though she's still waitressing in a restaurant, Stella neatly serves three plates at once: scrambled eggs and toast. She's added too much milk to the egg, but I pretend not to notice. She does everything too fast, doesn't measure anything. I glance between Ross and Stella and it confirms what I think: Ross isn't happy with the way the house is run, yet she does as she pleases.

Even though the eggs are quite terrible, I decide to be positive and ask Ross if he remembers the chickens we once had.

He barely looks at me. 'Yes,' he says.

'And the rooster, like the one on the Kellogg's Corn Flakes packet.' I smile, trying to engage my son in conversation.

'No,' he says. 'I don't remember that we ever had a rooster.'

I decide not to go into it, the details on how his dog got into the pen and injured the bird's wing.

I put more salt on the soggy eggs. The girls niggle each other, and I can't understand why. Ross opens his iPad and I think that is very bad manners, but he's obsessed with the weather, always searching for rain as if the radar will perform a miracle. Jemima lets out a pink open-mouthed wail, saying her sister has stolen her favourite horse swap card. Stella glares at Isobel and I can hardly bear all this carry-on.

'Stell,' Ross says, 'it won't be too hot in the yards tomorrow.'

She looks blankly at him.

'Pregnancy testing the spring calvers,' he says. 'The vet's coming.'

I understand the problem.

A moment passes.

'I'm not helping in the yards, Ross.'

My son leans back in his chair, frowning. He's about to say something, but Stella is quickly on her feet, an overly dramatic gesture, and we all stare at her.

'I've got twenty-four hours to get this thing done,' she declares. 'So. I'm letting you all know that under no circumstances am I to be interrupted until further notice. Isobel and Jem, you're old enough to get yourselves to bed. And Ross, I won't be helping with the preg testing or getting our children off to school in the morning. Whatever emergency occurs on this property, I will not know about it. And another thing, my darling' – she points at him – 'attend to your mother because from this moment on, I am unavailable to you all until the submission is uploaded.'

I bite my bottom lip and glance around to find something else to look at. Never have I heard anything like it.

Jemima says, 'Mum, but –'

Stella raises her hand. 'Tell your father.' And she turns and heads to the dining room.

Ross flicks his iPad cover shut. He slowly stands and follows her.

The shape of his body, the line of his shoulders. Ross is taller, but it could be Norman walking away from me.

The swing door closes behind him.

I look at the girls and they shyly look back. Jemima giggles, rushes from the table, plonks herself on the couch, opens her iPad and stares deeply into the screen. I am thinking of what to say to Isobel when she stands up, telling me she's going to the piano. She does play a lot; it seems a bit unnatural.

Ross and Stella must be having one of those whispering fights because I can't hear anything. Stella is in the wrong. This carry-on with the play isn't going to pay any bills. And now Ross, at the last minute, is left without help.

From my sitting position, I lean across the table and gather up the plates.

Then Ross is back in the room. I try to read his face: he's tight-jawed, definitely unsmiling.

'Have you had enough to eat?' he asks.

'Perhaps some toast. Is there any jam?'

There is no jam, only Vegemite and peanut butter.

Quince and apricot jams are my favourites. I've noticed the quince tree near the laundry has gone to the pack, infested with cherry slug and unpruned. I used to get on with things early, always up with the sun rising behind Mount Glencoe. Sunrises are quite beautiful here and it's been a very long time since I've seen one. I resolve to get up early and sit outside in the court-yard to watch the dawn arrive. I'll have a little conversation with Dot; sometimes I still think of the cruise we were planning and where we might be if she were still alive, which country we would be at now. And I'll think of Chester – that dry kiss in the hospital, his touch on my back the other night. It is true that Laura has more than her dead son to hold against me.

'What time is sunrise tomorrow?' I ask Ross.

'Why?'

'Just a question.'

He looks at his iPad. 'Six thirty-five.'

'Goodnight,' I say.

'It's only seven-thirty.'

'Doesn't matter.'

'You right there?' he asks, but he makes no attempt to lend assistance as I push up from the chair to my crutches.

'I'm perfectly fine.'

And I refuse his offer of a cup of tea, yet I would like one very much. I'm being contrary, but suddenly it is more important to get away from them all. From Stella's little speech ordering Ross to look after me. I hate it here, but don't know where else I want to be.

I recall the question Stella asked me at lunch in the café: 'Do you care about me?' And my tearful and devastating realisation – she is the only person concerned for me. Not Caroline. Not Ross, sitting there with his head in his iPad before I've even left the room.

I shut the bedroom door behind me and exhale with the utter relief of being in the sanctity of my own private space. It exhausts me to undress; the cautious way I have to move to protect my hip wears me down. I lift myself into bed thinking it would be convenient for everyone if I died. Yet I reach to the bedside table and take my rainbow of tablets: orange for blood pressure, yellow for arrhythmia, white for cholesterol and blue for pain.

Outside is the trilling call of a willie wagtail. And there are magpies too, four or five. The room is too light and I cannot sleep. It isn't hot or cold and I'm comfortable enough in the storeroom. I listen to the birds while staring into the ceiling, the hideous paper-and-wire light fitting. A white-browed scrub-wren has joined the choir. I drift away to the memory of a dark olive-brown woollen coat my mother made for me – the same colour as the wren. She adapted the pattern and gave it a belt, and a Cossack collar so I didn't have to bother with a scarf. My mother was full of surprises like that.

Stella

ROSS comes into the dining room and sits on the chaise lounge. Its green silk upholstery is two-toned because the afternoon light has bleached the lower end to nothing. He tells me the girls are asleep, and when I ask him about his mother he says she went to bed at seven-thirty.

'Did she take her tablets?'

He shrugs.

'You need to take more interest.'

'She said she was fine.'

'When she says that, she doesn't mean it.'

'If someone says they're fine, they're fine.'

He's drinking a beer, leaning back. I go and sit with him and he hands me the bottle. I take a mouthful.

He puts his arm around me. 'How's it going?'

'Crap. I'm exaggerating everything.'

'You'll be right.'

'Were you able to change the preg testing?' I ask.

'Now next Tuesday. No drama.' He takes the beer back. 'When are you coming to bed?'

'Don't know.'

'Can I get you anything?'

'Don't think so.'

He kisses my hair and stands. 'Night, babe.'

I'm left on my own with the staring dark eyes of the portraits. I love this room; its faded beauty feeds my imagination. It's a creative space like the old Robinson Street bakery, with those crumbling brick ovens, the floorboards that had carried a million feet.

I look around and imagine the Ballantines in their party garb, someone tapping a cigarette in the silver ashtray. Laughter; people holding glasses of wine. The fires roaring with split red box. But I'm not actually sure they were that cheerful – not if Margie and Caroline are anything to go by. In the end, though, it doesn't matter. I think we all pretty much want the same things: to be loved and have a special place.

I light the candles in a five-pronged silver candelabra – the one that Caroline didn't take – and place it on the table. I re-read and edit my answers before moving on to the question about the long-term outcomes of the project. That's easy: I want the Yellow Box Players to go on forever.

When I moved here from Melbourne in the winter of 2002, I was lonely but also happy to be with Ross all the time. We'd been miserable each time he'd left my place in Brunswick to come back to this farm that I'd never really seen and could hardly understand. That first winter, he showed it to me. Instead of taking the quad bike, we walked. Rugged up in coats, gloves and a double layer of socks in our boots, and with the chill on our pink faces, we tramped the paddocks, over rocks, through fences, across the creek. We sat and ate sandwiches, drank hot tea from a thermos and watched the cattle grazing with white frost on their backs, the rising mist and lacy clouds drifting slowly along the vast open sky. We checked pregnant cows, some with new calves standing on wobbly legs and nudging along their mum's belly, looking for their first drink.

I was pregnant too, with Isobel. She was born in the middle of October, just as the first perfect roses were blooming, and the rhododendrons and azaleas were out. It was then, being a mother, that I felt like I belonged at Maryhill; that I wasn't just Ross's live-in lover. I didn't change my name – I'll always be Stella Adams – but living in the big old house, walking down the hallways and entering the large rooms with a baby in my arms, it was like I was in the company of the other Ballantine mothers that had done what I was now doing. And yet, in all of the goodness, I missed the theatre, the process of creating something from inside myself.

In the few years I had been with the Robinson Street Theatre Group, I'd wanted to advance my career: do bigger productions, establish a reputation for myself, even work in London or New York theatre. But it didn't happen. Perhaps it was about timing. Because after I met Ross, in a way there was no choice to be made. He was the laid-back guy sitting in Dudley's All Day on his own, nursing a house lager, watching me. As his waitress, I asked if he wanted something to eat. I told him the daily specials. 'The lentil hamburger,' he said. Not quite love at first sight, but there was something different about him, and when my shift was finished and we went around the corner to the Lex Bar, I found out he really was different. A cattle farmer. I'd never met a farmer before, let alone one who ate lentils.

And so, with Isobel in the bouncer at my feet, I set up camp in the old dining room and starting writing *I Did My Best*, a story I'd been wanting to explore and tell since Mum died. I'd never written anything before, only ever produced and directed other people's work. It was a private thing, in a private space: an abandoned chandeliered room in an ancient house, on a three-thousand-acre farm, two hundred kilometres north-east of Melbourne.

It's after midnight when I answer the last funding question. Then I start going through CDs and photos of old performances, trying to work out which support material will make an impression. I re-read my CV, hoping it will impress them. The wind has picked up; the trees make a hushing noise – I could be close to the sea, hearing waves falling onto a beach. It's chilly and I drape the throw rug over my shoulders.

At 2 am I give in to tiredness. The chaise lounge is soft and comfy. I've slept on it before, sneaking a daytime nap in between jobs, kids and Ross. I turn off the lights, blow out the candles, lay the rug over me and sleep.

Carolling magpies wake me. I'm cold and stiff and go to the kitchen to make coffee. Diva is mewling at the back door, so I let her out. There's been a light rain, or perhaps it's dew. The birds are waking and I imagine them in the trees, nests, branches. The sun is rising; slashes of iridescent pink are cresting over Mount Glencoe. I put on Ross's coat and leave the house to bask in the solitude and watch the sky. The coffee mug warms my hands.

The sandstone path has cracks; moss grows in them. A long stem of dill pushes between the pavers and rock borders. Pink geraniums clash with red. The lavender is ragged. Hydrangeas droop and are yellowing from lack of water. It's been a dry summer, but these past weeks the weather has been turning. Ross is waiting for the autumn break when we'll get a good few inches to kickstart the pasture growth. I lean into a dark pink rose; the perfume is intense.

When I look up, I see Margie. She's sitting on the stone bench; the crutches are on the ground beside her. She's staring ahead, dressed in trackpants and only a light cardigan. She looks thin, the way she's hugging into herself to keep warm. She shifts her weight and I wonder about her pain.

She doesn't hear me approach. I take off Ross's coat.

She turns to me and speaks like we're in church, hushed. 'What're you doing out here?'

I reply the same way. 'I saw the sunrise from the back door and came for a better look.'

I tell her it's Ross's coat I'm draping over her shoulders because I know then she won't reject it. I sit beside her and we look forward. The whole sky appears water-coloured pink, grey and silver, and the sun's globe is gold. In the foreground are the ragged and overgrown vegetable boxes. A walnut and chestnut tree. Brown fairy-wrens dart between a tomato trellis and mildewed zucchini leaves. The basil has gone to seed.

I sip the coffee and am cold.

'Are you okay?' I ask.

'Not really.'

It's because it's quiet and beautiful and we are both looking forward – and because she's so desperately lonely – that she is speaking to me this way.

I say, 'I'm sorry that I'm so busy with the funding. It's boring for you, I know.'

'In some ways I admire you,' she says.

I'm stunned to hear this and want to ask why, but hesitate.

'Norman wasn't an easy man to live with.'

'In what way?' I ask, bracing at this first intimacy between us.

'He was demanding. Things had to be done his way.'

I press the coffee mug to my face, and we're both still looking ahead as if we'll break a spell if we turn and face each other.

'What if it wasn't done his way?' I ask.

'He'd get angry.'

Then she does turn to me, a direct, defiant gaze from her sad brown eyes. Ageing is a curiosity to me – I see it beginning in my own face – and I notice how Margie's sagging skin has formed wrinkles, especially around her eyes. The lines that moulded her features have worn into deep creases. I wait for her to say something, but all she does is glare at me, and I know she is telling me not ask her any more questions.

When she reaches down for the crutches, Ross's coat falls off her shoulders.

'Put it on,' I say.

'No, I'll go in now.'

I put the coat on and follow her up the path. At the step into the back porch, she holds on to the doorframe and struggles to pull herself up. She doesn't shy away or flinch when I lean forward to help her balance. The house is quiet; everyone else is still asleep. As she walks across the floorboards, the rubber stoppers on her crutches make an uneven and muted clomping noise. She closes her bedroom door softly.

I find Ross on his side, an arm exposed. His tattoo says something I don't think he agrees with now. It was an impulsive holiday thing and at least looks good: *All that I have to learn is within me*. He always sleeps so well – deeply, for hours of peaceful unconsciousness. I undress, lift the doona and climb in. Even in sleep he opens his arms for me.

Margie

IN my bedroom I turn many circles with the crutches. I sigh, squeeze my eyes shut and shake my fist. It is all rubbish. At my age. You'd think the struggle would be over, yet I'm in the frontlines, battling life. It never ends.

Fully dressed, I drag my body into bed, swallow two blue tablets and pull the blankets over me. The light coming through the hessian curtains is bright, but when I shut my eyes it's dark. I am determined to return to sleep, to fill time, to never wake up – or wake up to something different to this.

And I do.

There's a firm knock at my door.

'Margie?' Stella opens the door, hesitant as if walking into a cave. 'It's ten. And you're still sleeping.'

I blink and stare up at her face. She's too close and I pull back into the pillows. Even at this time of day she is wearing perfume, jasmine or lavender.

She opens the curtains then stands back, arms folded, and waits for me to sit up. 'Are you okay? Would you like breakfast in bed?'

She has hit a note: the luxury of breakfast in bed. I've only had it in hospital, yet I remember my mother sitting up with a pale-green tray, metal legs splayed across her legs, the dome of an egg in a cup, dry toast, a small pot of tea. Dad would say, 'Here you are, my-Lily.'

'No,' I say to Stella.

'Bad luck. I've already got the tray sorted. So stay put.'

But she doesn't leave and I stare at her.

'I've had two phone calls,' she says. 'One from the physio to say the X-rays were all normal and that you can now use the walker and resume your exercises.'

She pauses. I sit up.

'The rehab hospital in Wangaratta also called. They've got a place for you. I said I'd ask you. But they can only hold it till one this afternoon.'

I clench my teeth to keep my face still, to hide my shock and disappointment. Yet already I see myself there: the room is white and plain, with no adornments; it's a hybrid hotel room for people like me. The staff will be kind as they come and go from the room. I will be served scones and jam, shiny apples – better food than here – by cheerful people with dark skin.

'You don't have to go,' Stella says. 'When this funding crap is out of the way, I'll be able to pay you more attention.'

I don't like her free language, or want her charity or permission to live here in this house. So I will go to rehab. I feel something shrink – hope, happiness – that I know will never return. I close my eyes to stop the welling of tears.

'I know you're lonely, Margie. We've had stuff between us, but I think you should stay here. Ross will accept it. I'll talk to him.'

So that's it. My son is not happy with me being here. I am his needy, sad old mother. I will resign myself. Rehab first, then back to Bishop Street.

'I will take the bed at rehab,' I say.

'That's bullshit, Margie. You don't want to go.'

'I don't like your swearing.'

She smiles. 'Come on, Margie, say you'll stay.'

'Ross doesn't want me here.'

She sighs and shrugs, as if to say, *What can I do*?

'I think I should go, yes. Tell them.'

And suddenly it is a relief; I can see the freedom, the detachment; no expectations. There are advantages in being alone – you don't have to try.

'I want you to stay,' Stella says.

I shake my head.

'This is your home.'

'Not anymore.'

Stella looks tall from where I am in bed. 'I'm not letting you go to some sterile hospital when we can work things out here,' she says. 'I'm just crazy-busy until five today. But after that, it's you and me. Will I tell them you're coming or not?'

I will not tell her I want to stay. So I say nothing.

I push my legs over the edge of the bed. My feet don't quite touch the floor. I see the pilled ugly trackpants; how baggy they are.

'Margie?' she says softly. 'Tell me what you really want to do.'

'You decide. You're in charge, not me.'

'Okay.'

And she turns and leaves me, and I sit dumbfounded, unsure if I'm going or staying. Or if she's forgotten her offer to bring me breakfast in bed.

Stella

ROSS is a big lump on my dining chair and won't move. He is proofreading the application and working too slowly. Whenever he sees something, he asks me questions – annoying things like checking I have the ABN right. We've only got thirty minutes to upload and I can't handle it.

'Get off my bloody chair,' I say.

'Settle down.'

'It's my application.'

'You asked me to do this.'

'But not this slow.'

'You want it done properly?'

My breath is short; I'm tense.

'Go and find something else to do,' he says.

But I don't leave. I sit beside him, my hands flat between my legs, leaning in, watching.

He works through the pages, checking I've filled the required fields. He skips the irrelevant pages – I'm not Indigenous or working with an auspicing organisation. He reads the project summary and gives me a wink. 'I'll be going to this little show,' he says, then asks, 'Why do they want to know which federal electorate we're in, when it's state funding?'

'Beats me,' I say.

'Isn't Amber only seventeen?' he asks. 'Do you have a Working With Children Check?'

'She'll be eighteen by the time the production is on.'

'It's bullshit, all this suspicion.' He puts his arm around my waist and pulls me in as he scrolls down the budget template. It's balanced and too late to change anything now.

I frown. 'I've spoken to them and explained I'm uncertain about the marketing costs. I've put in five thousand, but I think it's too much.'

My arm is across his shoulder, and we're both staring at the screen, like we're expecting a tragedy, or a good ending – neither of us knows. He sees I've got every member of the theatre group's CV, the references from the council, the confirmation from the Benalla Town Hall where the performances will be held, what is donated in-kind and what is to be paid for. There is nothing Victorian Rural Arts will not know about his project. The detail is professional, yet extraordinarily bureaucratic.

'We're done,' Ross says.

He lifts himself out of my chair. And I sit. He stands back and watches me upload the application, the written proposal, budget, MP3 files, photos, support letters. It's all there.

We glance at each other. 'Send it,' he says.

The curser over *Send*. I click the mouse.

The internet isn't too bad today. We watch the upload. It takes less than five minutes, which is good for here.

'Call them,' he says. 'Tell them you've sent it. So they don't ignore it because it's late.'

So I do. And am told they can see it. I want some reaction, a hint that I will be successful, but I'm off the phone in a few seconds. I don't know exactly when I can expect to hear back.

'A coffee would be good,' Ross says.

I glare at him.

'You're in with a chance. Now go and make coffee.'

I grind beans then froth milk in a metal jug until I can't bear the heat on my hand. When it comes to coffee, I'm still a waitress in this house. I can do ferns and love hearts with the crema. Once I did a teardrop to let Ross know I was upset about something, and he pulled me onto his lap and let me talk through the problem. He says my lattes are the best, that he can't do them himself, yet I've never seen him try. But I don't mind; it's all part of the things we do – most days he makes our bed, and once a week he changes all the sheets and puts them through the wash. And he cooks half the time: mostly barbecues, although he does a good lamb roast.

Ross opens the dining-room door to the courtyard. I'm holding two mugs and teaspoons. We sit on the concrete bench. A Manchurian pear is turning, but only on the west-facing side where it gets the afternoon sun, so there's a panel of red among green, sparkling gold leaves at the top. The sun is warm and the sky is high; a few thin clouds are scattered. A helicopter is droning far away, getting closer. We look up and wait. I can't see it – the sound is confusing, it's everywhere, and not where Ross points. Then I see it, now passing high over the blue spruce, the rotors a dark, gauzy circle. I turn away before Ross does.

'Ambulance,' he says. I think of the accident that's happened somewhere to cause this emergency flight to Melbourne. And I bet Ross is thinking he'd love to be up there flying it. He knows the chopper model, everything about it.

Hospitals and patients – and I remember the call from rehab in Wangaratta. 'They said they had a bed for your mum.'

Ross nods, good.

'I spoke to her,' I say. 'She's staying here.'

He jerks around to face me. 'Don't be bats. Of course she's bloody well going.'

'No. I've spoken to her.'

'What the hell? Why didn't you speak to me? We'll never get rid of her.'

'It's till she gets better and can look after herself.'

'How long?'

'What's it to you? I'm the one who runs around after her.'

'Stell,' he says. I'm looking at his lovely face; he's got the first show of grey in his sideburns. Behind him is a soft pink rose with dense layers of petals; a butterfly flits by. 'Because she judges everything here. She's always belittled you and she does it now. And I can't stand the way she's always looking around. She hates our food. She hates the way we live.'

'Margie hates everything.'

'Then what the hell?' He raises his hands.

'She's got no one, Ross.'

He starts scraping the inside of his mug with the teaspoon to get the last of the froth.

'She told me your dad wasn't easy to live with. That she had to do things his way to keep the peace. What's that about?'

'I'm not going there,' he says.

'Tell me, I want to know.' My voice is hard, impatient – because he's still scratching the inside of his mug with the bloody teaspoon and it drives me crazy.

'Why are we even talking about this shit?' he asks.

It is the rolling of rubber on wood, or the hard puff of breath, that makes me turn. Margie is hurrying away, pushing the wheelie walker. Flat grey hair, the leaning line of her spine, her orange cardigan. In her haste to cross the veranda to the front door, she limps badly. Wisteria drapes along the eaves, its new shoots spring outward and its trunk winds around the post;

for more than a century they've forged into one strength, together holding up the veranda.

I hear the slap of the wire door.

'She heard us,' I say.

'I can't believe you knocked back the bed at rehab.'

'We should be looking after her.'

'Stell, you're not listening. She's better off with the professionals looking after her. Not you. And you've got to get on with all the work producing the play.'

'I don't like you for this.'

Ross stands. 'What the hell have I done?'

I stand too. 'I want you to go and sort this out with her, Ross. Tell her you want her to stay.'

'But I don't want her to stay.'

He has that defiant look – it's the shift of his eyes – and something seems to tighten inside him, making him taller, harder and indifferent. He puts his coffee mug on the bench and walks away. He will go down to the shed, or a paddock, to do some hard-jawed job that will fill his mind until he has reasoned all the arguments, and only then will we be able to talk.

*

Margie is sitting in the centre of her room on the wheelie walker's chair. The white paper-and-wire globe – bigger than a beach ball – is right above her head. Originally, I had thought this room would be a good place for me to write my play; its proximity to the kitchen and family room meant I could hear what was going on. But the dining room kept drawing me back. That space felt better. So even though I'd gone to the trouble of painting it, putting the light fitting up that I'd had in my Brunswick bedroom, I didn't like the vibe in here.

Margie has one arm behind her as if to relieve pain in her back. Her lips are tight.

There's nothing for it, so I ask her if she heard our conversation.

She dismisses me, a wave of her hand. 'Call the Wangaratta rehab people,' she says, 'and arrange for me to go. I don't want to stay another minute here. It was an error of judgement on my behalf to come in the first place. I don't fit into this household, not at all.'

'Margie –'

She raises the palm of her hand. 'Don't. Just call.'

I can't see a solution. She is hurt and determined, and if I was her I'd be the same.

My phone is in my pocket. I dial. The rehab administrator answers, and I explain that Margie has changed her mind and would now like to take the vacant bed.

There is a pause. I glance at Margie. Her eyes are wide, staring, waiting.

I'm told the bed has already been taken. I shake my head. 'Okay,' I say to the administrator, who tells me that he doesn't know when another bed will be available. But there are some in Albury, or something can be found in Melbourne. And if it's an emergency, the local hospital will possibly be able to receive her.

When I hang up, I tell Margie what I know. 'I'm not driving you two hours to Albury,' I say, 'or two hours to Melbourne when you've got a perfectly good bed here. The funding application has gone through. I can now look after you properly.'

She stares at the dull oak floorboards. Then slowly turns to the window as if she's heard something.

Margie

THERE'S an eastern rosella outside in the Japanese maple. Its song is quite different from that of the crimson rosella, but for years I had them confused. And I had the king parrot mixed up with them as well. The problem wasn't in identifying the species, but in connecting each song to the right bird because they must be sighted while singing.

I used to study birds while gardening: their voices, habits, breeding. I read various bird books and wrote my own lengthy notes. It was a private daily ritual to record what birdlife I'd seen in the garden each day.

Stella is leaning against the doorframe. She has a predicament; we all have a predicament. But I will not do what I feel like doing – implore her to let me stay. I am practised at controlling rage and despair. I've got decades of experience at holding it in, swallowing, feeling its weight in my chest, forcing myself to breathe. Early on in my marriage to Norman, I discovered that walking fast everywhere – doing my daily housework, gardening, meals, laundry – I could somehow escape my problems; that while I stayed on the move, my thoughts and feelings were hard to catch because I was distracted, I was busy.

But that is irrelevant and no use. I cannot move quickly anymore.

Ross is a disappointment. In fact, the whole business of motherhood has worn me down. Mark is dead. Caroline rarely calls me. And here I am, beholden to this woman who's wearing jeans with holes in them and a jumper that is too big for her, the neck falling over one porcelain shoulder.

My life has come to this. I feel my breath; it's even and shallow. I lick my lips and shift my weight in the seat. If this is a fight, I have no strength and few options.

I deliver my message to Stella. 'Tell Ross that in order to stay out of his way, I will not leave this room, except to use the bathroom, until another bed becomes available in Wangaratta. And I want your word that when that happens, you'll take me there immediately.'

'That's ridiculous, Margie. You can't lock yourself up in here. I think we all just need to chill out and take one day at a time. And don't worry about Ross.'

I will not be counselled by her. So I stand and twist around and push myself to the bed.

'This library book is overdue,' I say, pointing at Maggie Smith's face on the bedside table.

I hate these dramatics. Stella watches me sit down, swing my legs around and push back against the pillows. The sheets could do with changing, but I don't mention it. I lean forward and pull the bedding over me. And there: I'm in bed and here I will stay.

I close my eyes to let her know she is blocked out; for me she's not in the room. I wait for her footfall, the click of the door closing, but there's silence. Minutes pass and I'm sure she has somehow gone without making a sound, but when I open my eyes she's standing there with her arms crossed, looking out the window.

'I'll give the room a vac and quick dust,' she says. 'It'll be nicer in here for you. And maybe if I change the position of the bed, you could see out the window into the garden.' Then she looks at me, a shift in energy; her voice changes. 'Actually, I was going to put you in the other guestroom, Mark's old room – it's bigger and much nicer than in here. But I thought it might be upsetting for you. I've painted it and changed it around, and if you'd like I can move you in there now. The bed is queen-size and you'd be looking out at the climbing rose, and there's a really nice shade tree. You'd see the birds, not just hear them. Would you like that? It's quieter than in here and closer to the bathroom.'

I turn my head to face the wall. The idea of Mark's bedroom touches me greatly, that special place, and I cannot think of anywhere else I would rather be.

'Well?' She is looking at me, bending down. The neck of her jumper gapes; I see the soft sponge of her breasts above the cup of a hot-pink bra. She should notice this herself, pull it back and straighten up. But she is touching my hand.

I curl my fingers away. I don't want to be touched; even after her kindness I want to uphold a semblance of dignity, some poise, which only the appearance of aloofness provides. But she must see through me. She passes me a tissue so I can wipe my eyes. My tears are leaky and tepid, and I had not properly felt them, but there they are. I blow my nose.

A few minutes later, Stella brings me a mug of tea and a biscuit. She is hurrying, doesn't speak, just puts it on the bedside table with *The Weekly Times*. 'Give me half an hour,' she says. 'I'll make up the bed and give the room a quick going-over.'

And as she's leaving, I hear myself, so quiet and pathetically defiant. 'I still want to go to rehab.'

Then she is away. I hear the hum of the vacuum cleaner, but not for very long, not enough for a good going-over.

There is another bird calling now, too distant to properly hear. But if I had to guess, I'd say a black-faced cuckoo-shrike.

Jemima comes in and announces that the spare bedroom is ready.

'Good,' I say. 'Did you know this used to be my storeroom?'

'What did you store in here?'

'Bottled fruit and preserves.'

'What's preserves?'

I tell her, but she just stares at me as if I'm making it up.

'We didn't go to the shops like people do today,' I say.

'Why?'

It gets tedious, all this explaining. 'Never mind.'

I push the walker down the hallway. Ross is probably outside, but just in case he's somewhere in the house, I move as fast as I can manage. The floors are a disgrace, so I look up. The cornices have always been pretty, a design of leafy swirls – they need repainting, everything does; it was overdue even when I was a permanent resident here. And that's what is obvious to me: how much money and work is required to preserve an old place like this.

Stella and Ross's bedroom door is wide open. Of course, I know the room very well and don't want the memories, not now, not ever. I'm surprised to see that the old fireplace is exposed, with its scalloped oak mantel and inlaid ceramic brown tiles. The oil heater I put in after Norman died has been removed, the plaster pulled away, yet some of it remains as if deliberately cut into a curved shape. Whoever did this, it's not a good job. Their bed is unmade; a white doona plumps like a cloud. There are clothes on the floor. Shoes scattered.

I keep pushing myself down the long hallway, past the girls' rooms. The front door is ahead, panelled in red and green stained glass. I turn left.

Mark's bedroom is now the colour of avocado dip: a little too dark, perhaps, but the cream above the picture rail is a good contrast. The frayed fawn and crimson Persian rug that fills the large space between the bed and wardrobe was always in the family room, at the end where the television stands now. I find it disconcerting to notice things that have been moved around, as though I'm always trying to solve a puzzle. I recognise a green-cushioned cane chair from the enclosed front veranda and a glass-top table I've never seen before, with a lamp and an empty vase sitting in the centre. The double windows are open and the lace curtain puffs into the room with the breeze. The bed is against the back wall with a direct view outside. It is quite different to when Mark slept here, but similar enough. I lie on the crisp sheets and prop myself up on the pillows. It's quiet here, at the front of the house.

I exhale, and smile.

The piano starts.

My room shares a wall with the front room. The *tick-tock* of a metronome, and Isobel's fingers are racing through scales and arpeggios. Up and down the keys, the tempo increases. I'd not thought of this; perhaps Stella didn't either. The noise will disturb my peace and pleasure at being in this lovely private part of the house.

Isobel keeps playing without seeming to tire. I'm anxious and clench my jaw. When I was about her age I had piano lessons for a short while, but I don't have good memories of them: the teacher's stained teeth, gasping at my errors as she leaned forward and scrawled lead pencil on the sheet music, her little dog on her lap.

Isobel plays something classical, slow and even – the sound is wonderful – then shifts to a lower key and the mood of the piece makes me breathe in. Lower and higher notes together, and I close my eyes and think of birds. The tempo seems perfect, and she goes on and on.

A little trill and she stops. There is silence, and I'd like her to play it again.

And she does. I imagine her green-polished fingernails; her fingers seem to find the notes easily. I wouldn't have thought it was possible for anyone to play so well at her age. Tears come to my eyes again, and it occurs to me I'm emotional today. I dab my eyes and press, as if to stop bleeding. I've underestimated this child and incorrectly judged her because she's aloof. Perhaps she is like me, the way I separate myself as a way of protecting against anything I don't know or understand.

She is playing something else now; it's very slow, and I wonder if perhaps she's staring at the music, working it out. It's 'Ave Maria', I realise, and I'm pleased. She plays it too deliberately.

'Hi, Nan.'

Jemima is standing in my doorway, grinning, that shock of red hair.

I can hardly tell her to go away, so I smile.

'Look,' she says, coming to me. She opens the cover on her iPad, presses a button at the bottom, and the screen comes to life with a rocket moving in outer space, then a cartoon man walking in the air.

'What have you got this time?' I ask.

'An app that explains how the universe works.' She puts the iPad on my lap and tells me to 'have a go'. She's tried this before and I don't know why she persists.

'No, thank you.'

Her fingers are moving on the screen – as her sister's are moving across the piano keys through the wall – fast, with purpose. Planets spin and move. 'I'm making a solar system.'

'That's enough, pet.'

'Dad says you're negative,' Jemima tells me, sidling along the bed; she gives me a sly glance because she knows she's saying the wrong thing.

A burst of rising heat. I'm humiliated because a child is admonishing me.

But it is the unfairness of that comment that hits its mark. My son has been talking about me to his children. Stella will be in on this, too. And so judgement never ends, even at eighty. This isn't a surprise, of course. I just want to know when it's safe to be old and accepted for being flawed, stupid and human. For doing my best. I'm well past expecting anyone to acknowledge the effort and struggle. The several decades of work: the meals, bed-making, laundry, cleaning, running around – all of it while coping with Norman's peculiar personality and the cruelty he was prone to. How I've suffered, the secrets I have, the trap I've lived in – wanting to be me and never getting the chance. And the wash-up is I'm a negative person.

'Perhaps you've got something else to do now,' I say.

'And he says you take no interest in us.'

'In whom?'

'Me and Isobel.'

'Off you go now.'

She moves slowly; the flick of the iPad cover, a step and twirl, and she backs out of the room, looking at me as if daring me to say something. The little brat, but I admire her spunk.

I feel my weary old bones on the mattress. Through the window the gleditsia gently sways with the breeze. I planted it in the winter of 1986 on the first anniversary of Mark's death. No one else knows about this: it is my private memorial to him. It's a good tree selection because it provides shade in the summer and lets light into the room in winter. Shoots from the pink climbing rose along the veranda need cutting back.

I listen for birds, but it's Isobel I hear. She's playing a new piece, something familiar, and I vaguely think of a television advertisement, but can't quite place what for – perhaps a car or aeroplane. I hear a rising chorus, and see autumn leaves and flying swans. And then I remember a long time ago, in spring, when I spotted a lone black swan in the north dam. It stayed for about a month, then one day it was gone.

Stella

I'M walking along the dirt laneway that cuts through the property and ends at the cattle yards. Dust puffs from under my workboots. The tall dead tree on my right always reminds me of a statuesque mannequin wearing a skin-tight silvery dress; the black crimping around the hem is from a fire she survived. A branch is stretched upward as if she's in a jazz bar posing with a cigarette in a holder. One day the wind will push her to the ground, or she'll just collapse because it's her time – and if the borers haven't eaten her insides, then Ross will cut her up with the chainsaw and we'll feed her to the fire. There's enough wood in her to keep us warm for a whole year.

The track is dry, in parts deeply rutted from decades of cattle treading single lines that have been made worse by rain. Tufts of grass poke up here and there and along the fence line, especially at the base of every star picket. There are dry cow pats, dandelions, a broken bungee rope.

I hear a faint gas-gun explosion from over at Eddie and Dianne's walnut orchard. From here I can't see the cockatoos soar.

From down past the cattle lick-feeders comes the high-pitched whine of the tractor's drive-shaft working the pump that Ross is using to spray the blackberries. Then I see the red roof of the tractor cabin rising from the creek bed. That's where Ross is.

He said today was perfect for spraying, no breeze. That's a fact; everything is perfectly still. But what is also true is that we had a fight over his mother and he's not come back to the house for morning tea. So he is hiding down here in the tea-tree. And Margie is holed up in her bedroom; she only leaves for the bathroom and hasn't showered since she's been in Mark's old room. For three days I have been delivering all her meals on a tray. That's the problem. Ross says I'm not to do it anymore; he forbids me – for the first time ever, *he forbids me* – saying she's perfectly capable of coming to the table. But as I said to him, she refuses to join the family until he speaks to her and apologises.

'Apologise for fucking what?' He was wide-eyed, waving his hands, imploring me to tell him.

I counted the reasons on my fingers. 'For not making her welcome. For not making any effort with her. For basically being a rude, self-righteous prick.'

The sky is mostly white, as if covered by an enormous flat sheet. Circling above is a small prey bird, I don't know which one, but Margie would. Further along is the old stone ruin: the first Ballantine house. The two crumbling chimneys – one for cooking, the other for warmth – are a Ballantine monument, a legacy to the early settlement when the land was cleared with that Scottish determination I sometimes see in Ross – when he won't give in, even though he's hot, hungry and dehydrated. Beside the ruin are a peppercorn tree and a conifer that drops hundreds of pine cones that we collect each year for kindling. Whenever I'm here, I imagine William and Alice – as if seeing real-life ghosts moving around – planting those trees that are now towering, bedraggled, half-dead. I don't actually wave or speak to the ghosts, but I acknowledge them, an internal salute, a kind of nod that says, *Hello.*

At the creek I climb the fence on a strainer post, careful not to touch the electrics. I can't see Ross yet. Thousands of ants are busy scurrying in and out of a hole the size of a pea. It's snake territory down here near the water, browns and tigers. I stay close to the fence and follow a narrow track, probably made by the swamp wallabies that live in the scrubby bush and tea-tree. As I walk, crickets bounce from the track.

Up past the granite boulders, the tractor is in full view; a yellow 600-litre water tank is clevis-pinned on the back. The drive shaft drones. Ross is surrounded by tussocks, leaning in while he points the long rod attached to the hose and squirts the herbicide over the blackberries. He steps along, patiently working, pointing, spraying.

I take the backpack off and set it down in the shade of a tall, draping peppermint gum. I wait for him to turn. The hose gets caught on the branch of a currant bush; he jiggles it free, then looks up. He sees me.

Just watching him walk to the tractor – removing the safety earmuffs, opening the cabin door to turn off the crankshaft – I know there's been no softening in him. And trying to tell him that we are arguing over the welfare of his eighty-year-old mother somehow doesn't cut through. I don't like that about him, and told him so this morning. 'I thought you were better than this,' I said, flat-faced and meaning it.

I put tea bags in the mugs and open the thermos. Ross sits beside me; he's stiff in the back from all the bending. I don't look at him while I pour the water and add milk. He takes the mug from me. 'Thanks,' he says.

Ross and I never really fight; we're patient with each other and when something goes wrong we can mostly make each other smile.

'We need to sort this out,' I say.

He looks at me side-on. 'Run after her if you want, be her nurse, knock yourself out. Your choice, but I'm not playing her games.'

'Why do you hate her so much?'

He rolls his neck and looks up into the peppermint gum, its leaves like tiny draping fingers. 'I don't hate her. I just don't like her.' He tries to smile, as if that will somehow help explain. Then he sips the tea, and I realise he's got nothing else to say.

'What was your dad like with her? How'd they get on?'

I've heard a few things about Norman, snippets, never one complete story. That he was more of a farm supervisor than a farmer and, impossibly, his clothes never got dirty. That he used a leather strap on Ross once because he'd left a paddock gate open. And one time, Norman and Mark squared up to each other in the backyard, but Ross doesn't know why.

'Did your dad used to get angry with Margie?'

'Stell,' Ross says, 'just don't get carried away with all of this.'

'What do you mean? Nothing is resolved. Your mum has taken to her bed because you won't speak to her.' I know not to touch him. So I speak gently. 'Ross, I love you. But I don't get this. It shouldn't be a big deal your mother staying with us for a few weeks. I can't see the reason you can't poke your head through her bedroom door and talk to her about what you've been doing on the property. She'd love that. This is all out of proportion.'

'Dad had a temper, took stuff out on her.'

Magpies warble.

'Tell me,' I say.

He shrugs and looks around, as if distracted. 'Dunno – yelling at her, stuff like that. I never really saw; it was more hearing things. I'm pretty sure he used to hit her. Once in the kitchen, he had her arm up her back, hurting her. I can't forget that.'

'What did you do?'

'Mark was bigger. He was with me.'

Poor Ross, the smaller boy. He bows his head and breathes in. And all I can think is that I have been in this family for a very long time and didn't know.

'Did the police get involved?' I ask.

Ross laughs silently; his shoulders move. 'Ballantines don't go to the police.'

'So what are you going to do now with your mum?'

He looks at me, sad eyes. 'Mum and I never got on. That's not going to change just because she's living in the house.'

'Really?'

'Yes, really.'

'I don't understand.'

He tips the tea on the ground, it splashes, and we watch a tiny stream flow on the dry soil and pool by a dead leaf.

'Now what?' I say. 'Nothing's decided.'

'I want our life back, just us, you and me and the kids.'

'That's not possible until she's well enough to leave. In the meantime, she needs to be treated with respect.'

He stands. 'She doesn't respect you, Stell.'

He walks to the tractor, opens the door and turns the crankshaft back on.

So there I am by myself. I finish my tea, watching Ross drag the hose through the tea-trees. And I see Norman pressing Margie against the kitchen bench, pushing her arm up her back. She's bending forward, her legs and back braced against the pain. I hear her begging cries – or maybe she's silent. Her sons appear and see. Mark steps forward and does what?

My mouth is open with the shock of it.

Margie

LYING here, I've been thinking about the past, staring into the avocado-dip walls, watching the lace curtains move any time a breeze builds up the strength. Well, I have always had time to think, but not like this, here in this special room where there's space to breathe. Stella is taking care of things, so I have no worries. She doesn't linger but is efficient in coming in and out, filling the water jug, taking the empty tea mug away.

She is onto me about doing my exercises. I don't agree with the physio that my hip is fine, healing as normal; if it was I wouldn't limp so much. Yesterday Stella stood beside the bed, arms crossed, waiting for me to lift my right leg. I closed my eyes to shut her out and eventually she went away. And yet, I'm warming to her. I haven't been looked after since I lived with my parents in Benalla fifty-five years ago.

When I married Norman, it was a significant thing to happen in my family. I was considered special, chosen, the one who had succeeded and made them proud. Dad was the local bank manager in Benalla where the Ballantines did their business. There was always a fuss in the house when Freddie Ballantine had an appointment with Dad. Mum carried on about starching Dad's shirts, cleaning his shoes, brushing down his suit. Dad always left for work early on those days – to give himself time to prepare, straighten the pens on his desk, check things, write notes.

It's understandable, then, that I was caught up in the fame of the Ballantines, as much as in Norman's attentions. It has surprised me over the years that I wasn't more curious about who he was as an ordinary man. I was a pretty girl with a nice figure, attractive enough to turn heads. Back then my ambition in life – aside from travelling to England – was to marry and have children, so what was better than to walk down the aisle with a handsome bachelor from one of the biggest farming families in the district?

I had once fancied someone else and we'd seen each other regularly for a while. Laurie Mills was a shearer's son, the only boyfriend I had before Norman. We used to kiss behind the rotunda in the Benalla gardens, and even now I remember his lips were startlingly soft. I don't know what became of him because when my parents found out about him I was forbidden to see him or take his phone calls: 'Not Max Mills's boy!'

If I were to dream now, I would say that after I left school I should've kept on with my typewriting and shorthand, then gone to Melbourne and worked in one of the big legal firms or perhaps a bank. Or, if I had been brave enough, boarded a ship and gone to London. I wish I'd had the courage. When Susan, my school friend, moved to Melbourne to train as a nurse and sailed to England before she was twenty-one, my family seemed shocked, as if she'd done something shameful. And so I obeyed my parents and sat at a small desk at Ralph Wilson's Real Estate Agency making tea and typing up the descriptions of new houses and farms coming onto the local market. When I think about it, my parents never explicitly said I had to do anything: it was more about an unspoken correctness, about what was expected. Perhaps I'm passive by nature, and if I take on that line of thought it explains a great deal.

After our wedding reception at the Rose Hotel, Norman drove us three hours to Melbourne and we spent our first night together at the Windsor Hotel on Spring Street. Two days later, we continued on down the Great Ocean Road to Portland for a week at the beach. We had a nervous honeymoon, both of us awkward with each other, realising for the first time we were virgins, and strangers. Very quickly I learned that going with Norman to watch a Gregory Peck and Jean Simmons movie, and feeling his wet kisses in the front seat of his car, was entirely different to sharing a bed with him.

I hear cicadas in the garden beds. Their sound belongs to these long, warm and dry days, and the anticipation of rain. It is now the beginning of autumn and the ground is stone-hard. Freddie Ballantine used to say not to worry too much about rain until the Labour Day weekend in March – that it was a bonus if you got it before then, but that you should never count on it because it's natural to have dry spells this time of year. Freddie knew what he was talking about. So it's troubling that the *Weekly Times* says the forecast is for no solid rain until May. All this talk about climate change. It'll be worrying Ross. If he's not already feeding hay to the cows, he soon will be; the six hundred bales he cut in the Tully paddocks in December need to be carefully portioned because they have to last through winter and he won't want to buy any.

It's past seven and Stella hasn't brought in my evening meal. They might have been doing the preg testing on the cows today, but I'm not sure. The house is quiet and I wonder if I'm alone, yet Stella would have told me if she was going to be late, and left me a tray.

I make a play at doing my exercises, waggling my feet forward and back. Then lifting my right leg, holding, lowering. Then the other leg. I find it boring and tiresome, so I stop.

I start to feel that I'm definitely alone in the house, and it makes no sense. I sit up and face the door. I wait a little longer. Then I climb out of bed, cloak myself with the dressing-gown and push my walker down the hall. I can't help but see myself walking here as a young woman, strong and capable, carrying a baby on my hip or a laundry basket full of clean clothes to be put away. Now I'm struggling to walk those same steps. This strikes me as very strange, the young and old me, as I push into the family room.

And there's Dot's cat. The wretched thing is staring at me again, like Ross, also thinking I shouldn't be here. It stands and lazily stretches; its tail gives me a dismissive flick before it runs out to the back porch. I think it wants to go outside so I push across the room and down into the porch. It's waiting for me and, as I open the door, I give it a helpful kick outside. Yet I worry about birds; the cat should have a bell around its neck.

Tyres on gravel, a car pulls in. If it's Ross arriving home, I'm not in the mood to confront him. I hurry back across the family room and down the hall towards my room. My bladder reminds me I need the bathroom, so I turn right instead of left. I pass Ross's office. And there he is, sitting silently in the old sewing room that he now uses to pay bills and work on his computer. So he knows I'm here alone and has chosen to ignore me. I pause. He's wearing a t-shirt and jeans, and I see that tattoo on his arm he had done all those years ago when he and Stella were in Thailand. It's faded to a pale indigo.

Ross is staring into a large screen of weather maps that move. I hesitate, thinking I will speak. But words don't come.

'Ross,' I say finally.

He turns; he's unshaven and his hair is overdue for a cut. 'Yes?'

The muted light, the casual way he's sitting with an ankle over a knee, it could be Norman there. The resemblance between them has always unnerved me. And there it is, a thought that comes all on its own. I want it to be Mark sitting there, not Ross.

'Are you sorry for the things you said?' I say.

'I'm sorry you treat Stella so badly.'

'I'm sorry you don't want me here.'

All this saying sorry is ridiculous. It's not a victory having the last word because Ross is looking at me, strong and detached, as though I'm a stranger he pities.

After using the toilet, I return to my lovely room. The vase on the table is filled with gardenias, a gift from Jemima. I'm still struggling to rid myself of the dressing-gown when Stella rushes in, saying she's sorry to be so late. That she'd taken Isobel to her piano lesson then gone shopping with Jemima, who fell off a metre-high wall she was pretending was a tightrope. She landed on her right arm and they went to the hospital.

'A hairline fracture,' Stella says.

'Oh,' I say. 'Is she all right?'

Mostly I'm hungry and would like her to bring my evening meal. I know all about fractured bones. They heal; it takes time.

'Here,' she says, 'I got you these.'

She's gone before I open the plastic bag. I feel its weight before I look inside. There's a new pair of tailored black pants with an elasticised waist. A rather chic cream blouse with silky covered buttons and a line of gathering around the neck. Two nighties: one mauve, the other pale blue. And underpants, four pairs.

When Stella returns, I'm feeling the soft blouse; my thumb smooths over its little buttons, my eye taking in the gathering around the cuffs.

'We've got pasta for dinner,' she says. 'Do you want to join us at the table?'

She will see my stubbornness if I look up, yet she has done this very fine thing buying me new clothes, so I look away when I speak. 'I'll stay here.'

'Do you like the clothes?'

'Very nice,' I say.

Then she leans down, a soft quick kiss on my forehead. Her perfume brings to mind lavender. 'Good,' she says.

And this time I cannot look up because I'm suddenly very sad with grief, and I don't actually know why. But I see a flash of the pretty dresses my mother sewed for me – pinning the paper patterns onto the material, cutting the shapes with large sharp scissors, then stitching them up on her Singer treadle. I can even see her fingers effortlessly threading the machine; I recall the floral and lace pincushion, the yellow tape measure, and the smell of cotton.

The way the pasta sits dry and flat in the bowl, I'd say Stella heated it in the microwave. I press a fork into a square shape filled with spinach and ricotta, in a thick tomato sauce. It's a dish I've never had before and it's quite tasty. She's given me a glass of white wine, too – I think it's a riesling, but I don't know my wines very well. I would've preferred a brandy.

After Stella delivered my tray, she pulled the lace curtains back to allow a clear view of the motley pink hues of the evening sky.

I chew my dinner slowly and sip the wine. It's peaceful and quiet in the room. The cicadas don't bother me; rather, I enjoy their chirping song. There's a certain lightness across my shoulders; perhaps for this moment I am happy.

Outside the window, in Mark's tree, a pied currawong calls.

And I have some lovely new clothes.

Stella

MARGIE isn't at the dinner table, but she may as well be. We're all out of sorts here. Ross is silent, hunched and staring into his iPad while absently forking ravioli into his mouth. He's obsessing about the weather, the lack of rain – the long, dry days are now a problem. And I'm angry about the way he treats his mother. I'm not finished with him, not by a long shot.

Isobel is withdrawn and eating distractedly like her father. She's confused and offended because her piano teacher, Julia Zhu – a passionate woman with a grey buzz cut and red-painted lips who believes in Isobel's talent – told me this afternoon Isobel hasn't been practising enough: 'At fourteen she needs to be at the piano for at least four hours a day. Five or six is better.' Then, with a kind smile, she turned to Isobel. 'Sweetie, Lang Lang was practising eight hours a day at your age.' Isobel nodded. Then Julia said to me, 'We are working on her feeling for the notes.' In her next exam, performance flair and stylistic awareness are critical factors. Poor darling. She's only fourteen, and I'd say her introversion and reserve are locked in.

A sling holds Jemima's plastered right arm against her chest like she's swearing allegiance to God and country. She refuses to use her left hand, saying it's too difficult to grip the fork. So in between my own mouthfuls, I feed her too. And while I'm doing this, I think about Margie: the way she was caressing the new blouse, and how a few inexpensive clothes from Taylors could have such an effect on her.

So here we are. All I know right now is I'm tired and want to retreat to the dining room to read, or go to bed early. I need to recharge.

When the bowls are empty, my instructions to the girls are clipped and impatient. 'Brush your teeth, then reading in bed.'

Isobel says, 'No. It's only eight.'

'Do as you're told,' I say.

Ross stands, unfolding and rising to his full height, looking at me. There's a moment, the thought he's going to challenge me, to take Isobel's side. He sees the slow tilt of my head, daring him.

'Come with me, my little honeys,' he says. 'I'll read with you.'

*

Ross wants coffee. It's the way he's fidgeting while slowly pacing around the dining table. He will not ask me because there's this unspoken thing between us – I will not make coffee on demand because I'm not a waitress. It's about giving; my gift to him is making him coffee. And right now he knows I don't want to freely give him anything.

I've just sent an email to the theatre group to set up our next Monday-night meeting. Felicity and Owen have already replied saying they'll be there. In a way, a meeting is premature because the funding hasn't been confirmed, but I'm impatient and want to get some momentum happening, for us all to make this work.

Ross has his hands in his jeans pockets and is staring at the portraits. He stands in front of his father's.

'Your father was a complete bastard,' I say.

He turns and looks at me as if he's got no patience for my opinion. I take that as a challenge. So I go and stand between him and the portrait. Ross and I stare at each other, and I see he's all adrift, the searching in his eyes. Something needs to change around here.

I twist around to the wall and reach up. With my hands on the polished maple frame, I feel its weight. Then I lift up and pull Norman off the wall. Cobwebs coated with dust stay in the empty space.

'There,' I say, as I turn Norman's face to the wall. 'Tomorrow he's going out to the shed, maybe even into the rubbish.'

'Come here,' Ross says.

I don't move. 'What?'

He shrugs, and I see his need, but I can't reach out to him until he's done something that I think he might be incapable of.

'It was all such a long time ago,' he says. 'Please let it go.'

'Are you serious? Your mother suffered your father's abuse. He hurt her and made her afraid.'

'What do you want from me?'

'Be kind to her.'

'Stell, you can't make it better. We move on. I've moved on and I don't want her living in this house when she despises how we live. She's manipulating you, can't you see it?'

'A woman who caresses the buttons on a new blouse that cost forty-nine ninety-nine isn't manipulating me.'

We stand before each other, exhausted.

'We're tired. Let's go to bed,' he says.

I tell him about the repeating image in my head of his mother being pushed into the kitchen bench, her arm up her back, Norman degrading her.

'Was she crying?' I ask.

'Don't go there.'

'Was she?'

'For fuck's sake. I shouldn't have told you. I'm going to bed.'

The swing door flaps after him. I swipe the cobweb on the wall where Norman's portrait had hung. The blue Windsor wallpaper that hasn't seen light for half a century is bright, with bouquets in a layered pattern.

I've never kept anything from Ross before. Today, rehab admissions in Wangaratta called me when I was at Taylors holding up two blouses – deciding which one would suit Margie, worrying over the correct size, a ten or twelve – saying they had another bed for Margie and that I could bring her straight in. My secret. I refused it and told them not to worry. 'It's all going well now, there's no problem.'

They won't be calling again.

The chime of an incoming email, and I go to the dining table. It's Chester, asking if he can come around to discuss the set designs. He's got some ideas and would like to make a start.

And I think, because he knows Margie, it might be an opportunity to coax her out of the room, like a possum taking a bait.

Come for lunch tomorrow.

He replies straight away.

Love to.

*

In the dark bedroom I drop my clothes on the floor and lie down beside Ross. He's on his side, the rhythm of his breathing is slow and even, and I know he's sleeping deeply. And because he won't know I'm touching him, I roll into him and feel his warm skin. It's the safest place on earth, it's where I can dissolve, and sleep too.

Margie

THE girl who comes to help me shower is called Alicia. She's quite short, with heavy breasts that I think must be uncomfortable. Her fingernails are long, painted white and have silver glitter on them. All her actions are efficient. I'm a job unit, which means we don't talk and I'm just fine with that. She doesn't hold towels up for my privacy like Stella did, but because she's a stranger, and I'm just a body to her, somehow it's different.

I'm sitting on the shower chair and she's using the face washer on my back. It's a lovely feeling. I lower my head and notice how frail my body is – flesh and bones, lungs that breathe, a heart that beats – and I wonder how it all keeps on working. Then water gushes over my head, I'm under a waterfall, and I close my eyes so the shampoo doesn't sting. Alicia uses the flat of her fingers to slowly massage the conditioner into my scalp. She rinses, and the water stops.

'Got to get a wriggle on,' she says.

She tells me she has another appointment in twenty minutes in Kithbrook, that she's running late. She's too quick with the towel, so I assure her I can manage by myself. I prefer to take my time because I have no need to hurry. When she pulls her handbag off the vanity and shuts the door behind her, I slowly bend to dry my legs.

There is a small purple bruise below my knee and I don't know how I got it. I've always bruised easily, but they healed in the normal way, slowly fading from mauve to yellow. My fingers are light as I feel my neck, the slight tube-like rise of my windpipe, and I remember the bruises I've had there.

The thing is, when Norman was angry, mocking, backing me up against something, wall or bed, his fist raised, sometimes an open hand – I swallowed the shame because it was my fault. Of course it was. I'd failed as a Ballantine wife and needed to try harder. For years that was the only explanation I came up with for his brutal punishments. It didn't take much to set him off: a minor misdemeanour, such as not having a favourite shirt ready, or if the homemade ice-cream he liked had been eaten by someone else. Sometimes weeks would pass where Norman was relatively even-tempered, so I was often confused. I tried everything I could to keep things calm and settled, but whatever the riddle of his moods was, I never worked it out. Leaving him was inconceivable – I had children, no money, and nowhere to go. The threat of the public scandal alone was enough to make me endure. So I worked hard and tried to keep out of his way.

That all changed when Mark died. When he wasn't around anymore, I was prepared to not be around, either. I spent days and nights thinking of ways to end my life. Pills seemed easiest. The upset it caused when I did it, everyone thinking it was grief for the death of my son. And it was, but not only that.

I carefully stand and pull on my new black pants, buttoning the cream blouse. At first I ignore the mirror – only the centre is clear, the rest steamed up from my shower. I comb my hair without looking, only a brief glance, as proof that it's actually me there. Yet I'm curious about how the blouse looks, the gathering around the neck. So I raise my chin and lean in, half-expecting to be surprised, that by some strange quirk of light I will be beautiful again.

My secrets go deeper – into a private garden with a climbing clematis that trailed along a rusted corrugated shed roof into a Granny Smith apple tree. In spring the clematis pods grew, and when they burst the purple flowers were as big as my hand and wove among the apple blossom. During summer the vine sprouted; the apples ripened. By autumn the clematis flowers had withered, and the tree glittered with red, gold and brown leaves. In the coldest months the vine was bare, its tendrils stretched along naked apple tree branches. I watched those seasons come and go for ten years. It was one of Chester's sheds, a place where I knew love.

The location was far from his house, beyond a row of holly oaks, and hidden within a copse of tulip trees and flowering ash. In a nook behind the shed's back wall, which once may have been a stable, he built a bed for us – it had a dip in the middle, which didn't matter because it kept us snugly together. My offering was soft quilts and a pillow. The time we had there was urgent and always tender. The last time we met there was on the Tuesday afternoon before Mark and Justin smashed into the tree near Gall Bridge. Our ten-year affair ended then; we were too broken. The things I have suffered. In some ways, the moment of losing Chester was the worst. My soul craved him, but no further arrangements were made.

After the incident with the pills – the ambulance trip, drinking the black medicine and returning home – I moved from the marital bed to the enclosed front porch. I lived there for three years until Norman died. An unexpected benefit was being closer to the birds. Magpies, mostly: their carolling was constant from early morning and late into the night; even hours before dawn

I heard their song. They were company and heralded life, a new day. I found it was possible to exist under the same roof with my husband and be estranged. As long as there were meals on the table, laundered clothes in his drawers and wardrobe, and a pretty smile when we were in public, it was all right. After Mark died, Norman never touched me again. He knew my weapon.

I put my wet towel over the bathroom rail and return to my bedroom. Stella informed me this morning that Chester is coming to lunch today. The thought of it terrifies me. It's too much of an intrusion and I am unwilling to cooperate. So I do nothing. I wait.

Sitting in the cane chair, I feel self-conscious. The clothes Stella bought me fit very well. I still don't have my lipstick or the pink sapphire earrings. My thin hair has dried on its own without Stella's hands straightening and pulling it into position with the hairdryer. It is out of the question to ask her to fix it.

My hair was long and thick once, the colour of honey – mostly tied back to keep it out of the way. But it was too easily yanked, so for a number of years the most practical option was to keep it very short. My prison-camp hair was also a private statement about my suffering and grief.

Enough. It was all such a long time ago and it bores me to remember.

I listen for the birds, and there's no sound. I play with the left cuff of my blouse, straighten it. It's almost twelve and Chester will arrive very soon. Then Stella will present herself and demand that I go to the family-room table. Not to cooperate would be churlish, but really, all this carry-on tires me. This business of the play and Chester's involvement seems an odd quirk of fate. And what of Laura? I don't want all that fuss back in my life.

I stand and push my walker into the centre of the room. I'm anxious and wish for distraction, but don't know where to go or what to do. Stella gave me a crossword puzzle book, but it makes me feel like an old woman to sit here and try to nut out the answers. She asked me if I'd like a television set up in my room, and I think that would be nice, but I said no because I cannot go along with anything she suggests. I don't understand myself. If I could have anything, it would be a decent book. But I won't ask. I also recognise that I don't use my manners, *thank you* and *please*, because somehow that feels like giving in – but to what? I'm now unsure. The urge to cry comes to me and I cannot even do that.

The sun is warm through the window and it's now almost one. I can't hear any voices. Stella hasn't come for me. I listen for Chester's car and my thoughts return to that soft bed in the nook, with fragments of memories: our bodies together, the curve of his neck, him playing with my hair, his gentleness. Chester is beautiful to me. He loved me once. I know he did because he told me many times – and even to this day, I cherish those memories.

It's two o'clock. I'm tired now and can't be bothered with any of this. I remove my new clothes and fold them over the back of the chair, then put on the pale-blue nightie with wide bands of lace on the midriff and shoulders. It's quite nice.

I lie on top of the bed, pull the cotton blanket over me and drift to sleep.

Then Stella has her hand on my shoulder. She's telling me Chester isn't coming. 'His wife isn't well.'

Laura must have found out I'm here and caused a fuss. The notion pleases me.

*

Old people and their memories; it is so rich and big and no one would ever imagine. Laura in the hospital bed beside mine, with the curtain drawn around her; me talking to her, asking forgiveness on Mark's behalf because he had been responsible for the death of her only child. She ignored me until she was ready to speak, and it took me by surprise because in the hours she'd been sharing my room she'd not uttered a single word to me, but tormented me with the high volume on the television. We were settling for the night, it was dark, a thin, yellow light was creeping in from the corridor. Her voice was calm; perhaps she'd been preparing what she wanted to say all the time she was enclosed in her white cotton lair.

'I know you had a crush on my husband,' she said. 'You always put on that dreamy help-me look around him. But then you were married to Norman.'

Then she half-laughed.

My heart skipped and raced. I burned. And I stared at the plain hospital ceiling. I didn't reply.

Of course, what Chester and I did was wrong. Yet being around him made my skin tingle, my breath deep and slow. And I will say this: it was him as much as me. It was Chester, driving along Maryhill Road in his LandCruiser, who flashed his headlights and waved at me to stop. I was on my way home from dropping Caroline somewhere. The dusk light was bright yet flat. We leaned against my car, hugging into our coats, hands in our pockets, the temperature probably close to freezing. I have thought of this moment a thousand times; it's embedded in my brain. I can still feel his touch, the softness of it – the way he reached out and lightly traced my face with his finger. I closed my eyes. Such gentleness was almost too precious to bear. I smiled at him, tears wetting my eyes, and I knew he understood. 'If he ever hurts you again, tell me,' he said.

Whatever was going on between him and Laura, and why he cared for me, was never fully explained. But our slow dance started then, and it was still years before we met in the privacy of his work shed.

From behind the protection of the white curtain, Laura's voice seemed weaker. 'You Ballantines have always thought you were better than everyone else, strutting around the district all high and mighty. But everyone knew Norman was afraid of the cows.' She laughed, soft, as if to herself. 'Good thing Freddie got Keith in to run the place.'

It was too much. When I phoned Ross to ask him to come and get me, she was still talking to me, but I wasn't listening. Ross's phone was turned off. So I phoned Stella and begged her to get Ross to come for me. It was impossible to survive the night in that room. With all the upset, they gave me a tablet, drugged me, and as far as I was concerned it was a blessing. I floated into oblivion trying to make sense of Norman, who he was.

The clues were probably always there. Norman told me on our honeymoon, a vague, off-centre look in his eyes, that he hated farming: 'Hate it.' We were in the dining room at Florence House, roast beef with gravy and vegetables in front of us. I reached for his hand as if to comfort him. Not for a minute did I think he meant it, or think to ask what else he would prefer to do. Freddie and Evelyn had four daughters before him. He was their only son. All his life Norman had been groomed to take on the farm; there was never a discussion about alternatives. So my husband farmed and we were bound together.

Even though Norman always deferred to Keith Sanders to make the farming decisions, he still acted like the boss with his hasty strides, shoulders back, looking too clean and stern. It's true Keith decided when to buy or sell the sheep and cattle, move stock around, drench, fix fences, whatever. Laura was right. Before Freddie died he put Keith on, as if he knew what was to come.

It was never clear to me what alternative life Norman would've chosen if he could. I don't think he had much of an imagination. Every day he would sling a canvas bag over his shoulder packed with his morning tea: a thermos and tin mug, and a Tupperware container with a piece of sultana slice or pineapple fruitcake. At lunchtime he returned to the house and we listened to the ABC midday news while eating a hot meal, whatever I cared to make – which was what I knew he liked because pleasing him made things easier. The afternoon was the same as the morning when he went out again with his canvas bag. Dinner was always at six-thirty, never a minute later.

*

Stella is telling me that the quiche and salad she'd prepared for lunch with Chester is now being saved for dinner. 'What would you like in your sandwich?' she asks.

Her jeans are too tight, and the grey top she's wearing is too low, its buttons need to be done up a bit further.

'A salad with no cheese,' I tell her.

'You on a diet, Margie?'

I won't admit to her I'm feeling a little spongy; all this lying around with no activity isn't good for my waistline.

'Not really,' I say.

'Girl's gotta watch her figure, right?' She winks at me and I'm uncomfortable at the thought that this banter might lead to more familiarity.

And when she brings me the sandwich, just as I asked, I think I might thank her. I'm considering how it would feel and how she might receive it. But I don't get the chance because she drops a sheaf of bound papers on the bedside table and says, 'My play. In case you'd like to read it.'

I turn away, no.

'Margie, seeing you're here, living with us, how about you come to the Monday-night meetings in the dining room? Be a part of the group.'

Chester will be there.

My mouth is open and I can't quite close it. Stella wants me to join her theatre group. Of course I won't go, but even as I think this, I'm exhausted by my own paralysis. A theatre group. I have never seen a play. Although I recollect sitting far back in dim lighting, looking downwards at a stage, but I don't know where or what it was.

'Would you like a cup of tea?' she asks.

Actually, I would enjoy a small glass of brandy.

'No,' I say.

When she's gone, I pick up the plastic-bound script and feel its weight. *I Did My Best* is in big letters on the front cover. I flick through the pages. And there, on page 39 in capital letters, is the four-letter word. I slap the play shut, reach my arm out and let it drop to the floor.

Stella

BY nine Tuesday morning it's already thirty-one degrees; the wind is strong and there's no rain in sight. It's one of those days that makes me think about bushfire, yet it's March and should be too late in the season for us to be worrying about that.

I'm in the car with Isobel and Jemima at the Marion Road bus stop. Dust swirls off the ground. Dead leaves fly. The school bus is about two hundred metres ahead – and a box-leaf wattle is flattened across the road, blocking its way. The driver tells me she's called the council to clear it, and the girls say they can wait in the bus. But I hang around to be sure the truck arrives so they're not left stranded.

By the time I turn up at the cattle yards, they've already started the pregnancy testing.

Three white utes are lined up: the stock agent's, the vet's from Mansfield, and Ross's. The sky is clear blue. A dust haze rises above the enclosed braying cows. The air is so thick with flying dirt, the agent and his stockman wear dust masks. As they usher the cows and calves from the holding pen, they talk calmly, giving instructions as if the animals might understand:

Come on, up you go. That's the way. Go on, be a good girl. Sometimes they whistle in little bursts, as if that means something. The cows have been here enough times to know the routine – the few who don't remember get a quick single tap on the rump to prompt them. Calves are drafted into a large holding yard; their mothers are corralled in the pens. The chains jangle on the metal gates as the cows, in single file, filter into the enclosed steel race.

The rising dust isn't so bad in the work area. Ross has been doing my job as well as his. 'Tree across the road,' I yell, taking my place. He nods, gives a small wave. In minutes there's grime on my face and I'm already thirsty.

The cow at the front of the queue hesitates. Her eartag identifies her as M106. She's nervous at being confined, and I don't blame her. She lifts her head, sees the opening and makes a run for it. Ross catches her in the head bail and presses the lever down, making sure it's firm. Our vet, Hannah, slams the waist-high kick gate shut, lifts M106's tail and inserts the thirty-centimetre ultrasound probe into the rectum. Two seconds, and Hannah calls, 'Pregnant.' There's a vague outline of a foetus on the monitor that's sitting on the trestle table; Hannah sees it in the electronic monocular covering her right eye. Our vet is ten years younger than me, a smart and brave country girl who fulfilled an ambition. Her ponytail is threaded through the back of a cap that says *High Country Vet*. She's wearing blue overalls, workboots, and a shit-covered plastic glove up to her armpit.

Ross releases M106 and she trots out to the paddock, udder swaying. We glance at each other – Ross, Hannah and me – getting the timing right. I pull the gate open, and a cow enters the narrow testing bay. Ross locks her in the head bail. And while Hannah stands in, the ultrasound poised, Ross looks at the animal's feet, udder and general health. There's a problem this time, because he records her eartag number on his phone.

We keep working. A line of obedient black cows trails through. Twenty, thirty, forty. All pregnant. Then Hannah inserts the probe into a big old girl and shakes her head. A pause in the action, so I pour iced water from a thermos into a tin mug and drink as many mouthfuls as I can. I signal to Ross, telling him to have some too. He ignores me because he's distracted with everything going on: the cattle moving through, what Hannah's doing, calculating the result. Hannah reaches far into the rectum, past her elbow, feeling for the uterus to check for fluid and a foetus. She pulls out and goes in again, unsure. Perhaps she's like me, hoping to avoid what comes next. Standing back, she calls, 'Empty.' To set the cow apart from the others, I step forward and trim her tail with scissors. When Ross releases the cow from the head bail, the agent drafts her away from the main herd.

In this herd there's three hundred and fifty breeders, and we're done by lunch. Ross does the maths: ninety-four per cent pregnant. The 'empties' – poor girls, as if it's their fault – are going to market at the first opportunity. For three cycles, sixty-three days, they were with the bulls. Ross always says, 'They had their chance,' and he's not going to feed a cow who isn't pregnant or tending to a calf. Some are first-time heifers; others had a late calf the previous year. Then there are the old girls, those who've had seven or eight calves, and I think, for them, it's enough. Mostly I'm resigned to the pragmatic business of managing cows.

Ross and the cattle agent are talking beside the utes, deciding when to sell the calves. We're all filthy. Splats of shit and dirt on our jeans, shirts, faces. I'll be soaking Ross's and my clothes for a day before they go in the wash. My shoulder aches from pulling the gate open and closed.

Ross is concentrating, standing straight-backed, arms crossed. His felt hat is sitting back; his sunglasses glint in the noon sun. There's no rain forecast and not much feed in the paddocks or hay shed. The pregnant cows will lose condition if the calves aren't taken off them. The ABC news, just this morning, said we had the world's hottest-ever recorded February – partly from the El Niño, but also due to long-term global warming. It scares me, the responsibility of feeding animals if it isn't going to rain.

'Sale next Friday in Euroa,' the agent says. 'Prices will be good.'

Ross has already made up his mind. 'Let's do it.'

That means we'll have three days of hearing the penned calves cry for their mothers, while the cows bellow for their babies. Then they'll forget each other and weaning will be over. The cows will drift away from the yards to feed, and the calves will discover that silage, with its sweet molasses smell, is tasty.

Ross and the agent agree on a plan: how many pens at the sale, steers, heifers, Charolais and Angus. A group of Angus heifers will be set aside for China, and I wonder exactly where – whatever happens, I'm relieved there will be fewer mouths to be fed. It's the way it goes.

And so. My timing isn't good. When the agent and Hannah leave, and Ross is slugging back a litre of water – half of it wetting his face and dripping to the ground – I tell him I'm returning to the house to shower, then taking a run into Benalla to buy a television for Margie to watch in her room.

Ross's eyes harden.

The wind is still blowing dust, stirring the cows. Some are pacing the yards, wanting their imprisoned calves to be released, sniffing for them. It's noisy and distracting.

'This is bullshit,' Ross says. 'Getting her a TV just encourages her to stay bunkered in that bloody room. And I fucking hate these games she plays and the way she treats you like a waitress.'

I take a step back.

'She doesn't even thank you,' he says. 'Nothing. Zip. So just get over it. She's not staying.'

How is it possible to love someone – for life to seem perfect – then, standing in front of Ross, there's nothing there. This blockage, his lack of caring. I expect more from him and I decide I don't like him.

'I don't know you anymore,' I say. 'The way you treat her appals me.'

Something shifts; a shadow crosses his face. 'Don't do this now. I've got to bring silage down to the calves, move feeders and bring hay here for the cows.'

I turn away.

'Stell.'

His negativity towards his mother is too complex for me to understand. All I see are the tears that come so easily to her eyes, and half the time she doesn't even notice. Margie intrigues me. She's so unconvincingly stoic. And it shouldn't surprise me that she's still vain, that her appearance is so important to her. Old age seems a terrible affliction.

But I won't be going to Benalla because Ross and I always decide things together, and it's too upsetting and conflicting to disagree about this.

I look back at him and announce, 'You're a heartless bastard.'

Ross turns away first. And I drive to the house feeling heavy in my body, upset and hating that I just said that.

*

Margie is waiting for lunch, but I'd prefer to soak in the bath. I quickly wash my hands, make tuna salad sandwiches and take

Margie's to her with a cup of tea. She seems alert when I enter, sitting up like she's waiting to ask me a question.

'What?' I say.

As she reaches out to receive the tray, she says very seriously, 'Thank you for bringing me lunch.'

Then, as if suddenly shy, she turns and looks to the window as though something is very interesting out there.

I feel love for her, knowing the effort it's taken for her to say that.

'A pleasure,' I say. 'Would you like anything else?' I hear the tone of my voice – Ross is right, I sound like her personal waitress.

'No.' She glances at her sandwich and quietly repeats, 'Thank you.'

All this politeness, so I smother the moment by telling her about the preg testing, the percentage results, and the decision to send calves to the cattle sale on Friday.

'Ross is feeding out now,' I say.

'I think he's a good farmer,' she says. 'But what do other people think?'

'I don't know, Margie. What does it matter what anyone thinks?'

She looks out the window when she speaks. The gleditsia sways; the lace curtain lifts and floats. The air is warm. 'A local man worked here for many years, a good fellow called Keith Sanders. Freddie employed him because he knew Norman wasn't cut out to be a farmer. I don't like it that other people understood that.'

'What other people? I've never heard anyone talk about Norman.'

She ignores me and picks up her sandwich.

'It must've been difficult for Norman if he didn't like farming,' I say. 'What did he want to do?'

She shakes her head as if disbelieving she's said so much.

But I can't leave this undone. 'Ross knows what he's doing and he only has Eddie to help him when there are big jobs in the yards. So I'd say he's a good farmer.'

She nods, then bites into the sandwich.

I tell her that I'm having a bath.

There's so much about her I don't know, but I can now piece together fragments of her life with Norman. He was a reluctant farmer and angry man who could be violent. Ross said his father watched a lot of television – game shows with cued laughter and applause. I walk away from Margie feeling a yearning sadness for her – that she found herself living on the inside of Norman's troubled life.

*

Water pours into the bath; bubbles froth. I peel off my clothes and step in. Yard work is the only time I really do this, the slow thaw of soaking. My muscles need it and I've earned it. I close my eyes, feeling the warmth. But, anxious and still angry, I listen for Ross.

When he finds me he's holding the plate, eating his sandwich. He's forgotten we're in the middle of an argument, or he thinks I'm over it. 'How about I get in?' he says.

I sit up. 'No.'

He braces, takes a confusing step back. And he now doesn't want to be here.

He takes another bite, chews, and is half-turned away when I tell him I have developed a great affection for his mother.

'I love her. You don't know her story,' I say. 'What she's had to put up with.'

He laughs with no sound. 'Give me a fucking break.'

'Listen,' I say.

He pauses, looking unsure.

I'm naked in the bath and this isn't the place to meet him head-on with this conversation. So I pause, stand and reach for a towel. But in my hesitation, he's out the door.

'Not now,' he says.

'We have to talk this out.'

He's gone.

I relax back in the bath, let my muscles loosen. I drift into a memory, and in that embryonic state, I see Mum, Grace. She's on the phone while frantically mashing potato. Everything is urgent: getting dinner, and the apparently life-or-death problems of whoever she's talking to. She stabs a pointer finger out in front as if the caller is standing there. Sausages are spitting fat in a pan on the stove. Mum makes faces at me, waving and air-jabbing for me to attend to them.

I don't move because my stomach aches, deep and low. I'm scared and need her. At school I found a bloodstain in my undies. I think I've put the pad on the wrong way; adhesive is sticking to my skin. Mum is multi-tasking. She stops thrashing the spuds and rolls the sausages in the pan, while still talking to this person and gesturing to me to help. I want to cry. With the phone pressed between her ear and shoulder, she pulls out plates and serves dinner. There's a long backwards-and-forwards exchange about year-end bonuses and being over budget. Something about Sammy being a lying prick who for certain has fudged his numbers to max out. I don't know who Sammy is, but he's more important than me.

The call ends, and she turns to me. 'Why the hell didn't you get off your lazy backside and help with the dinner?' she yells. Normally she's beautiful, but now she's ugly, the way she squints and stares, her neck craned forward.

I stand, stooped with a cramp, and walk towards my room.

'No dinner for you, then,' she says.

I hear the clang of the rubbish bin, the scrape of a fork on crockery.

So, the bath isn't the balm I need. I dry myself off and dress, and the rest of the day falls into its routine. The girls step off the bus, climb into the car and come home. Autumn calving has started and Jemima goes to see an orphan. Isobel heads off to the piano and I wonder if it's a joy for her; it seems more of a self-imposed duty, something I don't understand a child having at that age.

A month ago she woke with a blood mark in her pyjama pants. We hugged and talked quietly, and she asked about my first period. It seemed right to share, but I didn't spoil the moment. The embrace I said my mother gave me was a lie; it was six months before she realised I was menstruating.

Margie stays in her room and receives my offerings of tea, a plain salted biscuit with cheese, and the local newspaper. She doesn't say thank you. Through the wall we hear Isobel playing a slow sonata; I think it's Beethoven's Opus 13. If I go in and watch, her shoulders will stiffen and she'll lift her fingers off the keys.

'How do you find the piano playing?' I ask Margie.

'She seems very dedicated,' Margie replies, and I don't know if that's a compliment.

*

I don't get a chance to speak to Ross until everyone else is asleep – the house is quiet and we're alone. Ross is staring into his iPad, moving his shoulders, uneasy. He's been withdrawn all evening; he knows what's coming and I won't let him avoid it.

The wind gently rattles the windows in their frames. The air is still warm.

I'm sitting opposite him, three placemats between us, the *Stock & Land* newspaper, Isobel's drink bottle. I lean forward, my hands in front, making a speech like an actor on a stage, telling him how it feels to lose a child. And how Margie had a tough marriage and then Mark died. That he should remember how it was for us when we lost Harry.

He slaps the table. 'Stop.'

I sit back.

'You don't know what you're talking about,' he says.

'Tell me, then.'

Ross looks sideways, as if to get the nod from someone else. He is tired; I feel sorry for that.

'Mum took an overdose after Mark checked-out. And when she came home from hospital, she moved into the front porch. For more than three years she slept there, till Dad died. I was younger than Isobel is now. She hardly came near me. Caroline wasn't living at home. Keith Sanders was more of a parent to me than anyone. So give me a break. Don't tell me you love my mother or how I should feel about her.'

I'm hurt because this is all news to me. All those precious times in bed at night when we've whispered our secrets and confessions to the ceiling. Those long-distance drives when there's been nothing to do but talk. I knew about the drink-driving brother. And that Keith Sanders was 'a good bloke who helped me a lot'. Ross went to his funeral a few years ago, somewhere down past Geelong in one of those seaside towns.

'I've had a gutful of this,' Ross says.

The chair scrapes; he stands. He looks sad as he leaves the room, and he's stiff in his back. A pause while he pulls on his boots, and the back door slaps.

It's past eleven and I don't know where he's going. I listen for a motor, some clue what he's doing.

Through the window I see him sitting on the concrete bench, the outline of him, arms tightly crossed, head tilted to stare at the sky. We've sat there together hundreds of times, looking into the vast universe, the shimmer of stars in the darkness, feeling the scope of things.

So that's what happened. Margie tried to take her own life. And for three years slept in the front enclosed porch; it's where we put broken-down things that really should be taken to the tip. The first time I saw that room, it did have the feeling of once being lived in. The little television angled towards the striped divan. The row of chairs. An electric heater. But I can hardly believe any of this. She's always been above the indignity of bad and shameful things. At least, that's what I've always thought.

Margie

SLEEP, when it comes, is always a blessing. During the night I'm thankful and surprised if I have more than three unbroken hours. When I wake I know the time by the tone and feel of light, the depth of silence, and my guess is almost always confirmed by the digital clock. Usually it's around 2 am when I first stir, but tonight it's not even midnight. Ten past eleven. I relax and breathe through the yoga exercise, visualising my resting body. This is what I learned from the classes I went to with Dot. Sometimes this helps me sleep. Tonight I'm impatient and go straight to my left foot, working through the toes, but my mind flits away. I'm hungry.

I sit up, twist around and put my feet on the floor. There's a lethargy in my movements as though I'm dragging something heavy inside me. It's no use just lying here, restless, thinking about random useless things. I went to bed too early, that's the problem. At 8 pm a breeze was puffing out the curtains, magpies were carolling, Isobel was practising a melodic piece over and over. I felt so confined in this room I even hoped

Jemima might pop in again to update me on a village she's building on her iPad. The point is, I confused boredom for tiredness.

I turn the lamp on. Stella's play is on the bedside table, but I resist picking it up. I've been reading it off and on and am almost finished Act One. My opinion is that the children are disrespectful, and I don't understand the mother, why she bothers trying to explain herself. The jokes seem far-fetched, but then I've always been a serious person so perhaps I don't understand them properly. And the vulgar language seems entirely unnecessary: to me, it's evidence of a mind too lazy to find a better word to express oneself.

So here I am; it's not yet midnight and I'm wide awake. I stand, pull my dressing-gown on and leave the room. Down the hallway, I push the walker to the kitchen. Two nights earlier I made this same nocturnal trek to the fridge, where I carefully pincered a cold sausage off a plate. Tonight I'm hoping to find the chocolate-chip muffins Jemima baked: she offered me one after dinner, but I declined. My steps are small and slow and I feel like a burglar. I could walk anywhere in this house with a blindfold on, but tonight there's enough moonlight to see; it illuminates the floorboards. And as I approach the family room I see the light is on, the door slightly ajar.

Ross's voice, so like Norman's – the cadence, measured and deliberate; the way he takes a breath or pauses between each sentence. I hear the word 'overdose' and it takes a moment for me to realise that it's me my son is referring to. I'm suddenly hot, as I was during the menopause years. I glance around, thinking I should return to my room, but his words keep coming through that small gap in the door.

They are discussing me and I can hardly breathe. She's imploring him to understand what it's like to lose a child. I don't know who Harry is.

Now Ross is saying – as though admitting to a shameful thing – that I slept out in the front porch for three years and hardly went near him. 'Keith Sanders was more of a parent to me.'

And immediately those desolate years return. Mark. Chester. The only happiness in the house was the fake clapping and laughter coming out of the mindless television game shows that transfixed Norman; his eyes eager with anticipation.

'Don't tell me you love my mother or how I should feel about her,' Ross says.

So Stella thinks she loves me. I'm warmed and horrified by this intimate revelation. Why would she think that?

She is naive. Ross is right to despise me. After his brother's death, and things ending with Chester, and not being able to endure one more minute of Norman, I did withdraw – not just from Ross, but from everything. Keith Sanders and his wife took Ross on, a casual arrangement where they often had him over for meals. One year they took him on a holiday to Queensland. Keith died a couple of years ago without me ever acknowledging his kindness to Ross, or his quiet acceptance of our family troubles and working discreetly within those limitations.

Ross is angry now, saying he's had a gutful.

My hip throbs, or I imagine it does. Sometimes I think it hurts, but when I concentrate it's more of a phantom pain that I strangely welcome. The more physically disabled I am, the less likely they are to send me away – back to Bishop Street, entombed inside those silent rooms. It suited me once to live in exile, allowing Ross and Stella to get on with running Maryhill. But there's no doubt I have an attachment to this place, which is quite different to anywhere else. Being in Mark's room is special. Listening to the birds here is different from how it is in town. I appreciate little Jemima's visits. Isobel's agreeable piano playing. And Chester is close, coming to the house for the indulgence everyone allows Stella to have with her play. And Stella herself, as inappropriate as she is, hasn't wavered in her service to me. Because she was a waitress in Melbourne, she does have experience in bringing food and taking away dirty dishes. But she also fluffs my pillows, checks if I'm too cold or hot and has a general demeanour of worrying about me – perhaps she missed her calling and should've been a nurse.

But I've worn out my welcome. Ross will insist I leave. Perhaps I should?

A chair scrapes; someone is standing. I'm afraid I'll be found eavesdropping, so I scurry towards my room like the frightened old woman I am. I pass the girls' bedrooms; their doors are wide open. I keep moving and now my hip really is hurting.

At the end of the long hallway, I hesitate. Ahead is the rarely used front door; red and green stained glass is on either side. To the left is the passageway to my room and to the right is the way to the enclosed front porch – the place where I retreated for three years, which included three long winters. Of course, I still ran the house, performing all the functions of a good housekeeper and gardener, but the porch was my sanctuary where I spent my spare time. Ross's grievance against me is legitimate because I didn't attend to him very well, not in the nurturing way of a good mother. My doctor wanted to give me pills for a depressed state. But I refused because in my own way I wasn't unhappy – more like relieved because I had found a kind of peace in my separation from the family. I wasn't capable of giving any more than I did.

If I return to my room I won't sleep; there's too much rattling around in my mind, things I must examine and put away again. So I push the walker towards my old haven. The doorknob is stiff and for a moment I think it's locked, but with a little shove it clicks and creaks open. I shut the door behind me.

The porch smells of trapped dust and mice. The cane blinds are raised and moonlight filters through the closed glass louvres. I feel for the light switch and flick it on, but the bulb must've blown.

I look around. Yes, I know this place. Three cane chairs with green cushions are lined up underneath the windows. The fourth one is in my room. My old 32-inch television is on the floor; reception was often poor because the bunny-ear aerial was useless and had to be constantly moved around – but I managed to watch Prince Andrew and Sarah Ferguson's wedding on it. A few times Ross came out and sat with me to watch the grainy images, but we didn't like the same shows so he stopped coming.

Against the interior wall is a waist-high built-in bookcase with old hardbacks collected by the Ballantines over the years. I have read all of them. Most were gifts to Freddie from Evelyn; the inscriptions are in blue ink in her fine cursive handwriting. I cleared the top shelf for my bird books and notepads, but it's now empty; they're all at Bishop Street. But the Irish poet's book is still here. I reach across and pick it up – the unclean feeling of mice – and hold it against my chest. I don't need to open it; the words come and still speak to me. *A cripple has to learn their own way of living.* That was me when I moved in here, and in many ways is still true of me now.

From outside comes the mellow piping of a butcherbird. I turn, but of course I cannot see it.

My old bed is on the left – it's more of a divan, upholstered in faded provincial stripes of pink, lemon and green. The folded pink quilt at the end was stitched by my mother and given to me when I turned twenty-one. I'd forgotten all about it. I leave my walker and shuffle to the bed, and sit. It's very soft and I remember how it felt to lie down on it, the spongy cushion moulding to my shape. Tonight is unseasonably warm; during the three winters I spent in this south-facing porch, it was bitterly cold. I had an electric heater, a hot water bottle, layers of thermal underwear and thick socks, most often a pink beanie with a small pompom. I managed well enough.

On the other side of the room, Ross or Stella has dumped things: an old vacuum cleaner, thick laminated cylinders, a stack of padded blankets, a leather armchair with only one arm. I remember that chair when it was in one piece; it used to be Freddie's office chair. Norman used it, too.

And so. Here I am in this old porch. This faraway room where I once found peace and rest. That Ross remembers this with such emotion shouldn't be a surprise.

And that leads me to an unwelcome memory of Ross, how he came to be. I didn't want more children after Caroline because submitting to Norman became increasingly intolerable; his demands were unspeakable. He would mock me, saying I was a prude – which, of course, was proven to be untrue because my experience with Chester was always intense and joyful in every way. In the end it was easier to surrender to Norman than be hurt. *And there they are, low-flying black cockatoos, their tiny beating hearts, and I imagine myself flying too, being free.* Ross was born in late March, just as the autumn calves began to drop. It only took one look at my new baby to see how like Norman he was: the shape of his eyes, his expressions, the brown curly hair. Mark was much more like me.

However, it's no good going on about the past; remembering doesn't change a thing. Part of it, I suppose, is about making sense of the decisions I made – and all that's left is regret that I ever married Norman in the first place. It took Mark's death to have Norman leave me alone. And Chester, too. He's a Catholic and said he was bound to Laura for life. Perhaps he loved her. I used to grind my teeth while pondering if a man could love two women at the one time. We never seriously considered that we'd have more than what we did. Divorce was also inconceivable for me. I didn't then and wouldn't now have the strength to withstand the public scandal. Besides, I had no money, nowhere else to go, and no training or skills except running a house. But, above all of that, my identity had been moulded here at Maryhill, and after twenty-four years of sharing a bed with Norman, I ended up in this strange enclosed front porch, my private sanctuary.

I ease myself off the divan and turn to the door. A visit to the toilet is required and a cup of tea would be very nice. Perhaps I'll find the chocolate muffins. Ross and Stella will be in bed by now, so I'll head to the bathroom, then on to the kitchen.

The moonlight guides me as I edge my way to the door, my hand along the bookcase till I grab the rubber handle of my walker. Then to the door. The knob is a little wobbly and I know it is stiff to turn. I twist and pull and it doesn't open. I try again and rotate harder. The door remains closed and I'm baffled. I turn anticlockwise firmly, determined that this is how the door will open, but it stays shut. Backwards and forwards I turn and twist and push in and out – I just need to find the way this door wants to open.

It doesn't budge. I stand back, breathing hard, trying to remember. No recollection comes of this door being a problem.

I think to call out, to bash the door and bring Ross or Stella to me. But I don't because I'm already a burden, and I don't want the fuss it will cause.

I go to the other door, which leads down wooden steps into the garden where the line of hydrangeas starts. It's locked, the snib shifts, the door opens and I'm now free to step outside. But the wooden steps are quite steep and I feel unsure. I place my right foot on the top step and it moves, rotten and unstable. Across the garden, a nursery-rhyme moon is at mid-distance. The wavering rustle of leaves, the flickering of insects. The birds are sleeping.

I step inside and shut the door. Then I go back to the interior door, and I twist the knob once more, inhaling, hoping that it will simply unlock. It doesn't move.

The glass louvres are stiff to open, but I persist with the top ones along the length of the room. Even in this sallow light I see cobwebs, the shapes of dead blowies, a thick film of dust. Cool air comes in with the breeze. It's pleasant.

I need the toilet and know this is going to become a problem.

I lower myself onto the bed and look to the familiar white slats of the ceiling. Dark mouldy patches stretch from the windows all the way across – possibly wood rot from a leak in the roof. In the years since I lived here, not much has happened in the way of maintenance. But I consider that even if Ross and Stella haven't kept the place the way they should, they've made a nice family, the farm is managed properly, they are getting on with things. And Chester is, too. He's grown a moustache and is involved in Stella's play.

It occurs to me I've been left behind. And I drift to sleep trying to make sense of that; it's important to gather up the lost years and understand.

*

It's still dark when the first magpies warble. I half-squat in the far corner and relieve myself beside Freddie's old office chair. It's disgusting, and I blame this humiliation on Ross and Stella for having a faulty doorknob. The inside of my legs and the hem of my nightie are wet. I hate the feeling and have nothing to wipe myself with.

I return to the divan. It's cooler now. I pull the old quilt over me, with its foul stink of mice. Eventually I return to sleep, sometimes twisting my right hip at an angle to ease the pain. I dream and smell the perfume of roses; perhaps I am in a garden, but I don't open my eyes.

Stella

WHEN I wake it's still dark, the first silvering of dawn. The ceiling fan gently whirs. Ross is collapsed in sleep; his arm hangs over the edge of the bed. I lean across and kiss his shoulder, and he doesn't stir. He came to bed after me; we've not spoken since he left the house last night to sit on the concrete bench and stare into his own thoughts.

Through the bay window I see a single radiating star in an inky sky. It's beautiful and surreal, like I'm in a movie looking at something supernatural. In that moment of awe, the story of my life flashes before me and I feel very lucky to be standing here. Magpies carol. The air from the open window is cool and welcoming, but I know it's going to be another hot day. Mid-thirties all week and no rain – yet leaves are turning red, orange, gold. The grapevine climbing the pergola is almost fully red.

Yesterday's clothes are on the floor where I dropped them. I reach down, shake them to be rid of any spiders or bugs that have hidden there overnight, and put them on. Ross doesn't wake. I shut the door quietly behind me.

Diva is loitering at the back door and I let her out. In the kitchen I empty the girls' schoolbags and read their notices. Jemima's homework is to create a musical instrument out of recycled materials. School photos are being taken today, so I'll do something special with their hair. I unpack the dishwasher, wipe the benches. I like the morning quiet, being the solo witness to the waking house, the creaks, the birds, the strengthening light.

Victorian Rural Arts hasn't notified me yet about the funding and I'm anxious to check my emails, though it's not even business hours. Any day now.

The kettle boils and I know Margie will want a cup of tea too. I leave the tea bag in so she can remove it when it's at the right strength. Up the hall, I turn right towards her bedroom. Her door is open and I'm surprised by this. I walk in and see her bed empty and unmade. Her walker is gone. She's not in the bathroom. The girls are still asleep in their rooms. I stride down the hall, peer into the front room, then through the house, my dining room, the family room. I'm confused.

Outside into the garden, I circle the house. The glowing star is now barely visible in the pale sky. At the pergola, I hear the distant blast of the gas gun over at Eddie and Dianne's. A kilometre north, across the boundary cypresses, I see thousands of cockatoos scatter like snow in a storm. They'll settle in the eucalypts and poplars along Maryhill Road. And wait. The battle will go on and on until harvest in April, the birds' tenacity matching our neighbours' resolve to make a living.

Margie isn't on any of the concrete benches. I go down the path to the cars and towards the sheds. Perhaps the laundry, but she's not even in there.

Back in the house, I'm looking around expecting to see her, an apparition in every corner, doorway, sitting on a chair patiently waiting for me to present her with the cup of tea. I do another circuit inside the house. Margie is missing.

I wake Ross. He turns, looks at me.

'I can't find your mother.'

'Jesus,' he says, stretching, rolling onto his back. 'She'll be around somewhere.'

'I've been everywhere, inside and out, even down to the sheds. I don't know what to do.'

He sits up. 'She'll turn up.'

'We have to find her.'

'I'm onto it,' Ross says. He throws the covers off and walks to the bathroom, and I hear the long stream of his piss. He dresses without talking, unhurried and unconcerned. So I leave him and scout around the house one more time, staring inside every room, believing I've somehow missed her the first time.

I peer under Margie's bed; she might've fallen.

'What the hell?' says Ross from the doorway behind me. 'You think she's hiding?'

I turn, expecting him to smile, but he's grim-faced.

'She's not in the house,' I say.

'I'm having breakfast then I'll take a run around on the bike.'

The girls get up, one then the other into the family room, both quiet, sleepy and expectant, wanting their morning hug. Ross attends to them because I'm turning in circles. I'm impatient with him, snappy because he should be outside by now, looking for Margie; she's wandering somewhere, pushing the walker. She's had enough and is trying to escape from us. Then I think of the dams and the bush down at the creek, all the places that are dangerous for children and perhaps old people, too.

Finally, the back door slaps behind Ross. Then the groan of the quad bike, the sound fading as he trails away. I wonder if Margie has a special place on the property, somewhere she might go. The garden, the birds.

Then I remember the front porch. I go back up the hall, then right at the grand, glass-panelled front door. I turn the knob; it's stiff so I push and twist. A little jiggle.

The door opens and shoves in against Margie's walker. A whiff of mice and mouldy dust; something else, dense and thick like a toddler's wet nappy. It's cooler in here than anywhere else in the house. Margie is on the day bed, lying on her back, mouth open. For a terrible moment I pause, waiting for the rise of her chest. I lean down to feel her breath.

'Margie,' I call.

She opens her eyes. 'I've wet myself,' she blurts.

I blink.

She struggles to sit and I help by pushing from behind. With a heave and gasp, she's on her feet, taking three strong steps before she hesitates and drags her right leg as if partially paralysed. I've noticed her do this before, and the sigh that comes with it – as if for a moment she's forgotten then suddenly remembers her injury.

'What are you doing in here?' I ask.

'Just taking a look. The door wouldn't open.'

And she's pushing her walker back up the hall to her room.

*

When the girls are on the school bus, hair braided for the class photos, I deliver Margie her porridge with sliced fresh figs from the garden and a dollop of honey and yoghurt. I've also made her a fresh mug of tea.

I set the tray before her and she pours milk over the porridge.

'I was frantic when I couldn't find you,' I say.

She doesn't look at me or acknowledge me in any way, like she's deserving and I'm a servant. This is not new, but I'm now paying a high price for my kindness: Ross and I aren't looking at each other properly, and neither of us can fully breathe because of it.

I've had enough.

Margie picks up the spoon.

'I think you should say thank you,' I say.

She glances at me, a worried frown.

'I went to the garden and picked those figs for you specially. I've made you a fresh cup of tea just as you like it. I wait on you hand and foot, and I think the least you can do is show some appreciation. It's good manners.'

Her hand trembles when she puts the spoon down. Poor woman. She's so defiant yet vulnerable, and I can't bear to see the fright that has come into her tired brown eyes.

I sit on the green-cushioned chair.

She stares at the food on the tray and I know she won't touch it. She'd rather go hungry.

'Margie.'

She glances at me.

'I need your help. It's time we got real.'

She turns away, looking at her clasped hands.

'Ross is angry with me for allowing you to stay here. But I want you to know I'm more than willing for you to live with us. I know you've had a difficult time in some parts of your life, and at your age someone should be supporting you. But you need to help me. How are we going to sort things out with Ross? We're usually so happy here, Ross and me, but since you've moved in, it's not been great and I don't understand.'

She lies back into the pillow and closes her eyes, blocking me out.

'Open your eyes, Margie. You're too old to be playing games like this.'

She doesn't move.

I stand up and say, in a quiet voice that I hope sounds caring, 'Ross told me that his father used to hurt you. When he was a boy he saw you pressed against the kitchen bench; Norman had your arm up your back. And Ross thinks other things happened between you. He heard fights. You being smacked about. He heard crying.'

With her eyes still closed, she shakes her head and says, 'None of that is true.'

Tears leak from her eyes.

'But, Margie, why did you move to the front porch, then? Why didn't you sleep in the same room as your husband after your son died?'

Her lips quiver and move like she wants to say something – like she's practising vowels. I wait, but she remains silent. Surely she'll speak or open her eyes. Seconds pass and I can't bear to see her struggle.

I surrender. And smooth her hair, as I do with the girls when they need comfort.

'I'm sorry,' I say. 'Let's forget about all of that old stuff. Please eat your breakfast.'

I lightly kiss her forehead. Then tell her that I'm going to help Ross feed out some hay, and that I'll be back for morning tea.

She opens her eyes before I leave the room, but she stares ahead and I wish I could say something that would matter to her.

All that comes is something that matters to me. 'Have you read my play?'

A little shake of her head.

*

At the hay shed, Ross is in the tractor loading 350-kilo bales onto the long trailer. He stacks four on the base and three on top and keeps one suspended on the tractor forks. I sit behind the wheel of the ute, pull the seat forward, change into first gear. I slowly accelerate and feel the heavy weight behind me. I'm not sure where we're headed so I follow him.

Inside the tractor cabin, he bounces on the seat when he crosses a dry gully and bumps on the track. He'll have the air-con on and is probably listening to Life Matters on Radio National. I tune in, too. Ross opens gates and I swing wide to get the trailer and load through. Young heifers stand in a herd, staring, inquisitive. By August they'll be four hundred kilos, joining weight. Ross will put a couple of Angus bulls in with them – both bred to sire small calves. On the radio, the presenter is talking about teenage computer-game obsession; it seems unique to boys who spend hours or even days locked in their bedrooms playing elaborate wargames. I drive down the track, past the yards and through another gate, and by now I'm glad I've got girls.

Ross has set the feeding cradles in a long row, twenty metres apart. I pull up beside the second one. He lowers his bale into the first one, then out of the tractor he finds the end of the hay netting and pulls it away. The cows are grazing in the distance, searching for feed near the dam and swamp gums, and in the tussocks. They see the hay – perhaps they smell it – and start walking, then running, a dust veil behind them. Very soon there's a frenzy of cows around Ross as he's pulling the netting away. He's calm, keeps working. Back in the cabin, he tips the forks, and the bale falls nice and loose into the cradle.

I open the window, feel a breeze. The Life Matters host asks if a child becomes antisocial as a result of too much solitary time, and I think of Isobel.

The cows look all right; their black coats shine like polished shoes. The gas gun at the walnut orchard fires again; a pause – then a fluttering white shadow appears above the cypress. I feel the release of weight, a lightness, when Ross lifts a bale from the trailer. Handbrake off, clutch out, I drive forward to the next feeder. We know the routine. In fifteen minutes the eight bales will be swarmed, and by lunchtime the cradles will be empty. Cockatoos will eat the leftovers.

When Ross and I are back at the shed, it seems churlish not to be talking, being normal with each other. But Ross is out of the tractor, talking on his phone. He turns his back on me and I feel insulted.

I wait.

He shakes his head; whoever he's talking to, there's a problem.

Under an open shed, I sit on an old wooden bench. At my feet are offcuts of fencing wire and a tangle of bungee ropes. The tyre on the wheelbarrow is flat. A stack of twisted star pickets and rolls of old barbed wire are waiting for the next tip run. Always stuff to do.

Ross walks further away, now leaning on a gate, still talking.

He knows I'm waiting for him; perhaps that's why he seems in no hurry to get off the phone. I don't like it that he now seems to be enjoying the conversation.

I look across at the chook pen and remember when we had hens. I was intent on them being free-range so let them scavenge around the place, leaving their droppings wherever they pleased. Until a fox took them all, six in one go. It remains a mystery: did the fox come and go with each kill, or was there a pack of foxes? I lost heart and never replaced the chooks.

Ross is walking to the machinery shed. He's off the phone and not bothered with me. I won't be ignored, not like this. I wanted to simply have a chat, try to connect, but now I'm instantly bloody furious.

I walk fast. 'Ross.'

He glances up, and recognising from my tone of voice that trouble is coming, he turns away and removes the fuel cap on the quad bike. He picks up a jerry can.

'Is this how it is?' I ask.

He looks at me. Puts the can down and straightens up.

My hands are on my hips.

'I'm not fighting with you,' he says.

'Well, just so you know, I'm fighting with you. If you don't care about her, then you don't care about me. That's how I see it. So sort it out.'

He puts the yellow funnel in the bike's fuel tank. And picks up the jerry can. As I leave, I hear the gurgle of unleaded as it pours.

'Wait,' he calls.

Something in his voice.

Ross is standing at the shed door, telling me it was our stock agent on the phone. 'He said Chester's wife, Laura, died yesterday when her heart gave out. And he's got some paddocks going for agistment.'

I shrug, digesting the news. I didn't know Laura; only ever saw her a couple of times up at the local shop. A straight-backed, unsmiling woman who never made eye contact with me. And already I'm thinking about how this news affects me, the distraction this will cause Chester in making the sets and organising the lighting.

'I said no to his paddocks,' Ross tells me. 'He wants too much.'

My husband holds my gaze, and I wonder if I've gone too far. He's never pretended to have any affection for his mother. So what right did I have to bring her into our home?

*

That first lentil-burger night when we walked to the Lex Bar, Ross told me he wanted to be a pilot. A dreamy look on his face when he talked about landing on foreign tarmacs, being far away, independent and happy. He'd just qualified as a commercial pilot and flew for pleasure some weekends.

Somewhere along the way, I understood the pressure on him to farm Maryhill, that it wasn't negotiable. Yet after my first meeting with Margie, it became complicated. Ross was caught trying to manage the farm while spending too many nights with me in Brunswick. Margie chased him on the phone with questions and accusations. Sometimes it felt like stalking.

He was driving up the Hume, that long stretch between Seymour and Euroa, when he phoned to tell me he'd made the decision to quit the farm and apply for a pilot cadetship. 'You only live once,' he said.

Qantas didn't get back to him. Cathay accepted him. So, we were confronted with settling in Hong Kong and me being on my own for stretches of time. I wasn't sure.

Isobel changed everything. The pregnancy test line turned a faint blue. We both stared at the strip, then to each other, and grinned. Perhaps I panicked, but I didn't want to raise a baby alone in an unfamiliar city with Ross coming and going. I couldn't visualise it.

Ross gave up his dream for me. He said he wanted me to be happy; that on the farm we'd be together every day, raise our kids, and 'maybe reclaim something'.

'Reclaim what?' I asked him.

'Don't know. Just do things the right way. Be happy.'

Our first day in the house, we lit the candelabras in the not-yet-claimed dining room and ate chicken tikka with rice. I was four months pregnant, so we toasted with green tea and danced to JLo – the dark eyes and milky white faces of the portraits staring at us.

*

Around five, when it's a little cooler, I put on my straw hat and go outside. It's been a couple of days since I watered. The tips of the azalea leaves are browning, the hellebores are wilting, and a general lethargy infuses the garden. I drag the hose around the front of the house, twist the nozzle to spray and prepare to stand patiently while the plants drink. An ibis glides low over the house, its legs stretched behind; a galah follows as if they're in chase.

I've still not heard about the funding and I'm convinced I've missed out. Already I'm thinking about the cancellations, the let-down; that I'll invite everyone here for a barbecue so we can regroup. All that practice and no opening night – well, not one it deserves. The play deserves a proper theatre, so I won't produce it for an audience in a dull community hall with crap seats. One benefit is there'll be no need for Chester to make the sets now: he can bury his wife in peace.

Pointing the hose at a camellia, I think maybe next year I'll try again for the funding, take my time so I have a better chance. Perhaps it's natural after disappointment to start thinking negatively, but I wonder if the Yellow Box Players is up for discussion; does the group want to keep going? Although, Felicity is keen for us to do Patricia Cornelius's play *Do Not Go Gentle*.

Parrots have been nibbling the succulents; their edges look like chipped green glass. There's yellow spot on the roses, yet the blooms keep coming. At the end of the path, the branches of a pink crepe myrtle and bright orange rosebush entwine. I move to a rhododendron; its leaves are yellowing. I count to fifty, guessing that's enough time to be standing there, but the watering meditation is entering my body and my mind drifts to *I Did My Best* – the actors on stage, Felicity and Owen doing their lines, Amber strutting with her hands on her hips, Noah getting the timing of his jokes right, the violin being the perfect segue to the next scene.

The grapevine surrounding the pergola is turning to autumn. This is one of my favourite places to watch the leaves change, to follow the seasons. I move around and point the hose onto a bed of daphne and gardenia. I see Margie's walker at the bottom of the pergola steps. She's inside, her head down, reading. This is a nice place to sit; it's warm and sheltered. I twist the nozzle shut, drop the hose and go to her.

There are dried red and brown leaves on the floor; the breeze tickles them along, like they're being pulled by an invisible thread. Pieces of a pink plastic tea set are scattered in a corner, an undressed Barbie doll close by.

Margie looks up. Alicia helped her in the shower this morning; her silver hair is soft, probably due for a trim. She's wearing her new clothes and I think she looks very nice. An image of a younger Margie comes to mind – if only she'd smile.

Then I see. It's my play she's reading.

She knows I've seen it, yet closes it and puts it on the seat beside her, then pushes it along like it suddenly belongs to someone else.

'What do you think?' I ask, pointing.

'I don't know about plays. It's interesting, the way the people are told exactly what to do and say. I thought they'd make it up, at least some of it.'

'No,' I say, 'it's very controlled, that's the thing. The actors have to memorise all their lines.'

'I would prefer to read a book,' she says.

I'm a bit over Margie and what she'd like. Sure, she's made some effort, but it's too little, too late. Her lack of gratitude and warmth now irritates me; it's annoying that she seems unwilling to cooperate, smile or show me any appreciation. She didn't eat the porridge with the figs that I delivered to her room this morning. She's contrary and stubborn – and I think perhaps people don't change, that Margie is a difficult woman and I should leave her to herself, back in Bishop Street. Meals can be arranged. There are home services for the elderly.

Then the words are coming out of my mouth. 'You seem to be doing pretty well. I think next week when we see the surgeon, I'll discuss with him when you can return to Bishop Street.'

In her sad brown eyes, a silent pleading as if she's asking for something but can't speak. I can't bear to look into her face.

I turn to continue the watering. Then I remember. 'Something's happened to Chester.'

She stares at me.

'Ross had a call this morning. Yesterday his wife, Laura, died. Apparently it was her heart.'

I don't expect Margie's reaction. She drains white and turns away, pressing her hand to her mouth.

Margie

LAURA is dead and I can't imagine a world without her presence. There were times I was obsessed with her, the woman Chester shared the intimate parts of his life with: bed, bathroom, meals. Just a simple thing like drinking a cup of tea together, something we never did. I know they sometimes went to the movies, and on holidays to visit her sister and brother-in-law in Cottesloe. Once in the local paper I saw a photo of them dancing together at an arts fundraising event, both laughing. It really is too complicated to sort out – being the third person in their marriage, secretly sharing her husband's body, and his mind. Chester was like a drug I needed to survive. Of course, it was wrong. I did try to feel guilt and shame, but I loved him too much to ever regret it.

Stella is dragging the hose to the salvia and hellebores near the laundry. And how dare she? The way she just stood before me, wearing those shorts, announcing that when we go to the surgeon next week for my check-up she's going to discuss with him when I will return to Bishop Street. 'Meals can be arranged and other support.'

I'm nothing. Something to be discarded when I'm no longer wanted.

In my heart there's a wrenching ache, a feeling of grief, and I can't quite put anything in its right place. Is it Laura dying, the absence of her, my nemesis? Or is it the prospect of leaving my old home again? I think they are entwined and that somehow my chance for happiness is here. I stare into my hands, the spots and veins, thickened joints. My wedding ring is as smooth as a stone found in an ancient river.

Not long after Norman and I married, we were on a Melbourne tram headed to an eye specialist appointment. An elderly couple sat opposite us holding hands, fingers with arthritic joints and wedding rings, comfortably linked together. I've never forgotten the natural affection between them – I wasn't yet thirty years old and already craved what they had. Beside me, Norman had his arms folded, awkward in himself but staring out the tram window, excited, as though he'd discovered some missing thing and, if he had another life, he might like to discover this city. I knew then that I didn't understand my husband and he probably didn't know himself. But the elderly couple opposite knew exactly who they were.

I have some difficulty wiggling my wedding ring over my knuckle. It eventually slips off. I study it, the dull gold, and the illegible smudge on the inside that was once the jeweller's insignia. And without a thought I lift my arm and throw it backwards, behind me somewhere in the garden. I don't turn to see where it's landed, but it'll be somewhere in the agapanthus – and very fitting because I never liked them, either. They're too common.

And so. I'm no longer a respectable widow. That grand gesture has set me free. I stare at my left hand and waggle my fingers like I'm Isobel playing the piano. Fifty-five years that ring circled my finger and it's left a deep indent. Here I am sitting in the pergola, looking down at the hem of my silky cream blouse, knees together, the tips of my black shoes. I don't know what this means now, Laura dying and Stella wanting me to return to Bishop Street.

The laundry door slaps. Ross and Jemima step onto the path. She's carrying a filled calf-feeding bottle. They're going to feed the abandoned twin: a bull calf named Justin after a Canadian singer. She showed me a video of him on her iPad, a nice-looking young lad. How does Ross know how to be a good father? I'm too old to understand things and it feels exhausting to try. All I know is he didn't have a happy childhood. But I don't feel great remorse because I did what I could manage. What more could anyone have asked of me? I've thought more than once I should feel resentment towards Freddie and Evelyn for their knowing intention to marry their only son off to a naive young woman who was for certain going to have a difficult life.

I splay my hands before me and see the vacancy where my wedding ring was for so long. For more than half a century it was a burden to me. And from somewhere inside, this upwards feeling of happiness flows over and I give into it and lift my arms as high as I can, clench my teeth, and smile. Actually, I would prefer to have a good howl.

Stella

I'M breaking a cooked chicken apart. The salad is already made; canned chickpeas and sweet corn have bulked it out. As I work, I'm making plans. The phone calls I'll make to relocate Margie back to Bishop Street. The aged-care services. Her doctor. She'll need a cleaner and gardener. Her mail will have to be redirected. Perhaps by now new neighbours have moved into Dot's old place; I'll introduce myself. I find the wishbone and set it aside for the girls. Margie's tray is ready; a tea towel is a tiny tablecloth. A glass of water for her to take her tablets. I remove the crystal vase. It's taken almost three weeks, but I've had enough of Margie. She won't be getting a fresh rose tonight.

Ross is sitting on the couch listening to Jemima read. Diva is cruising around looking for a place of interest. I can't hear from this distance, but Isobel is in her third hour at the piano. Another thing to worry about; her dedication isn't enthusiastic.

And there. Margie is at the kitchen door. She smiles; her lips quiver. 'Perhaps I'll join you for dinner,' she says.

She looks diminished standing there, trying to please me.

I can't bear to see her hand tremble on the walker. Pleading eyes. That's all it takes.

I am kind. 'Margie,' I say, 'it's great you're eating with us. Take a seat, I won't be long.' I glance at Ross, wanting him to help me with her.

He is pointing into Jemima's book, helping her sound out a word. 'Un-scrup-ul-ous.'

It's strange not taking a run down the hall with Margie's tray. She sits in Isobel's chair, and when Isobel arrives I wink at her, saying she can sit on the other side of the table.

There is no pretending this gathering over our evening meal is easy, that we are a functioning, happy family. Margie is an unwelcome guest. Ross eats silently. The girls answer questions with minimal words.

It seems Margie is suddenly aware of all this. She puts down her knife and fork. 'I'd like to apologise,' she says, wiping the sides of her mouth with a tissue. 'For the trouble I've caused. And thank you for having me. I appreciate it very much.'

We stare at her.

She looks at Isobel. 'Tell me, dear, what are you playing at the moment? I do enjoy listening to you.'

Isobel chews and stares at Margie. We're all silent, watching, waiting, and I think she won't answer. Then she swallows and says, quietly, 'Mozart, Concerto No. 21.'

'You seem very devoted. What do you want to do when you grow up?'

Isobel stares at me, wanting to know how to answer this impossible question. Her glasses have slipped a little way down her nose, and I resist reaching out and pushing them up.

'Who knows, Margie?' I say. 'There's a long time for her to decide.'

'But all this piano playing. It's lovely' – she looks at Isobel, smiles – 'but do you have any friends?'

'Of course,' Isobel says.

As if relieved to hear it, Margie gives a little chuckle and smiles across the table. Then, looking back to her food, she chases a chickpea around the plate with her fork.

Nothing further is said. Ross digs into his food, staring down at the table like it's a deep unfathomable pool. The girls are themselves. But I can't bear the tension, or Margie's floundering helplessness trying to fit in. I want to say something to her, to everyone, but no words come.

I let it be, but it kills me, and I'm angrier with Ross than ever because he doesn't try.

Later, in Margie's room as she settles in bed, I fluff her pillows and offer to bring a cup of tea. She isn't looking at me, yet she's softer, smoother in her movements. Isobel is back at the piano, Mozart.

'Thank you,' I say.

Now Margie looks up. 'Why are you thanking me?'

'Because you helped me. You made an effort. It's a step.'

She looks away again; her hands shake. I revert to being her nurse, straightening the bedding, pretending to tuck her in. Tears leak from her eyes and she dabs them away with a white hankie. I put my hand on her shoulder, lean down and kiss her cheek. She doesn't move or acknowledge my gesture until I'm about to step away – then she reaches up and pats my hand, as if it's me who needs comforting. Her mouth is slack with mute crying.

I see her wedding ring is gone and I lightly brush the naked spot with my thumb. 'Margie?' I whisper.

She shakes her head and flicks her hand to the door, telling me to leave her.

There's a terrible ache in my chest, like I'm separating from a distressed child. But I close the door anyway because she wants me to go and I need to spend some time with Isobel, to see what's going on with her. And there's Jemima's recycled instrument project. Plus, I want to look at my emails and think more about what I'll do when we're told we've missed out on the funding. And of course, there's Ross.

*

I grind beans and froth milk to make Ross coffee. It's not a gift: tonight I'm performing a function because it's a habit. He's emotionally deficient, and while the espresso is flowing into the cup, I question if he's on the autism spectrum and wonder why I've never thought this before. But I'm sick of the ratty conversation I'm having with myself, so I pretend everything is normal and take him the latte. He's in his study and I place it on a ceramic coaster on his desk.

On his laptop screen are satellite images like unravelling white cartwheels.

'Storms are building on the South Australian border,' he says. 'We might get some rain overnight.'

He seems light and cheerful about this – of course he is – but more than is warranted given how things are between us.

'I've got washing on the line,' I say.

I leave him, pacing down the hall, out of the house to the clothesline. It's been flapping in the heat for two days and now it's an emergency. The air is muggy; the sky is pink, grey and low. I imagine I hear faraway thunder, yet there is no sense of rain yet; it's still not reached Victoria. At the magnolia, a baby rabbit watches me unpeg and yank sheets off the line, and without folding I push them into the cane washing basket like they're garbage.

Then Ross is there, unpegging, taking his time, folding before he places anything in the basket.

'What'd you make of your mum over dinner?' I ask.

'Not much.'

I'm throwing the girls' shorts and t-shirts in the basket, and it's not because of pending rain, more like I'm just wired and anxious.

'There's no hurry for her to leave here,' I say. 'She's making an effort and she's very upset.'

'Since when don't I get a say?'

'Since you let me down and became a complete bastard.'

With the clothesline still half-full, he drops my folded jeans in the basket and says he's going to the shed to sharpen chain-saw blades.

I watch him walk away, the familiar shape of his body, shoulders, the line of his back, jeans resting low. I have the thought to call out, to apologise, but I don't because I've just told him the truth.

*

If you can measure the loves we have in our life, Ross is by far my biggest. But he's not the only man I've loved. There was someone else when I was seventeen, after I quit home and uni, and sat at a table in the old bakery on Robinson Street that soon became a theatre.

Erik Kozlov was thirty-three, bloody gorgeous with his scary blue eyes, and had a creative energy that was so powerful it sucked me inside him – until four years later when he spat me out, saying I was 'too trusting'. It took some time to understand that he actually meant I was naive and immature.

He left me for an Italian sculptor, chain-smoking Marie, and a gig with the Sydney Theatre Company. From there he moved into experimental theatre in London. Sometimes I sneak a look on Facebook. He's now in New York directing *The Moment*. The reviews have been very good. And he's still with Marie. They did me a favour, though I didn't think that at the time.

I'll give him this: he taught me a lot about theatre – directing mostly and being courageous enough to own my creative concept. He often wore white clothes like a messiah, and that's how the theatre group saw him – a man walking with an outstretched arm, telling us what to do, laughing.

*

Around 10 pm, I'm in my dining room filling in time until Ross comes inside. The not knowing about the play's funding makes me feel insecure. And I'm thinking that if the money doesn't come through, that's all right. I feel a strange detachment.

For years I've been thrashing this story to death and I'm sick of it. I'm troubled by the scene where Ruby and Jack accuse Grace of leaving them for three days and nights when she went to a work conference and didn't leave a note or any money: 'and hardly any food. We were orphans.' It's not true. It was only one night. Tommy was eleven, I was thirteen, and we got ourselves to school, and home, and nothing went wrong. And Grace says, 'Your father was supposed to be home. He forgot you, not me. So go and accuse him!' The story isn't mine anymore; it's taken on a life of its own and should be renamed. It's the production that interests me, the creative process, the actors, not my story. It's fake.

I'm depressed. I miss Ross and want to talk to him about all this junk swirling in my head.

The back door opens. Boots off and he pads in his socks through the family room, up the hall, and goes straight to bed without coming to say goodnight to me. That's something to take notice of, his rejection, and I'm unsettled that he's avoiding me. Ross never does that.

I consider possible responses. Perhaps I'll sleep in here on the chaise lounge. Maybe I'll grab my handbag, drive away and spend a couple of days in a small motel eating chips and watching TV. Or slam our bedroom door open, flick on the light and start yelling. All the options feel good. A small voice tells me to settle down, that I'm tired and should go to bed.

The hallway is dark, but I don't put the light on – I know where to touch the wall and feel for our bedroom door. I slink in. In the bathroom, drinking straight from the tap, I swallow a couple of paracetamol, hoping they might somehow knock me out into a solid sleep. Lifting the cotton blanket, I lie beside Ross. His body is heavy on the mattress, his breathing steady, so I know he's asleep. I drift away, too.

*

The digital clock says 4.31. It's raining. Or perhaps it's wind chiming through leaves. I lift onto an elbow, crane forward and listen. Yes, it's drops of rain, hesitant and soft. I lie back on the pillow. A cool breeze drifts through the lace curtain.

'Ross,' I whisper, 'it's raining.'

He sighs, rolls onto his back, listens. Then, reaching for his phone, he opens a weather app. His hands and face are illuminated. A slow exhalation, his shoulders relax, and he shows me the green radar, like algae creeping across the northern part of Victoria. Orange and red tell us that the whole distance from Bendigo to Shepparton is getting soaked. With his finger he follows the arc of the rain moving east. 'Looks promising,' he says.

We lie together, hearing the firm splats on the roof. The rain is everywhere: on the lawn, the garden, across the paddocks, washing the dust off the backs of cows, spitting heavily into the dams, spilling into the gullies, feeding into the creeks, tunnelling underground and flowing down to the flats. We're lying still, breathing in the cooling air, relieved.

In that lovely dark and private space, I can't quite gather up the stuff going on between Ross and me and make it important enough to not move across and lean against him. He receives me as if he's been waiting.

By the time the first glimmer of sunlight cracks through the blinds, I've forgiven him for not being perfect, and myself too, and everything else outside our bed. We whisper that we love each other.

And when the first gas-gun shot fires across the walnut orchard, we step out of bed and everything seems better somehow.

Margie

EVEN though it's raining, Ross and Stella still feed the cattle. They've got their all-weather gear on and just soldier out the back door as if the sky is clear. Her hair isn't covered and she doesn't seem to care, which strikes me as unusual – and I can't say why, except I wouldn't like the frizz the rain would cause me. That's one thing I didn't have to worry about: working outside on the property. When I first came here Freddie helped Norman, then Keith Sanders, and Mark. I kept up with the morning teas and lunches – my pineapple fruitcake was always popular; sometimes I made a coconut and raspberry jam tart. But Ross and Stella work the farm on their own and just bring Eddie Bain in for the yard work.

I stand at the family room's open bay window. The damp heat is quite pleasant. I can't see any birds, but I expect the rosellas will be enjoying themselves somewhere, preening and washing in the pools.

So. I've got nothing else to do except wait for Ross and Stella to return, and after that there will be more waiting for I don't know what. The rain is lovely, though.

The breakfast dishes are stacked in the dishwater; its door is wide open. The benches are covered in toast crumbs and tiny globs of jam. This is something I can do. I leave my walker, and the soles of my slippers make little sucking sounds as I walk to the sink. When I look down, nothing is obviously to blame, but I suspect spilt jam. The floor needs washing. Yes, this is the exact spot where I endured Norman's punishment when his tuna mornay wasn't heated properly. That pitiless shift in his eyes signalled danger.

'You seriously expect me to eat this?' he said.

'Heat it up yourself.'

Foolish me. I'd just given him a reason to hurt me. He twisted me around and bent my arm far up behind me. Pain is pain. I clenched my teeth. He wanted me to apologise, but I wouldn't, which enraged him further.

'Stupid man,' I said.

'What did you just say?'

Many times I wished I was as strong as he was so I could fight back.

Then the boys were at the kitchen door – and Norman, now with one arm around my neck, the other still forcing the fracture of my humerus, hadn't noticed our witnesses.

Mark rescued me. He jabbed his father in the ribs with his elbow, making Norman grunt as the air left his lungs. After some shoving between them, Norman sidestepped and hurried outside. Mark disappeared up the hallway. It was Ross who stood there watching me, pale-faced, wide-eyed. He was only ten years old, so I pretended everything was all right and just got on with scraping Norman's mornay into the bin.

Stella puts saucepans in the dishwasher; surely that's unnecessary. I lift them out and wash them in the sink, dry them, and open and close cupboards, looking for their place. I wipe the benches. The floor really needs attention, but I can't manage the mop and have no idea where it is.

Ross and Stella still haven't returned. I put the kettle on and, while I wait for it to boil, I open the swing door and walk into the dining room, free, without my walker. I'm careful on my feet. The feeling is light; perhaps I'm leaning forward as if still holding the thing.

I never really liked this room, yet Stella has made it her own, and it's now what I'd call bohemian with her stacks of bound plays and files, and a television and printer on the table. This is where the theatre group will come on Monday night. Chester, perhaps. But there will be a funeral, of course there will – although there was no mention of it in the local paper.

I hear the back door open and, as I turn to leave, I see a blank space. Norman isn't on the wall. He's gone. I look around, but can't see his portrait anywhere.

Then Stella is there, her hand on the door. I'm embarrassed that she's caught me in her room.

But she smiles. 'I'm going into Benalla to shop. Want to come?' She follows my gaze to the darkened square on the wallpaper. 'Norman was a bastard, Margie. Let's not pretend he wasn't, and I don't want to be looking across at him.'

'Where is he?'

'Nowhere for you to worry about.'

I stand, confused, and can only study the dull veins in the oak floorboards, trying to understand what's going on. This woman has taken Norman off the wall; his stature has been removed and that's all he ever had. I'm not making excuses for him, but then I suppose I am. It's just that he wasn't born to farming and had no say in it and lived a miserable life. But then he made my life wretched, too. And the sums start adding up – how it was for the children.

'You'll like the drive,' Stella says. 'We'll have a coffee.'

I think of her unflinching declaration that she'd be speaking to my surgeon about my return to Bishop Street. But that's not until next week. So this is something else entirely: it might be all right.

At the same time, we both realise I don't have the walker with me – evidence that, yes, I can be independent. So I limp, just lightly, though I doubt she's noticed my antics because she's already turned to the door and says we are leaving in ten minutes.

A single magpie carols. The rain has eased. And the idea of a daytrip satisfies me. I feel loosened and relieved. But I don't think I can get ready in ten minutes.

*

We are in the main street; I know it well enough – the distance between the pharmacy and bank, then across the road to the post office. Stella drops off one of Jemima's drawings to the picture framer, which is a couple of doors down from the second-hand bookshop that I sometimes used to go to. Stella seems to know the man who does the framing, it takes no time because she tells him to decide what to do. Then we head over to the new place on the corner for coffee. I've seen it before and thought of it suspiciously, with a vague decision to never go in there.

But first Stella drives around to show me the new street art: people's faces on buildings that are quite striking, and surprising because I don't know why buildings need to be painted with faces, particularly sad, pleading ones. But when we pass by, I'm still thinking about them, wanting to understand the questions in their expressions – especially that of the girl in the centre with the blue background. From her haunting eyes, I can't tell if she's brave or afraid. Up at the greengrocer, a painted red-bellied black snake covers the whole side of the building. It's very confronting; even a small one would have been unnerving.

In the café, Stella orders a latte and I copy her. I would normally have tea, so I'm now a little anxious about what I've done.

'Do you want something to eat?' she asks.

'No.'

She orders a slice of lemon tart and says yes to the cream. I don't know how she does it, eating sweets and keeping her nice figure. I try to avoid eating between meals and rarely have dessert. Lemon tart was Mark's favourite, so I used to bake it often. And so, a wedge of tart arrives with two forks and Stella hands one to me. She digs in and I am expected to join her.

Then the coffee is on the table; the froth on top is a picture, like a fern. In two even movements, Stella sips the coffee and cuts into the lemon tart. I feel outside myself and glance around, insecure. It's not normal for me to copy others, especially not her. So I concentrate on the coffee. It's too strong and needs more milk. I take a pinch of the tart, but its flavour doesn't mix well with the coffee.

'You want some water, Margie?'

That's exactly right, and I say so.

Stella seems cheerful, and I feel the separation of years and life between us. I'm ancient. She's young. It's very strange we're sitting here together. It wasn't supposed to be like this, me with her. I married into local aristocracy; the Ballantines had a reputation, an image to uphold. Yet here is my son's wife, Stella, whose blonde hair is tangled high on her head, bits hanging down like an egret's wing plume. Square-shaped copper earrings hang from her earlobes. Her silky blouse gapes; a black bra strap shows. She's the type of female that men like. Ross certainly does. So does Chester – the memory of him laughing with her when she strolled from the back porch into the family room. The image of it still crushes me. Things I thought were certain are now in a muddle. I'm lost.

'Taylors have a sale on,' she says. She's clutching her big heavy bag and lifting out of her seat.

I take a sip of water. 'But I don't need anything,' I say.

'I've been washing your bras. So I'm telling you, you do.'

I feel quite confused. Yes, I know my undergarments and clothes are old, but for a very long time I've had a strict habit of not buying things. Norman wanted receipts for everything I spent and I still think that way. And in 1991 when the wool market crashed, I had to tighten the budget even more; everyone did. Aside from all that, what's the point of buying new things that will never get worn out?

'Norman's long gone,' Stella says, 'and not here to tell you how to spend money. You deserve some nice things.'

I wonder how she knows this.

*

Stella walks along the shopfronts, pausing to wait for me. If I wasn't with her, she'd already be at the next place.

We need to cross the road and stop at the roundabout. Cars advance with such purpose, it's as if they don't see us. There's a gap, and Stella says, 'Okay, let's go.' And I push the walker across the road as fast as I can. Her arm is like an extended swallow's wing, ready to help, and I do appreciate it.

Inside Taylors, I know where to go. For fifty-five years I've been coming here; occasionally I bought something.

Stella is staring at my breasts. 'What size are you?' Then she's holding up a bra, saying I need to try it on.

A prim-looking assistant appears. Stella pounces, asking for something that'll be comfortable and easy for me to clip. And just as I'm being ushered into a change room, she steps away and skims her fingers along a rack of black underwear. I've never owned a black bra or pair of underpants; it always seems wrong, as though only a hussy would wear such garments.

Then there's the memory of me being a loose woman. Somehow it wasn't me who was with Chester, but this other audacious *femme fatale*. It is with that thought I admire a pale-pink bra; it's lightly padded and has tiny flower buds embroidered into the cups. The size isn't quite right so I'm given another one. Somehow wearing it makes me put my shoulders back. I turn to see my profile in the change-room mirror.

'It also comes in black, skin-colour and white,' the assistant says.

I choose pink, but when Stella learns this she finds the skin-colour one too and says we'll have them both. She's carrying black stringy underwear that have tangled on small plastic coathangers.

Stella isn't finished with me yet. She's gone to the clothing section and holds up a navy and white dress with a matching navy patent-leather belt. It's the sort of thing I'd wear to a wedding.

'Try this on,' she demands.

I'm unwilling to take off my clothes again, but then I see she's also got a quite nice slate-grey blouse, the same colour as the back feathers of a fan-tailed cuckoo. I return to the change room and Stella waits outside the curtain, wanting to see.

When I appear wearing the dress, she clasps her hands under her chin and studies me.

'You look gorgeous,' she says. 'But you could go a size smaller.'

'I don't want it tight,' I reply.

The blouse is very lovely, with a collar and pleats in the back so it shapes quite well.

When I try it on, Stella is full of praise, and so is the assistant. The two of them convince me that I should buy the dress and the blouse. But there's this terrible restraint in me, pushing back into an old place where I know this spending is wrong.

Through the curtain, Stella tells me to hand everything to her. I do as I'm told.

'I'm taking them to the counter,' she says.

I think to protest, but I like the clothes very much. It's exhausting, all this pulling off and putting on of clothes, so I sit on the walker's chair for a rest. Yet I have to go and pay. I hurry with my buttons and slip into my shoes – but by the time I'm there, Stella has already handed over her credit card. She's also put in two pairs of pantyhose.

'But they're my clothes,' I say, now frantic about what Ross will say with all the expense.

'Half the cost of a small heifer.' She winks. 'Don't worry.'

We head to the car. It's parked out the front of the shoe shop, and without hesitation Stella walks in and I follow. She's wearing red leather thongs and loose khaki cotton pants that hang below her knees. I assume she wants more suitable footwear, but then it's me who's sitting down to have my feet measured. And I leave there with a spongy pair of black runners that do up with two velcro straps, and a comfortable pair of gold-buckled tan flats. I have a debit card and the pin number is the year I was born, so it's never forgotten. Together the shoes cost more than two hundred dollars, but I'm very happy with them.

A lightness has spread through me that could very well be nausea from the excitement and doubt about buying new things. I wear the black runners out of the store. I feel as though I could walk a mile.

I ask Stella if we can go by Bishop Street so I can get a few things. It seems she's not in a hurry today because she just nods and drives back across the bridge. She passes my hairdresser and the police station, then takes two left turns and a right, and we're in my driveway.

There's a white VW in Dot's driveway, and a child's bike is on its side on her front lawn. New people have already moved in, and even though she was my best friend I'm still a distant observer of all this change. I knew that her daughter, Ashley, had put her house up for sale. It depresses me, this noticing of time passing. I imagine Dot and me on that cruise, the forward, gentle movement of the ship with us sitting on deckchairs, a vast blue sea stretching all around. By now we'd probably be home again and back in our old routine.

It has only been five weeks since I left here in an ambulance and my house looks more than empty: it's forsaken. The garden beds are ragged from a long summer with little rain; the lawn is patchy. The plane tree leaves are heavily scattered across the driveway, paths and lawn. It's a job I quite liked doing, raking them up and wheelbarrowing them to the compost bay down by the garden shed.

A spotted pardalote flits from a salvia. There have always been birds here, but I've never seen a sulphur-crested cockatoo or a bird of prey – I don't think there's enough feed for them in the town; they prefer bothering the farmers.

The front door key is stiff in the lock, and Stella ends up working it out. Inside the house is warm, stuffy, with a restrained feeling as if it's been waiting. She sits on a kitchen chair while I go to my bedroom. I don't want to be long in case she gets the idea I should return here sooner than necessary.

In the left-hand drawer of my dresser is a small heart-shaped black lacquered jewellery box, which belonged to Freddie's mother, Elizabeth. I take out the earrings. She had some very fine things; wool prices were very good back then. It was she who last decorated Maryhill and did all the entertaining in the dining room. Of course I never met her; she died before I was born. Freddie was the first of her eight children. Two other sons fell in the Great War. Louise, her youngest daughter, married an important man who sold antiques for a famous company in London called Sotheby's.

Stella is on the phone, using her soothing voice.

I've got my lipstick and the jewellery box, and stand and wait.

'Bye,' she says into the phone. 'See how things go.'

Back in the car she is very quiet, an inward look, as if she's thinking about something. It's not until she indicates to go onto the Hume Freeway that she speaks. 'That was Chester on the phone. The funeral is tomorrow and he doesn't know if he can still work on the play. I'll have to think of something else. Bugger that.' She smacks the steering wheel with the heels of her hands.

At the mention of Chester, I stare out the window. After the rain there's no dust, yet everything is yellow and dry down on the flats. A P-plater passes at high speed, well above the limit. I'm noticing all these things, even though inside I'm ready to die, too. Perhaps Chester will come to my funeral as well. My hand is on the armrest, and I wonder what will happen if I undo my seatbelt, open the door and let myself fall out. I'm seeing and feeling it – the slamming into the gravel, the air knocked out of me, my body brutally crushed and destroyed. It's not dying that bothers me, but what if I live?

'Did you know Laura very well?' Stella asks.

'No, not really.'

She glances at me. 'Everyone knows everyone up here.'

I'm feeling agitated and rub my hands together like I'm putting on hand lotion. 'Not necessarily,' I say.

'But wasn't Chester and Laura's son Mark's friend? They died together in that crash?'

'It was a very long time ago,' I say, closing my eyes so she stops talking about Chester and Laura.

At home Stella hangs my clothes in my wardrobe and puts the shoebox with my new gold-buckled flats at the bottom. She slides the door shut. I'm sick with worry about all the money we've spent. And I consider what a folly it was to buy them, some ridiculous idea that I should look my best for Chester, who is so devastated by his wife's passing he cannot now work on the play. I am ridiculous. At my age, for heaven's sake, I still can't get out of my own way and find peace.

*

The next afternoon Stella walks into my room with my lunch on a tray: an avocado, ham and tomato sandwich, a small bowl of red grapes, and a cup of white tea. She has worked out just how much milk I like and has it the right colour. She's all dressed up in a fitted black dress that comes to her knees, and the tan and black high-heeled ankle boots that she seems very fond of. Her blonde hair is brushed and flows around her face and shoulders; her lipstick is magenta – there's a rose just like it beside the magnolia not far from the pergola.

'We're going to Laura's funeral,' she tells me.

I'm beyond surprised and have nothing to say.

'We'll be back before dinner. The girls won't be on the bus. I've made other arrangements. Will you be all right?'

I stare at her, and stop breathing. I want to ask why. *Why are you going to Laura Sullivan's funeral?*

The faint blast from the gas gun, a signal I need to take a breath.

There's pity or sadness in Stella's eyes, and I think she is about to ask a question when we hear Ross calling her from the hallway.

'In here,' she calls back.

'We've got to go, come on.' Ross glances at me, perhaps with a slight smile, but it all happens too quickly to tell. He's fresh out of the shower, his hair is damp, and he hasn't shaved for at least two days – yet I think it's deliberate, as if it's the fashion to go around looking untidy. His charcoal-coloured suit fits snugly, and he's not wearing a tie with the white shirt. I think to tell him he should wear a tie to a funeral, but I remain silent.

When Stella leans down and kisses my cheek, his eyes widen as if seeing something that surprises him. 'Enjoy your lunch and have a lovely afternoon,' she says, traipsing from me to my son, then stretching out her hand to him. He clasps it and they disappear through the door.

It takes a few minutes for me to settle down after they leave. Her perfume lingers, perhaps blending with whatever after-shave Ross is wearing.

A sticky fly is pestering around the cling-wrapped sandwich. I shoo it away and decide I will not sit in bed like an old frump on the afternoon Laura is being farewelled from this earth.

At the wardrobe I pull out the grey shirt and black pants. I put them on. The tan shoes are quite comfortable. Then from the jewellery box I put on the pink sapphire earrings; my fingers tremble pushing on the clips. In the bathroom I brush my teeth and pull a wet comb through my hair. The shirt is lovely and I believe that I look good enough.

Without the walker, I unhurriedly wander the house, looking for a place to settle. I quite like having the run of the house. After that good soaking rain, the house seems to shift into itself as if settling down; all the trusses and joists are getting comfortable again after a big upset.

In the sideboard cupboard, I discover bottles of wine beside tall and squat bottles of spirts, brandy, tequila, whiskey, gin. I find a glass and pour a good shot of Jack Daniel's. In the kitchen I add a little water. The cat is on the couch and I don't want to be near it. There's a magazine on the table, and I take that with me through the swing door to the old dining room and sit on the green chaise lounge. I hear a white-naped honeyeater and a yellow-rumped thornbill in the garden, perhaps a fantail, too.

I open the magazine and find advertisements for cruises. I follow the arrows that circle countries.

Laura's funeral will now be underway. I picture the crowd; there won't be many there. Yet Ross and Stella have gone, perhaps out of respect to Chester for his involvement in the play, although that seems a weak motive to me. The service will surely be at St Joseph's, the Catholic church in Arundel Street. Religion was behind Chester's commitment to her, his devout belief that his marriage couldn't be dissolved for any reason: *till death do us part*. He was always resolute, even though the conflict was bizarrely obvious – rejecting divorce, but enjoying and accepting the sin of adultery.

I close my eyes and sip the whiskey; it heats my throat on the way down.

*

It was only when Laura visited her mother in Geelong or caught the train to attend a botanical drawing class in Melbourne that Chester and I saw each other. Sometimes months passed between our meetings. I would wait for his note to arrive in the letterbox at the top of the driveway, formally addressed to Mrs Margaret Ballantine in a sealed envelope: audacious, vague and illegible enough not to cause suspicion, and always signed with the single letter C – all of it clear enough to me. And, anyway, I was the only one to collect the mail.

I don't know how to describe the attraction between us; a glance that somehow communicated desire. In 1975, I saw him in the supermarket carpark and he asked me to have coffee with him. I was too shy, surprised and afraid, so I said no. But from then on I looked for him – up the street, in the shops, driving along the roads.

It was on the oval sidelines, watching our boys play football, that we spoke again. A cold winter's day, but a clear sky. We stood side-by-side, hands in our coat pockets. Our spouses were elsewhere, so we were just two parents watching our eleven-year-old lads play. It was in the third quarter, while staring forward onto the footy field – kids running and collapsing into a scrum, a whistle blowing – that Chester mentioned Laura was in Geelong visiting her mother, and perhaps I would like to have morning tea with him sometime in the coming week.

How shocking of him to suggest it. Lovely Chester. What a terrible, foolish thing. I glanced at his profile, the line of his neck, the navy collar of his coat – all of it was somehow familiar.

'If you'd like,' he said, turning to me with a roguish smile.

Chester was very handsome. I don't know how I answered, but it was agreed that we would meet two days later, on the Monday morning. And to avoid any neighbourly suspicion or detection, he suggested it might be best if I approached his place from Hoskins Lane, and he'd leave the back gate open.

At exactly ten that Monday, I entered his house, Laura's home. It was the one and only time I ever went in there. The house was rustic, made from natural timbers and stone. The central room had a feature wall of local granite with a firebox in the centre and a cavity to store logs. He'd built the house himself, he said. Everything was neat and the furniture was much more modern than in my home.

On the walls were botanical drawings of fruit in identical frames: a red Bartlett pear, a medlar apple, a quince, a pomegranate and a blueberry. When I asked him who had painted them, he didn't answer. Later, when I thought about it, I realised that of course Laura was the artist. How odd it seemed, then and now, that he didn't own up to his wife's talent, as if mentioning her name would somehow break the bubble we had enclosed ourselves in.

We didn't drink tea or eat the butternut snaps he'd put on a plate. Somehow we just stepped towards each other, and within a few quick minutes retreated to the sleep-out, a room unprepared for us. The mattress on the pine bed was bare and covered with plastic bags of old clothes and a box of wire coathangers, all of which we quickly removed. We flapped a white flannelette sheet loose to float down for us to lie on.

It remains my most precious experience, his arms around me, our twin breaths, and just being loved, sincerely. And it was, shall I say, the first time I had known pleasure.

Afterwards, my head against his shoulder, he held my hand and kissed each fingertip and had something to say for each one: 'Margie is gorgeous. Margie's got a beautiful body. Margie's skin is like velvet. Margie is strong and courageous. Margie is a special person.' And when he finished with my left hand, he did the same to my right: 'Margie has beautiful eyes. Margie is my adored lover . . .'

I lived on those words and memorised them every day, until one day I stopped because it hurt too much, and because our sons were dead. And what was the point of it all, anyway? Waiting for his notes, frequently being disappointed and finally, whenever he beckoned me, sneaking around like an eager whore, when afterwards all he did was hitch his trousers and kiss me goodbye until the next time.

*

The whiskey has made me sleepy, so I kick off my shoes and lie on the day bed. Magpies are carolling – and, as I drift to sleep, I think Laura's body will now have left the church. I see Chester, the grieving moustachioed husband, shaking hands in that sincere way of his, holding the wrist with his left hand, 'thank you so much for coming'.

And I decide I hate Chester, and it blossoms in me and feels very good.

Stella

AFTER the funeral we want to stay out and have dinner at the local pub with the kids. Except Margie is at home expecting our return and her evening meal. We all feel it, a silent resentment that our fun is taken from us because she is waiting for us.

We buy Chinese takeaway. And as Ross powers us up the mountain – sugary red sauce leaking from the plastic containers, rice sweating and bulging, and Isobel and Jemima gorging themselves on prawn crackers – I try to explain to them how it must feel to be Margie, old and alone. But my voice falls flat. I'm tired of the story myself and want her to be more positive, brighter, different to who she is.

I think of my own mother, Grace, and consider that I wanted her to be someone other than who she was. And here's a question: what opinion will my girls have of me when they're adults? Already, I have my answer prepared for them: *this is who I am and I'm doing my best*. But my mother said the same thing to me and I judged her harshly. When she died I was still angry with her, and right now I'm sad. Perhaps I'm depressed because I've just seen Laura Sullivan's solid oak casket put inside a hearse and driven away. Poor Mum. I was too hard on her, and I whisper 'sorry' into the air, to her memory.

And so I resolve once again to be kinder to Margie.

At home it looks like we've rehearsed it, the way Ross gets the plates, Isobel clears the table and Jemima puts the forks down. But only for four.

'I'll get Margie,' I say. 'Set another place.'

They stare at me as I leave the room.

Margie is sitting straight-backed on the cane chair, like the matriarch she thinks she is, wearing pink lipstick that is too bright for her. For a weird moment I think she must be going out somewhere, in the grey blouse and black pants, the tan flats on her feet.

'We've got Chinese,' I say.

'Who?'

'Chinese takeaway for dinner.'

She's on her feet. 'Dot and I used to go to Tamarind Thai regularly. I quite liked the sweet-and-sour pork. I'll need a fork because I don't use chopsticks.'

She pushes the walker down the hall, yet she looks spritely enough, as if forgetting her lame leg.

Ross has a beer. He's poured a glass of white wine for me.

The food by now is lukewarm, a bit soggy, but we're ravenous and there's too much food on the table for five. I take Margie's plate and serve her. She stares at what I give her, like it's beyond Chinese food, more foreign than that. Perhaps she's never had crispy-skin chicken or king prawns with ginger and shallots. Ross offers her a glass of wine and she surprises us by saying she'd prefer a beer.

Margie is in a good mood and seems interested when Jemima shows her a photo of a guitar she plans to make out of recycled material.

'What's the point of it, pet?' Margie asks.

Jemima grins. 'For school.'

'But you can't play a cardboard guitar.'

'We're having an orchestra.'

Margie can't fathom what Jemima's said, so she turns her attention to Isobel – yet she seems even more perplexed by her. She knows only one question to ask her – that is, what is she now playing? And the answer is always unfathomable: a Chopin ballade, a Mozart sonata, a Prokofiev piece.

So it's Ross and me that Margie speaks to. There's lipstick on her front teeth when she reminds us again that she and Dot used to go to Tamarind Thai once a week. And with the mention of Dot's name, one thought links to another, and she's telling us about the cruise they planned to go on and that today she saw a magazine advert for one just like it. Then she looks at Ross and tells him about the problems Freddie Ballantine had with the titles when he bought Tullys. She thinks this is very important information that Ross really needs to know. He necks his beer while listening and I know he wants her to be quiet.

When she stops talking, there's a hush in the room. We want to eat and be light among ourselves, but Margie's presence stops us. It's like we're back in church, at Laura's funeral. And so I talk about the funeral, telling Margie that about a hundred and fifty people were there. 'Laura's sister and her husband from Perth are staying with Chester for a few days,' I say. 'It's good he's not by himself.'

Margie puts her fork down and sits up.

'Did you know she was a botanical artist?' I ask. 'We have one of her pieces in the front room. A persimmon.'

'Yes, I know she painted fruit and flowers.'

There's a definite shift in Margie's mood; she seems distracted and starts fidgeting with the edge of the placemat. I notice again the thin gold band is missing from her left hand.

'Are you okay?' I ask.

She nods, then slowly rises from the chair. With the walker, she pushes towards the hallway. I watch until she's out of sight, then glare at Ross to let him know I'm unhappy he's not talked to his mother. He shrugs, as if to say, *What the hell did I do?*

Like Ross, I want our life back, how it was before she came to live with us. I'm finally resigned to speaking to the orthopaedic surgeon about her returning to Bishop Street. I've got a list of services and things she'll need. Margie will be all right; somehow she always is. And she's more mobile now, moving better, and I wonder if she even needs the walker, but then I don't want her to have another fall.

*

The girls are in bed and Ross is in his study, drinking his coffee, looking at cattle prices, markets, weather, god knows what interests him half the time. I pour a good slug of Jack Daniel's and go to the dining room.

I log on more out of habit; it's something to do. I open Outlook and wait to see what drops into my inbox. I sip the whiskey, feel the lovely burn. Various newsletters, and a chain of community messages on a CFA dinner auction. I reply, saying we'll all attend and also donate six bales of hay with a reserve of three hundred dollars on them; we do it every year.

I sip my whiskey, glancing at the portraits, the missing Norman – and raise my glass in defiance because he's now covered in an old blanket, hidden behind the tool cupboard in the tractor shed.

An email from Felicity asks if I've heard about the funding; I reply saying no. A message from friends over on Barry Mill Road, Erin and Steve, inviting us to dinner on Saturday the ninth; I answer saying we'd love to. I delete a catalogue for kids' clothes.

Then. I stare.

Victorian Rural Arts have snuck in, they're about six emails down, and I'd missed it.

I know the funding has been rejected. So when I open it I'm prepared, braced, ready to be devastated and spend the night getting drunk, deciding what the purpose of my life is if I can't even get this gig up. But it says:

Congratulations, the Yellow Box Players have been granted six thousand dollars.

There's a long unnecessary spiel on why my request for fifteen thousand was rejected. Six thousand is enough.

I stand, raise my arms and explode the air from my lungs in a happy scream. Already I know how the money will be spent. I need Chester to do the sets because he'll do them expertly and cheaply. We won't advertise in the local paper but will do black-and-white posters, put them up all over town and everywhere else. We'll post regular Facebook updates.

Ross is rushing to me; the swing door opens. 'Jesus, what?'

I tell him.

'Bloody beauty, my darling.' His arms are wide.

And I fold into him and do this sort of crying-laughter while he gently rocks me from side to side.

*

Monday morning, Margie asks me what time the theatre group meeting is. Then she asks me again after lunch, but this time she wants to know who is coming. I tell her, yet she looks at me like I've not answered her properly.

Later in the afternoon, I discover her napping in the pergola; her lipstick-painted mouth is slightly open. She's wearing the grey blouse with the black pants and runners, and she looks smaller, or perhaps more compact with clothes that fit properly. It's warm and a pleasant place to sleep.

My play is beside her, and a pen and ruled pad. At first I think she's taking this very seriously, writing notes about what she's reading. But it looks more like a letter: there's a salutation at the top; whole lines have been filled with her spidery cursive lettering. There's scribbling out and tiny words in the margins. For fear of waking her, I don't step forward to see who she's writing to; perhaps Caroline or some relative she still keeps in touch with.

I leave and make tea for us, and when I return she's awake, staring across the garden. I follow her gaze and see three red-breasted robins in a row on the fence. The lipstick she's wearing isn't as bright as the birds, but even so I must get her a lighter one. She turns to me and doesn't smile – Margie rarely smiles, but I know she's not unhappy I'm there. She takes the tea from me and blows into it, checking the heat. There's something going on with her, more than just the clothes. She's less sullen and more alert. The pad is now facedown, and I'm curious about who the letter is addressed to.

'Where are you up to?' I say, pointing to the play.

'Everyone is worried that the pizzas haven't arrived. The son has opened another beer and is in trouble.'

'Act One, Scene Eight,' I say.

I sit so we can face each other, and I ask her what she thinks of Grace.

'She's distracted with a magazine and doesn't listen to what she is being told. She's quite frustrating.'

I nod, pleased. 'And are you enjoying it?'

'It's all right.'

I wonder if Margie just doesn't know how to make conversation, or is it that she can't give in to me for some reason?

'Is Chester coming tonight? To the theatre group?' she asks, like she's accusing me of something.

'I don't know. Why?'

She seems to want to say something else, the way she's shifting in her seat.

'I'll phone him now and find out,' I say.

And my thumbs are in Contacts and I've pressed his number before I notice her hand is to her neck, and she's shaking her head.

He doesn't answer. But I leave a message, saying I'd love to see him tonight. 'But of course I understand if you can't make it.'

Margie is gripping the mug with both hands, leaning forward as if she's cold.

'Are you coming to the meeting yourself?' I ask her.

'Perhaps,' she says.

'I'd love it if you would. Given you're reading the script.'

She shrugs lightly and tries to smile, a closed-mouth effort. And, as I turn, I hear her softly say, 'Thanks for the tea.'

*

We eat an early dinner of reheated lasagne so I can get organised for the theatre group. Ross takes the girls up to Tullys to see if a cow has accepted her twins and to give Isobel some more practice behind the wheel of the ute.

At seven-thirty Felicity arrives with a bottle of prosecco; 'to celebrate,' she says. And Noah walks in with Amber, and they're standing close in a way that makes me wonder. Holly enters with her arms wide and does a little dance. Owen is himself, shy and self-conscious; he only ever seems relaxed when he's performing. The backstage helpers stride in, Mandy and Justine. We open the bubbles and I cut slices of a flourless chocolate cake I made with figs, a shot of brandy and espresso.

We clink glasses and hug, Owen too, and I think we all want to be here. The group is working.

The swing door opens. Margie steps through without her walker, standing straighter; the new bra gives her a good shape. She's changed, now wearing her navy dress with pantyhose, and the brown flats and lovely earrings I've not noticed before.

She glances around the room and towards the back as if looking for someone, and I know it's Chester she wants to see. She's wearing the dress and walking freely to impress him. Perhaps I'm wrong.

I introduce her as our new member, and because the prosecco is finished I rush to the fridge for a bottle of Lilly's Lane sparkling. She takes a glass from me, but even with all the cheer and warmth around her, she only nods, with a thin-lipped smile, and takes a seat. She refuses a slice of cake.

Margie stares as we cluster together and sing Madonna's 'Give It 2 Me'. Owen's got the best singing voice and carries us. He wants our next production to be a musical, but I only do drama. We always sing together to get our lungs open and minds focused. We shake our arms, twist, stretch and bend our bodies. We know the routine.

Only then do we read through the first act; the lines are paced well, the beat is right. Noah's more confident on the violin. Amber's lines are great.

Felicity stumbles over saying 'fucking bullshit' and asks if it can be changed to something more family-friendly. I hesitate because I understand where she's coming from; but the answer is no, and I explain that we have to be true to the character. So she says it with exaggerated fury and we all laugh. Margie is stone-faced but continues to read along.

Holly gives us an update on the poster and tells us she's got another story in the local paper. Amber is going to update the Facebook page every day. Already we have more than eight hundred followers.

We decide to meet again on Sunday for a full run-through.

‘How’s Chester going?’ Felicity asks. ‘Is he working on the sets?’

‘He’s started on them,’ I say. ‘And if he can’t keep working on it, Ross said he’d finish them, but he’s not very handy with a circular saw.’

Margie stands while I’m passing around the budget updates: printing, ticketing, hall hire, canteen supplies, miscellaneous. She bows her head and, almost in a whisper, says goodnight and leaves quietly. We all watch the swing door noiselessly flap. Something is wrong, but I can’t leave the group to go to her.

Margie

BACK in my room I sit at the small table. I like the feel of this navy dress, so rather than take it off and put on my nightie, I leave it on. And the pantyhose holds me in firmly so I can pretend I'm in better shape around my middle. It's nice to remember how my body once was.

I turn the lamp on. The letter I'm composing to Chester is before me. My handwriting has been inelegant since my Grade One schoolteacher forced me to write with my right hand, though I was born left-handed. Over the years my script has become delicate long lines and small curves, like the footprints of a silvereye. I've noticed Isobel is left-handed and has been allowed to write her natural way.

I've been drafting this letter in my mind for a few days, ever since I heard of Laura's passing. An envelope arriving in Chester's letterbox from me will no longer present a difficulty for him. The communication between us was always one-sided, from him to me when he dropped an envelope into our letter-box. I suppose I'm reaching out to him, wanting to reconnect for no other reason than perhaps we can discover a proper friendship. I would like that very much.

Chester's face is before me, as though I'm talking to him. I read the words that I've already written on the lined pad and see I've been free in my disclosures, saying things that are too private and after all these years are best forgotten. I've scrawled out words and made a mess of the page, so I'll have to rewrite it. Perhaps I won't send it at all.

Since returning to Maryhill, Chester, I've been thinking about many things. How I suffered with Norman. The loss of our beautiful boys. My happiest memories are with you . . .

I hear the caw of a raven. The mournful sound comes through the open window and makes me sit back. It's only a bird; even so, I feel unnerved. I pick up the pen, turn to a fresh page and, in my blue-inked clawed handwriting, I write the first thing that comes to mind.

I was hoping you'd be at the theatre group meeting tonight. Stella's play is quite interesting. It makes me think of my own children. Ross had it the hardest . . .

Aah-aah-aah. The raven is in the gleditsia outside the window. Mark's tree. I can't see it in the mass of leafy green fronds. A blowie darts around the lamplight and across the table. I slap at it, but miss. I wish for a cup of tea, but I won't go down the hallway now. I persist with the letter.

Today, I saw an advert for a cruise in the RACV magazine. I've always wanted to go to England.

Even as I write this, I know I'll never go anywhere on a ship. But I visualise Chester with me on a big liner, the two of us sailing away. In the early days of our long affair, he said he'd like to kidnap me, that we'd drive off together, never to return to the tableland. But we couldn't leave our children, our reputations. Maybe we were cowards.

Of course, I'm a stupid, senile woman. These thoughts. It's just that now, after all this time, we are both free.

The idea of rewriting the letter and giving it to Chester excites me, but I'm unsure. So I fold it and tuck it away in the shoebox in my wardrobe. Then comes the worry of it being discovered, so I look around for another hiding place. Stella is in and out of my drawers with the laundry. Perhaps under the mattress? Or should I tear it into little pieces? But, in the end, I leave it where it is, and go to bed.

Stella

EVERYTHING on my phone is telling me Ross wants me. The radiate ringtone, his name on the screen and his photo: grinning at me across the table in the beer garden at our local, with that relaxed expression, the light in his eyes.

I ignore it.

Pressing my lips together, I'm not convinced that the old trick of blotting my painted lips on a tissue and reapplying the lipstick to make it last longer works. Leaning closer to the mirror, I paint on another coat. Joli Rouge.

Ross phones again. He really wants me. There's a predictable pattern to these things: most often I'm needed minutes before I'm about to walk out the door, showered, dressed, lipsticked, focused. Today I'm taking Margie to see her surgeon.

I answer.

'Bringing a calving heifer to the yards,' he says.

'What's wrong with her?'

'She's stopped trying. I tried Eddie – he's not answering.'

'Smart bloke.'

I'm already reordering the morning. 'There in ten,' I say.

In the ensuite I change out of my linen pants and t-shirt, then pull yesterday's work clothes from the laundry basket. I tie my hair up, out of the way.

Margie is sitting at the family-room table, waiting for me, inscrutable.

'Want to come?' I ask. 'We're pulling a calf.'

'What about my appointment?'

'We'll see how we go.'

She stands, and I'm now moving fast.

'Meet you at the shed,' I say.

The calf puller is leaning beside a pallet stacked with bags of annual rye grass seed. It's a boat winch bolted onto a heavy iron plank. I heave it onto the tray of the ute. A litre bottle of vegetable oil. Nylon straps with metal hoops. It's been a while since we did this so I stand and think, *What else?* Gloves.

I've got the ute up to sixty before we turn to the yards, dust flying. Margie is stiff, holding the armrest.

'Have you ever pulled a calf, Margie?'

'That was men's work. Keith Sanders took care of things like that.'

It reminds me of Norman, that he always had someone else do all the work.

At the yards I position the ute so Margie can watch without getting out.

The heifer is caught in the head bail, standing calmly. A broken amniotic sac, pink and grapefruit-sized, bulges from under her tail.

Ross is all business, securing the winch in the race, loosening the strap and pulling it forward. Then he rolls up his sleeves and I wet his hands with oil. I lift the heifer's shitty tail. We're like doctor and nurse.

As Ross pushes his right hand and forearm into the cow's vagina, he tells me he doesn't know how long she's been calving. 'Might've started anytime overnight. Touch and go.' He's feeling for the head, front hooves, checking everything is in the right place.

'What?' I ask.

'Seems all right.'

Ross nods and I hand him a strap. He pushes his hand and arm back inside the poor young cow – strains, grits his teeth, neck tight, turns his wrist, and he's got the hoof forward and with his left hand tightens the strap above the hock. Same for the second hoof. But the first strap loosens and drops to the ground.

'Shit,' Ross says.

My fault; I should've held it tight. We start again. I'm holding the cow's tail up as he reattaches the first strap, then the second. He fastens the winch hook to the straps, and I move back into the race and look up, waiting to be told to start winding. The calf's black front legs are partly out, two pearly hooves pointing straight, straps taut on the winch line.

'Go for it,' Ross says.

I wind, easily at first, but the tension builds fast. I know Ross is keeping the angle of the winch line downward, controlling how the calf will fall. The heifer, birthing her first calf, stands compliant, silent. I've got no clue what it's like for her. The calf needs to be born. I glance up and see the front legs and calf's nose, a long pink tongue. I keep winding.

'Head's out.'

It's much harder for the shoulders. Ross yells for me to hurry up.

'Fuck off,' I shout back, breathless. I'm going as hard and fast as I can. We've talked about swapping places because he's stronger, but I don't like being so close to the action in case the cow drops to the ground or kicks, or the calf doesn't present quite the way we expect.

Both hands now, another turn, another, another. I'm heaving for breath.

And then there's lightness. The easy flop of the winch handle. The calf slithers from its mother's warm insides. Head, shoulders, hips, it crashes to the ground. Steam rises from its wet, warm body. Mouth open and nostrils flared, taking in first air.

'Alive,' Ross calls, already pulling the straps off its hooves.

He drags the calf close to the head bail. It's all big bones and slimy hair, long in the body and hollowed out – too big for its mother to push out. Seconds old, and the calf is already raising its head off the ground. I lift its tail: a boy. Good. They're worth more at market because they weigh more.

We step out of the pen. Ross opens the head bail. The new mum comes out, sniffing. And there, after four steps, she puts her head down, makes that lowing sound and lovingly breathes in and licks her baby, glancing at us with a warning in her eye to now leave her be.

I lift my face. Ross kisses me lightly on my Joli Rouge lips.

'Back at lunch,' I say.

A heavy watery gush. We turn. The placenta has come away. On the ground behind the heifer is a mass: glistening pink membranes, cotyledons, bloody fluid. She temporarily diverts her attention from the calf and starts eating.

At the ute I pull the bloody and shitty gloves off and toss them in the tray. Margie watches my every move.

Behind the wheel, I turn to her. 'Don't worry. A quick shower. We'll make it.'

Margie

ABOVE the cattle yards a wedge-tailed eagle is being chased by two magpies. The eagle's wingbeats are slow, making it vulnerable to attack. I've never seen anything like it. Perhaps it is injured, and I wish for my notebook so I can record this remarkable thing. The pursuit carries on while Ross and Stella winch a calf from an exhausted cow. The eagle is immature, less than five years old – I know this because the back of its neck and wings are pale gold. And, not for the first time, I admire magpies for their courage and community; presumably they are protecting their territory.

It is only when I hear Stella's foul mouth, yelling the four-letter word at Ross, that I turn to them. The calf drops to the ground. It looks alive, so this will be worth being late for my visit to the surgeon.

Out across the lower paddock and a copse of eucalypts, I look for the magpies and eagle. They've gone now, over the rise towards Tullys, and I feel a terrible sadness for the plight of the eagle, yet uplifted that I saw such an extraordinary and rare thing. I remember seeing three magpies chase a fox across a paddock once, swooping low and determined.

Ross and Stella kiss on the lips, so I don't understand what her vulgar language was all about. Then she's back in the ute, driving up the laneway like a crazy person. We bump and sway and any moment we'll crash into the fence. I'm holding the armrest for dear life. She thinks we'll be on time for my appointment, yet she's going to have a shower.

We pass Chester's place on Black Wattle Road. The tinge of red on the row of lilly pillies is berries. Crimson rosellas are feeding on them; a cuckoo-shrike dives in. My mother used to make a very nice lilly-pilly berry chutney.

Smoke is coming from Chester's chimney, which surprises me because it's not cold enough yet for a fire. We pass Hoskins Lane. For ten years I manoeuvred the car between those weathered pine posts and past the rusted gate Chester had left open for me, always expectant and elated to be meeting my lover at his work shed, our private world – and I see how it was all those long years ago when I drove down there like a brazen fugitive daring anyone to catch me. And on the way out, I'd often be weeping with the misery of not knowing when I'd see him again. I wonder about that younger me and feel deep sadness for her. It would've been wonderful to have lived a life knowing that kind of happiness as a standard way of being, like Laura did, like most people seem to. Like Ross and Stella do.

The letter I wrote yesterday is safely hidden in the shoebox in the bottom of my wardrobe. I wonder what Chester's reaction would be if I dared to rewrite it neatly and post it to him. But these are dangerous thoughts connected to long-gone fantasies. The past cannot be resurrected and brought into the future, not after all these years. Writing the letter was cathartic and I'll destroy it first thing.

Stella is pressing buttons on the steering wheel. Then the car is filled with the sound of her phone ringing, and not for the first time I'm in awe that it works when the phone itself is actually in her large handbag. No one is going to answer and I wonder how she will hang up.

Then Chester's voice is inside the car – the way he drawls his name as though it's two words: *Ches-ter*.

Stella is cheerful and talking into the windscreen as if he's on the bonnet. She smiles at him when she says, 'What's with the fire on a day like this? Are you all right?'

'I've cleaned the chimney, checking to see if there's a blockage. I can tell you're in the car. Where're you off to?'

And she tells him she's taking me to Wangaratta, and he must know I can hear because he says hello to me.

I stare around, unsure where to give my reply.

Stella carries on before I work it out. 'No pressure on you, Chester, but the play is only three weeks away and there's work to be done on the sets. Ross says he can try to do it. What do you think?'

I grip the armrest and stare across the valley, down at the row of windswept golden poplars winding beside the creek. An echidna waddles along the side of the road.

Chester is hesitating and I cannot think what his problem is. Most of his farm is agisted, and if he had time for this before Laura died, then surely he has more time now.

'I'm planning on going to Perth with Laura's sister and brother-in-law,' he says. 'Stay a couple of weeks.'

Chester and Laura used to holiday with Julie and Ian at their place in Cottesloe. Chester is being selfish: Ian sails a forty-two-foot yacht off Fremantle – that's the attraction, not a need for consolation. Sometimes the visits were reciprocated with Julie and Ian coming to the tableland. I was never told directly, but I believe they all went on daytrips, sometimes to Melbourne.

Chester always reported that Julie and Ian were dull. There was the time I was having a quiet lunch by myself at Minnie's in Benalla, and the four of them walked in and took a table not two metres away. Chester positioned his back to me. I sat there unable to finish my sandwich, while they talked and laughed among themselves. That day Laura wore a very nice fitted tweed jacket in the colours of an olive whistler, and her fair hair was brushed across to the side and behind her ears. For a short time afterwards I experimented with doing my own hair that way, but it didn't suit me.

Even though I don't want those distressing memories, I'm struck with renewed resentment that Chester is going to the west, carrying on as if Laura was still alive.

'I understand,' Stella says. 'It'd be good for you to have a break.'

'But perhaps I'll hold off until the play is out of the way,' Chester says.

'Are you sure? I feel I'm putting pressure on you.'

'I'd only do it for you, my Stella.'

I know Chester is smiling, flirting and being himself, the foolish old rogue that he is. And Stella is grinning back at him through the windscreen. Her sunglasses are very modern, large like Jackie Kennedy used to wear.

'So, Chester,' she says, 'would you like to come to dinner one night this week to discuss it all? Especially the dimensions of the back shelving. And I'm uncertain about the kitchen layout and how we'll organise the water.'

We are now on the Hume Freeway; flat monotonous double lanes stretch to the horizon. I rub my finger where my wedding ring once belonged – its absence makes that little part of me feel strange. Something is missing, which reminds me I am alone.

'How about tomorrow night?'

'Lovely,' Stella says.

They agree he will come over around seven and bring a bottle of wine. Then she presses a button on the steering wheel and he's cut off.

It is thrilling and unbearable to know Chester is coming to dinner. So I decide then that I should return to Bishop Street as soon as possible. For the next twenty kilometres, while Stella swoons at that soulful female singer's voice, I put myself back in my house. Another winter is coming and how will it be without Dot next door? She used to drive a little silver Honda; that's how we got around. Now I'll be housebound. Some of the old folk have gophers, but they look ridiculous whooshing along the footpaths. There is the retirement village, but I am loath to live in a commune of old people, everyone with their aches and pains, knowing each other's business.

I'm caught up in myself; this long-gone business with Chester is unsettling. The expectation of contact with him brings a baffling sensation of joy and despair that I seem unable to cast off. If I return to Bishop Street, I won't see him again.

And the children have become an unexpected pleasure. Jemima has been showing me how to press buttons on her iPad so I can look things up. Last week she showed me how to press a blue square called Safari that changes the screen. Then at the top she typed in a question I had about the difference between a female scarlet robin and a female flame robin; I've often mixed them up. She told me to lightly touch a button, then the whole screen suddenly changed again and filled with lines of information and photos. I was astonished. She did something to make the scarlet robin start singing. I could hear it. The same for the flame robin. Seeing and hearing them like that, it was so obvious how different they are, yet for years I'd been confusing their calls.

Isobel worries me. She practises on the piano as if she's got nothing else to do; as if she might be lonely. A pretty girl hiding behind those dark-framed glasses, I suspect she doesn't have any friends. I do enjoy listening to her, and a couple of times I've sat in the front room and watched her hands move across the keyboard. She concentrates very hard and doesn't seem to mind me being there; I know to remain quiet and not ask questions. It's not natural for a child to be so driven, and I think Ross and Stella should pay more attention to this obsession she seems to have. At that age, Caroline was outside with her horse, or at a girlfriend's house – that is, until she became interested in boys. I found a packet of contraceptive pills in her underwear drawer when she was only sixteen.

'Are you all right?' Stella says to me.

'Of course.'

'You seem upset about something?'

And so I take a deep breath and clasp my hands and do my best to appear myself. I look ahead, not just up the freeway but also into my future, knowing that Stella is about to speak to my surgeon about putting me back in Bishop Street and I have no say in it.

*

The surgeon is half my age and it is Stella he talks to, not me, as if it was her hip tendons he repaired and joint he replaced.

'So how's it going?' he asks.

'Not too bad,' Stella replies. 'In pain for the first fortnight, three weeks, but in the past week she's picked up. Do you think, Margie?'

'I'm doing quite well,' I say.

He tells me to stand, to stretch my right leg to the side, forwards, backwards, to lift my knee. I don't know if I've passed his test, but he tells me I can sit down.

'Do you need anything for the pain?' he asks.

I would like some more blue pills, but I will not ask in front of Stella. Sometimes if I take one in the middle of the night it helps me go back to sleep, but Panadol also helps, so I'm not sure what's going on. I think it's all in my imagination, that every pill is a placebo and I should try to do without them.

'I'm fine,' I say.

Any moment Stella will ask her question about me returning to Bishop Street. I stare at the green leather inlay on the surgeon's desk. Alicia still comes to help me shower, but the truth is I can probably manage well enough on my own. It's the shopping that will be a worry, getting up the street. And the housework and garden. Cooking for myself again will be a pleasure. I feel the shallow rise of my chest, breathing, waiting.

'When will I bring Margie back?' Stella asks.

'Three months,' he says, telling her that I should continue with the physio for the time being and that exercise in a swimming pool would be a benefit.

She gathers up her bag and stands.

Nothing is said about me going to my house, and I feel indignant because decisions have been made about me and I don't know what's going on.

'But I'm returning to Bishop Street,' I say.

They look at me.

'Do you want to?' Stella asks. 'I thought we'd wait a bit, until the play is over.'

I can't stand it, being at her mercy. One minute I'm going, the next staying. I hear the false conviction in my voice. 'I would like to return to my home as soon as possible.'

'It's just there's a lot going on right now, Margie. I won't have time to organise everything. Can't you wait until the play is over?'

I stand as straight as I can, poised.

The surgeon looks at a pad on his desk.

'It's only another three weeks,' Stella says.

My mouth betrays me with a sudden weakening, the urge to weep. I'm confused. No one wants me.

'Do I have a choice?' I say.

'Margie, stop it.' I look at her and she's smiling. 'Three weeks is nothing.'

She waves at the surgeon and goes to the door.

I follow.

So it is decided, without me answering, that I will be at Maryhill until the play is finished.

As I'm clipping my seatbelt on, Stella turns and says, 'Hell, Margie, your place is so bloody depressing. It's not only the play – I just can't see how I can leave you there.'

I don't mean to, but I nod.

*

When we're on the freeway, with an esky and a boot full of groceries, her chatter roams from one topic to another. One minute she's telling me Ross is taking Jemima to have her plaster cast removed after school. Then, would I be up to making dessert for when Chester comes to dinner tomorrow night? And can I please proofread the flyer and media release she has written for the play? 'Any suggestions you've got would be great.'

'Very well,' I say.

She takes the short cut up through the logging plantations. Since the deluge, the road is rutted and potholed. It's not worth driving here for the sake of fifteen minutes. I don't know why she does this. A wallaby lopes across the road in front. A fallen gum tree has been chainsawed and pulled away for clear passage.

She's thinking about something and I can't imagine what.

'This morning when you and Ross were pulling the calf,' I say, 'there was a wedge-tailed eagle being chased by two magpies.'

'Really? Above our heads?'

'Yes. Then they disappeared over towards Tullys.'

'That's awesome.'

As if to prove how special a day can be – I'm not going back to Bishop Street – out in front of us, above the pines in the clear white sky, two wedge-tailed eagles slowly glide on upswept wings, circling, and I can only suppose there's a rabbit below, a possum, or perhaps an injured kangaroo.

I point them out. Stella stops the car in the middle of the road. We stare up through the windscreen, through the gap of trees, and watch them for minutes until they drift away.

Stella

AFTER dinner I remind Jemima that her recycled-material guitar is due at school in the morning – as if she doesn't already know this. I'm sick of the project and tell her the easiest instrument to make would be a handful of rice in a plastic bottle with a lid. Maracas! She whines, telling me this isn't allowed, that it has to be made of at least five things. I'm sidestepping to the dining room to print the play's promotional material off when she starts crying.

Ross is reading his iPad. He turns to me deadpan and says, 'Rock. Paper. Scissors.'

We've done this many times, but I'm not in the mood for it. I'm tired and want out. Tonight, though, he's doing our BAS statement and updating the stock records. So I go along with it. On the count of three – he puts his hand flat as I open my fingers. I win. He loses. That quick. If it was the other way around, I'd insist we do best out of three.

Without complaint, he goes with Jemima to the back porch bench to build a guitar. I hear him say he's got a length of poly in the shed that will make a good neck and irrigation taps that are the right size for tuning pegs. And Jemima, cunning child, is now quiet and standing back, allowing her father to build the whole damn thing. 'We need a small box,' he tells her. 'That's your job. Find something for the body and soundboard.'

I push through the swing door with a glass of red wine. It's cool in the dining room and I think about a jumper, but shrug the feeling off. All the beds now have an extra blanket. Ross and Eddie have been chainsawing and splitting fallen peppermint and blue gum, and some stringybark eucalypts. The woodshed is already half-full, and when it's full I won't care about the approaching cold months. In many ways, I prefer those closed-in grey days and icy winds to the relentless dry heat and dust.

I open the *I Did My Best* Word file and print the flyer, poster and media release for Margie to proofread. I think they're okay; it's simply an experiment to see if I can engage her, help her feel connected to our theatre group. That's what the Robinson Street Theatre was for me when I was a troubled seventeen-year-old: a quiet and simple oasis. Well, it was that before I climbed into Erik Kozlov's bed and let him do what he wanted. I suppose everyone has things in their life they're ashamed of. But it's more about sadness, that I was so vulnerable then. I know what loneliness is.

Mum stares back at me from my laptop screen. She's the signature image for *I Did My Best*, an angled sepia photo of her lovely face – head tilted slightly to the right, eyes wide and steady, lips curved, perhaps a smile. She's on everything. I feel a pull in my heart and a vacancy, the reminder that the writing and producing of this play has gone on for too long. I'm done with it. Other plays are calling me. *Ghosts* by Henrik Ibsen looks interesting. Alexi Campbell's *Apologia* would be brilliant. And I'd like to write another play, something on patriarchies and how a capable, independent girl feels about them.

The printer is on the other side of the dining table. While I wait for it to click to life, I look across at the portraits. The picture frames are all different, each of its generation: walnut fretwork with gold inlay, a fussy pattern in tarnished silver, rosewood with raised leaf clusters, and plain gilded oak. The empty space where Norman once hung throws all the others out of balance. I wonder, then, if it was my right to take him down and hide him away. Perhaps it should have been Margie's decision about what should be done with him. She might've wanted him to hang at Bishop Street. I'd not thought of that.

The printer clunks, paper slides.

Shoulder first, Ross bashes through the swing door.

'Jesus,' he says.

My open mouth, a waiting question.

'Check this out.' He pushes folded pages into my hand.

'What?' I ask.

He whispers, 'A letter from Mum to Chester.'

'Chester?'

'Read it.'

I look sideways at him. 'Where'd you get it?'

'A shoebox.'

'What shoebox?'

'Jem said she found it in the bottom of Mum's wardrobe.'

'Did she ask first?'

He shakes his head.

'What the hell?' I say.

'Just read it.'

Ross has lost his usual calm: he's wired, his fingers move, a slight quiver around his mouth.

I sit in my tasselled, red-cushioned chair and unfold the letter. Ross leans behind me. Margie's handwriting is familiar, spidery with loops and long lines. If you could guess someone's personality by their handwriting, you would expect this writer to be creative, flamboyant. It's too untidy for Margie.

From the appearance of the paper, the way it's set out, my impression is that it's the letter she was working on in the pergola yesterday. It's wrong for us to be reading it, and I'm scanning, not taking anything in.

'There,' Ross says, pointing. 'Mum and Chester.'

Then I do read.

. . . you kissed my fingertips. How precious that was.

I feel the distressing weight of Maryhill's history; in this house, in Margie, her kids – and the whole business with Chester, only a few kilometres down away on Black Wattle Road. And what was going on there between Chester and Laura? They had a good marriage, so everyone said at her funeral, over and over. Chester was too choked up to properly speak. His face was blotchy from crying.

This news about Margie is unreal, and I feel insecure at the deceit people are capable of, like nothing can truly be known or trusted. That feeling I always had when Dad was still living at home and Graham would visit Mum. 'Only a good friend,' she'd say. Then Dad left, and Tommy barricaded himself in his room. I remember one day, close to Mum's death, watching Graham bend over her bed, his body racked with sadness, and Mum's hand pulling through his hair. Funny. In all the years I've unpeeled Mum's life for the play, I'd not considered that dimension. Grace as lover.

Well, then. Margie and Chester.

I turn a page.

That time you made me a birthday cake. Lemon icing. Thank you again. It was such fun, wasn't it?

Ross's breath is warm and fast on my neck.

Living with a violent man was my terrible misfortune. Now our spouses are both gone . . .

I lean in closer, as if that will help me read faster, but I'm missing words, worrying that any moment Margie will push through the door and demand to know where her private letter is.

. . . the idea that after all this time we can become proper friends. It would mean a great deal to me.

'Shit,' I say.

After the first page, the letter doesn't flow: topics shift before one thought is complete. She wants to go on a cruise to England. She thinks Isobel plays the piano too much and has no friends. Words are scribbled out; arrows lead to sentences in the margins.

'Where's the shoebox now?' I ask Ross.

'Painted purple, with a sound hole in the lid.'

'I'll just drop this letter in the back of the wardrobe, like it fell out.'

'She won't buy that.'

It happens. A sound, the sense of something, and we're looking up as Margie pushes and huffs through the swing door. I thrust the letter onto my lap under the table.

She is standing in her dressing-gown: pale, hunched, thin-looking.

We all stare, paralysed.

No one speaks.

Margie's lips tremble when she says, 'The shoebox in the bottom of my wardrobe has been taken. There was something inside it that belongs to me.'

I cannot tell her the truth. The exposure will destroy us and I can't deal with the fallout. The theatrics. Margie's pious demands to return to Bishop Street tonight. We are not grown up enough for this honesty. Sometimes it is necessary to lie.

'It's here,' Ross says. He tugs the letter from my clasped hands. Four strides and he rests it on the table in front of her.

She glares into his face with startled, sad eyes, demanding the answer to an unspoken question. Her hands are shaking.

'Yes,' he says. 'We've read it.'

It's a bullet to her heart. Margie lowers her head.

'Don't worry about it,' he says. 'It's in the past.'

'You can't brush this off like that, Ross,' I say.

Margie turns to me and I tell her we already knew Norman was a total bastard, although we're still shocked by those details. 'And as for Chester, that really isn't a big deal. Not to us. Only to you. And I apologise that we read your letter.'

She leans forward and holds on to the edge of the table to support herself. There's a kind of desperate yearning in her expression, something that she wants to say but can't.

We are all confused now. I take a gulp of wine and stand. The moment ends when she clasps the letter in both hands, gathers herself straight and leaves us. We watch the flapping swing door.

'What the fuck?' I hiss at Ross. 'Why did you tell her we read it?'

'Because we did.'

'What now?'

He shrugs.

'Go and speak to her,' I say.

'What can be said about any of that?'

'I want you to step up.'

And there, a shift in him, he's taller and turns to face me. 'You think I don't get any of this,' he says. 'Wrong. It's just that I don't want to go there. It's a choice. I'm happy with my life and I don't need or want to get involved. End of story.' His hands are up, as if pushing me away.

My husband has just echoed how I feel about going over my past, trying to understand my mother as though that will somehow make my life different. In the end, Mum's life provided me with a creative challenge and obsessive occupation, but I can't say getting to know her changed one thing. It's only Ross himself, our life and future that make me happy.

'I'm sorry,' I say.

'Didn't think the old girl had it in her. Screwing Chester.'

'He's coming to dinner tomorrow night.'

Ross smiles. 'Getting better all the time.' He picks up my wineglass and drinks.

'Get your own.'

He does. And we sit on the chaise lounge with our wine and look across to the end of a sunset. Beyond the garden, in the mid-distance, there's a shimmering red line along the hill crest; above it the sky is flat and grey. We've still not solved the problem of Margie. I don't know, but perhaps Ross is right that what happens now is up to her.

Margie

MY hands tremble as I press the silver blisters and pop out the last of the blue pills. Ross and Stella have read my letter so it's a good thing only two are left, otherwise I could very well take the lot. What does it matter if I go to sleep and don't wake up? It would be a mercy, for me and everyone else. Blood is surging in my ears, throat, chest – perhaps I'll die of a heart attack. But in the meantime I need a safe place to hide and the tablets will take me there. One mouthful of water, a hard swallow, and they are on their way.

In bed I curl on my side and pull the bedding around me like a cocoon, with my ancient head peeping out. Stella has changed the sheets and put on an extra blanket; it feels the right weight for these cooler nights. The room is not dark yet, the red glow of the setting sun throws a soft light through the lace curtains, the floorboards are the colour of molasses. When I close my eyes and enter that private bedtime space, I hear the ringing *purr-purr pip-pip* of a grey shrike-thrush.

I breathe and concentrate on the yoga relaxing exercise. My right foot. Left foot. Calves. Knees. Legs. My breathing is even, in and out, in and out. I feel myself drifting, letting go.

But something yanks me back to wakefulness: the look on Stella's face, the tiny crease between her brows, as she said, 'I'm shocked to read the extent of Norman's abuse.' This is where their concern lies, not in my involvement with Chester – yet I would've expected it to be the other way around.

Suddenly I have an image of Norman, a random memory. He's at the head of the dinner table with me at the other end, our three children at the sides. We all eat quietly except Norman, who chews loudly. He holds his knife and fork out in front like weapons and tells me he can't find the television guide.

'Seen it?' he asks.

'No,' I say.

'You?' he says, looking at the children.

They look blankly at each other, then back at him.

'I want it now,' he says to me.

There is nothing more important. I leave the table and look under every cushion, through the mail and in the rubbish for the green newspaper that lists his favourite TV programs. It is nowhere and I can't avoid his rage. The details were carried out during the course of the evening.

Was that the evening he left the house and didn't return for a fortnight? 'Fishing,' he said when he came home. Although there were no rods in the car, or offerings of trout or cod.

These memories are boring and from such a long time ago. I roll over and sigh. It's not as though every day or week I was cowering in a corner or bent over with him behind me. Not at all. Sometimes months would go by and all was calm. That's the point: it was all so unpredictable that I was on edge, never knowing what was going to set him off.

Enough. I return to the peaceful yoga, wishing I could remember the pose's name. It starts with the letter S. Breathing in, I focus on my left leg. Breathe out. Breathe in, right leg. I exhale, thinking about Chester's silly moustache and the way his eyes crease when he smiles. My mind is tricky because it switches to the recipe for a baked lemon tart. That's what I'll make tomorrow for dessert when he comes to dinner.

It will be unbearable with Stella and Ross there, and I burn with the shame of them knowing my secret. How dare they read my private letter.

Still, I consider the ingredients for the tart. There are plenty of lemons hanging on the tree; I see them every time I go out the back door. But it's the butter and eggs that worry me, and I wonder if Stella has them in the fridge. I fall to sleep feeling anxious because Stella probably doesn't even have plain flour.

*

A magpie wakes me, a sweet morning reveille. The curtains puff with the cool breeze. Then a sick feeling in my belly. My body aches from a night of strange and tense dreams. My letter to Chester is everywhere, in my mind and body, in the bed with me, the whole room. I stare into the avocado-dip wall and breathe in my humiliation. I don't know what to do. I think of Stella calmly telling me, 'Norman was a bastard . . . and Chester, that's not a big deal. Not to us . . .' She thinks she understands.

My bladder forces me out of bed. I shower and wash my hair. It needs cutting and styling, and I hope Stella will take this problem in hand. She does Isobel's and Jemima's hair nicely, and the other morning I saw her in the back porch running electric clippers up Ross's head. He was drinking coffee while she was buzzing around him, then she had a comb and scissors like a real hairdresser.

I'm first in the kitchen, and in that open space I feel exposed knowing Ross or Stella could appear any moment. I make a cup of tea, and toast. I'm looking in the pantry, hopeful there's jam, when Stella rushes in. She stops, hesitates, then steps forward and embraces me. She's wearing a cotton dressing-gown, and I can feel the shape of her.

I stiffen.

'How are you this morning?' she asks, still not letting me go.

'Fine,' I say, pulling back.

We step away and she stares at me. No make-up, her skin is clear, no wrinkles. I feel old and ugly.

'I've not slept,' she says. 'I'm so worried about you.'

'There's no need for that.'

'I'm so sorry we read the letter. Please forgive us.'

I feel the rise of tears, so bite my lip and look to the back porch as if someone has called me.

She touches my arm.

I take a breath and talk through the window, beyond the porch. The vine needs pruning. 'It's all a very long time ago and private. I don't want it to be raised again. Ever.'

'There are counsellors who specialise in domestic violence. I was thinking about making you an appointment. You know, so you can talk to someone about it.'

'Why?' I ask.

'If you felt the need to write it down . . . Perhaps you need to discuss it with a professional.'

'I will not discuss or mention any of this ever again, to anyone.'

'Would it help if I went with you?'

Her audacity stuns me. 'No.'

'You seem resolute.'

'Do you have plain flour?' I ask.

'I can't imagine what it was like having to live up to all that Ballantine status bullshit.'

I wince at her language. 'I was thinking of making a lemon tart for dessert tonight.'

'Are you sure you don't need any help?' she asks.

'I know how to make a lemon tart.'

She stares back at me. 'Will it be awkward to see Chester?' she asks. 'Do you want me to cancel dinner tonight?'

I want her to be quiet and not force me to answer her prying questions. Instead I force a smile. 'My dear, do you have a flan tin?'

She grins, almost a chuckle, and I hate her for it, as if she understands something. Then she bends low into a deep drawer, pulling out muffin trays and cooling racks; it is a mess. Her dressing-gown gapes open, and on the soft mound of her left breast, an inch above a pink nipple, is the name 'Harry' in tiny calligraphy. A man's name tattooed on her breast, and I am stunned, not least because of the pain it must have caused to have it done. And she isn't wearing a nightie.

Unembarrassed, she wraps herself up again in the dressing-gown and gives me a choice between a round or rectangle tin. The rectangle will do nicely, and I take it from her. 'Thank you,' I say.

She turns from me and shakes muesli into a bowl, drops some blueberries on top, and then adds a dollop of yoghurt. So this is what the rice milk is for – I had wondered. Stella pours the pale brown milk into the bowl, takes a spoon from the drawer and walks out to the dinner table. But the room is too quiet and, when I check, she's not there. So I am alone, standing in my old kitchen with the task of making a lemon tart, and I can't think of anything else I'd rather do.

Stella

ROSS slowly gets out of bed and stands. He sighs and straightens up. It's as if the top and bottom of him somehow don't quite fit together. His back has flared up; any little thing can trigger it, and it's worse from a night in bed. The only emotion he attaches to the pain is resentment for the inconvenience. He'll keep lifting and straining and bending until he's moaning flat on the floor.

He dresses like an old man, one hand on the bedside table for balance, pulling on dirty jeans. I don't know how he can stand the feeling against his skin and tell him to put on a clean pair.

'In the yards this morning,' he says. 'No point.'

I sit in bed with my muesli; a splash of rice milk blots the sheets. 'Your mum seems happy about Chester coming for dinner. She's making a lemon tart.'

'Whatever,' he says.

'She called me "my dear", and smiled.'

'About time.'

He's shitty. It's the sore muscles and damaged ligaments around his lower back, and it's also crunch time to decide about buying more hay or selling cattle, and the always waiting fence repairs, and having to check the pregnant cows to see if there are any problems. And the promised rain missed us and we've only had forty millimetres this month, which is less than half the monthly average. But mostly, I'm guessing, it's Margie and her letter that have transported him back to his life before me.

I know how unsettling it can be when you're faced with all the old crap in your life. The only thing Ross has talked about from his childhood that brought light into his eyes was the model aeroplanes he made: 'Had them hanging from my bedroom ceiling like baby mobiles.' I wonder about grief and repressed memory and all the things I read in magazines and Facebook feeds that talk about dealing with issues.

But then, Ross is all right. I know him, so I leave him be.

He comes to the side of the bed and wants to bend down to kiss me before he leaves to go outside, but can't stoop that far. So I sit up tall and crane my neck and we meet halfway – an everyday, taken-for-granted, lovely kiss.

As he's walking to the door, a thought comes and I say it. 'Maybe they'll hook up. Your mum and Chester.'

'Don't be bloody ridiculous.'

I feel chastised. Even so, I finish my breakfast trying to picture the long-past affair between Margie and Chester – secret plans, the terror of being caught, and meeting near a purple clematis that grew long enough to reach a Granny Smith apple tree. Sounds nice. But I can't quite put Margie in the picture, a lustful woman having illicit sex. My god. Margie having sex at all.

I close my eyes and watch the sun bloom on the inside of my eyelids, pink and purple – and I think the idea of 'mother' is so embedded in my brain, it's impossible to see Grace or Margie as ordinary women, like me.

*

When Chester arrives, Ross is checking water levels down at the pump. Margie is nowhere to be seen, although a perfect lemon tart sits on a white plate, waiting to be presented to the table. A Chopin ballade floats in from the front room.

Jemima is sitting on the couch staring at her iPad. If I ask her what she's playing, she'll say Ace Maths, but I doubt that's true. She's shrewd, or inventive, and all I can hear is bird calls, so god knows what game she is playing this time. If her school marks weren't so good, I'd worry.

Chester steps inside, and there's always this thing with him, the way he puts his splayed hand low on my back as I walk ahead, as if this is his home and I'm the guest being ushered to the family room. And as we go, I explain I'm running late because I've just emailed the play's flyer to everyone on the database.

'You make yourself right at home,' I say.

When I turn to the kitchen, his arm tightens around my waist, as if this is our real greeting and not the one we had at the back door. A light kiss on my cheek, and I pull away, feeling that's too much touching. Yet Chester's always been a charming, flirtatious poet; the only difference is now I know he's not the harmless old bloke I thought he was. And about when I open the oven door and the heat hits my face, I realise I'm not too keen on him anymore.

The potatoes are looking good, broccolini is lightly steamed, fig-infused balsamic vinegar is waiting to be drizzled.

I've not showered.

'Give me five minutes,' I say to Chester.

Down the passageway I phone Ross. I'm annoyed he doesn't answer so leave a blunt message. Before I enter our bedroom, I hear the hairdryer so keep going and find Margie in the main bathroom. She's leaning into the mirror with Isobel's roll brush, her arms configured strangely as she tries to style her hair.

There is no time to waste. 'Give it to me,' I say.

The way she sighs and drops her shoulders it's like she's been expecting me. She looks relieved.

'I'm getting you some velcro rollers,' I say. 'You put them in when your hair is semi-dry; an hour later you take them out and just comb. Easy.'

I work the brush, drying, shaping. It takes a minute, such a small effort, and there's a difference in Margie, in her stature, the slight lift of her chin.

'I've not showered yet,' I say. 'Can you go to Chester? He's in the family room by himself.'

She turns away as if she's got other things on her mind.

'Offer him a glass of wine,' I say. 'I won't be long.'

I sound ridiculous, telling her how to attend to her old lover, but I'm as nervous for her as she appears to be. Margie is wearing the fitted black pants with that first blouse I bought her, the cream one with covered buttons and a line of gathering around the neck. And the new light pink lipstick I bought her, and the square-shaped pink sapphire earrings. She looks very nice. But the weight of their past feels too tragic and reminds me of a scene in AR Gurney's play *Love Letters*. I don't think I can stand to see them at the table together.

A quick once-over in the shower and I'm out in a minute. Jeans, a white linen shirt, dry-shampoo, hair up. My tan and black boots aren't right for home entertaining, but when I scramble through my shoes looking for inspiration nothing seems right so I zip them up.

When I stride from the hallway into the family room I'm expecting to be needed, but Ross is with Chester, the two of them standing by the window necking beers. Margie is in the kitchen, my kitchen, looking the part with a striped apron on. She's got the roast beef out of the oven, lifting it onto a tray.

I reach for the packet gravy.

She touches my arm. 'Let me.' The tiny weight of her hand, such a normal gesture.

It's as if she's moving to an inner music as she sprinkles plain flour over the pan juices, then whisks, adds salt, a splash of red wine from the thirty-dollar shiraz I bought at the local bottle shop. I pour myself a glass. And it all comes together, the two of us moving about, putting plates out, carving the meat, serving the vegetables and pouring the gravy without one word spoken between us.

She takes off the apron.

At the table I stand back to allow the seating to take care of itself.

Margie hesitates; Chester looks around. They are uncertain and sit opposite each other. I push Jemima's chair in to bring her closer to the table. Ross points to Isobel to put her knife and fork down until we're all ready. Wine is poured. Bread is buttered. We eat.

No one speaks because there is too much to say, or not say, and perhaps Ross isn't aware of the vibe – and maybe it's just me feeling this is all too awkward. But Ross chats about the banalities of local politics, something about the consolidation of under-utilised amenities. And then he's on about the lack of rain, as if somehow talking about it will make it pour buckets and fill the aquifers and make the springs flow and turn the dry dams into beautiful flat silver lakes. Margie seems astounded to hear her son speak so many words at once, as if it's a surprise that he's so articulate. And I don't blame her – in the weeks she's lived with us, Ross has been a brooding pain in the arse at the end of the table.

But I'm very pleased with him right now, the way he's carrying us all forward, making it easy. Chester is himself again, talking about the floods in 1993, the evacuations, and the homes and businesses that were damaged. Margie sits primly, cutting into the meat, eating small mouthfuls, listening to their every word. Sometimes she nods as if what's being said is important or she's in complete agreement.

I try to picture them together, young and naked, beautiful bodies, and I suppose it was very intense, the secret, the anticipation. I'm guessing it must've been good sex to risk your whole life and security over. But I still can't imagine Margie pulling at Chester's clothes, kissing his face.

Ross laughs at something and I've lost the thread of conversation. And now I'm back in the moment and not completely happy because this dinner is supposed to be about the play and the set designs.

'Chester,' I say, 'thanks again for agreeing to help with the sets.'

'Pleasure,' he says, smiling.

Ross tells me they are spending Wednesday together to finish them off.

'No running water in the sink,' Chester says. 'You can't have the plumbing.'

'We'll just use a filled kettle and pour from that,' I reply, gathering the empty plates, taking them to the kitchen.

I return with the lemon tart, making a grand statement that Margie baked it. She smiles like a shy girl as Chester looks down at his hands. And I realise he's not spoken to her once during the meal, hardly glanced at her. She cuts and serves and passes – as her hand slightly trembles across the table – the first slice to Chester. The two of them now have reason to look directly at each other. Chester is being polite, a slight nod, and I think, *Poor Margie*.

We all tell Margie the tart is delicious. And it is. She offers seconds, and only the girls say yes.

As Margie serves them, Chester stands. 'I'll be off now.'

'Coffee or tea?' I say.

'No, thanks.'

Something is wrong and I don't know what. It's Ross who rises from his chair and walks Chester to the back door. Margie's mouth is open and round, as if to say 'oh', while she watches Chester leave the room without a backward glance. The silver cake server in her hand is midair. And whatever is going on, I am infuriated by Chester's rudeness.

The girls disappear down the hallway.

'I can't quite get used to his moustache,' Margie says to me.

I wish for the intimacy of friends so I could ask her about the past – how long they were together and how they got away with their affair. For a strange quirky moment, I think she might go along with it: the relaxed dip in her shoulders, the way she's just put a dab of lemon filling in her mouth with her finger.

'How did it feel having him here tonight?' I ask.

She stares to the side, perhaps remembering.

'I mean, you used to be at this table with Norman and the kids,' I say, trying to prompt her. 'And tonight Chester was sitting opposite you. It must've been strange.'

'Yes, it was. Very strange.'

Margie's back is straight as she turns to leave. Her limp develops when she enters the hall as if she's somehow wounded.

Margie

I feel so lonely and something else. Stella watches me leave the room, so I straighten up, my back tall, chin raised – my I'm-a-Ballantine pose. Over the years, this proud mask has been a safe place for me to hide behind, a necessary refuge. But disappointment makes me limp as I enter the hall, giving in to my right hip and letting it do what it wants. Perhaps my limp has become more of a habit than about pain. Everything in my being hurts to varying degrees, so I wouldn't know how to distinguish one ache from another. One thing I'm certain of: I'm a foolish woman and I think I always have been. At my age, you'd think I could step away from myself and be clever, or wise. Something. The gold buckles on my shoes, left, right, left, out in front as I navigate this dusty hallway to my room.

When Stella finished styling my hair and sent me to greet Chester, 'offer him a glass of wine,' he turned to me as I entered the family room.

I went to him, smiling. There he was, my Chester, with his expanded forehead, crinkling brown eyes, greatly deepened cheek lines, unsmiling mouth. But it was his grey moustache that put me on guard – the way he wears it so confidently, as if mocking me, reminding me that many years have passed between us.

'I'm so happy to see you,' I said, reaching out my hand.

He took it fleetingly, as if reluctant to touch me. As if we were unfamiliar with each other. As if I didn't know the secrets of his body. His appendix scar. The pink birthmark on his right thigh, the size and shape of a small strawberry.

He took an awkward step away. 'How are you?'

The insincerity of his polite question was a shock.

'Very well,' I replied.

He smiled, not at me but to himself, as if embarrassed by the situation, the two of us there. Alone. Isobel's fingers sent Chopin quietly through the walls.

'Is there something wrong?' I asked.

He stared at me.

'I'm not here for you,' he whispered.

I couldn't have heard correctly.

A turn of my head. 'Pardon?'

His hands spoke this time. Out flat, a cutting movement. 'I'm only here to help Stella. Not here for you.'

His words were a face slap. I flinched. And dashed to the kitchen, wishing I was quicker with words and had something to say, a clever retort that even now I can't think of. All I could do was put on Stella's apron and let my face burn as I pulled the spitting roast from the oven, disguising that I was already hot.

Now I limp past the bathroom and remember Chester's pity, that knowing expression, a small, cruel smile that I don't understand. He kissed my forehead at the hospital, didn't he? Each step I take is a chant to my age: *Eighty, eighty, eighty, eighty . . .* I remember a day when I was almost half this – Ross had just started school – and our affair was new, passionate and intense.

I was on Maryhill Road and saw Chester driving towards town so I followed him, flashing the headlights so he would pull over. I wanted to look into his face, hear loving words of reassurance. And he did pull over and said, 'Don't get unhinged or this won't work.' That was the first time I saw that knowing look, the clever half-smile.

All I have ever wanted is to be loved. And if I can't have that, then peace.

I close my bedroom door and for the first time since I returned to this house I have a gentle feeling for Bishop Street – that is my place of belonging, not here. I think of going on without Dot and see an image of myself eating alone at Tamarind Thai.

To help me sleep, I drift with the memory of a bird – the powerful owl with golden eyes that twice appeared beside the henhouse in the ancient conifer that Alexander Ballantine would've planted sometime around 1920. From the bird's imposing height and unflinching stare, I presumed it was waiting to take one of the chooks. For months afterwards, even years, I searched for it in the weathered tree, and sometimes willed it to return, but it never did.

*

In the morning I stay in bed, waiting for silence, the signal that the girls have gone to school, Ross has left the house and Stella is most likely in the old dining room. Around nine I get out of bed. It feels lazy to lie in for this long, but I can't be bothered with the early morning chaos of everyone rushing.

The firebox has been lit in the family room, the first for the year. The vent is closed and the fan is on. Wood is stacked in a cane basket. I make a cup of tea and stand in front of the heat and feel warmth seep into my bones – there's nothing nicer than having your back to a fire. I see the image of Chester in this room last night, the cruel, upward curve of his lips that was once a rascally smile. The urge comes again to return to my little life in Bishop Street, to be away from this humiliation.

I listen for Stella's footfall, but the house only creaks. The cat stares at me from a lounge chair. I push the swing door open and peek into the dining room to see if Stella is there. Empty. Up the hall, I glance into the rooms. Her and Ross's bed is unmade; the doona coils like beaten egg whites. The girls' beds have been roughly made, their clothes on the floor – you'd think everyone abandoned the house in an emergency.

I wait for Stella to charge through one of the doors and I can't relax until I know where she is. It dawns on me then that I have developed an attachment to her. Her presence provides a sort of confidence and security.

Outside, I expect to find her in the laundry or garden. Then I notice her car is gone and try to remember if I was told she was going out. I feel disappointed that wherever she is, she's not taken me with her or told me what's going on. She always does. So I start to worry.

The morning drifts slowly. I deadhead the roses, always listening for Stella's car up the driveway. The secateurs need sharpening and I can't find the diamond stone. The tinge of smoke in the air reminds me of long-ago autumns, the arrival of walnuts, figs and apples. The air is fresh, but Stella's gardening coat is warm. Sometimes I rest on the bench. And in the course of two hours, I see a dozen different birds, including a white-browed scrubwren and, I think, a white-eared honeyeater.

By lunchtime I am very anxious. Ross and Stella don't have a landline, so I can't phone her to find out where she is. My heart is beating fast with too many terrible imaginings.

I go inside and push a log into the firebox. And wait with my hands clenched in senseless panic.

The back door bursts open; boots drop on the floor. Ross appears wearing socks. I breathe in, expecting something. He's in a rush.

Three strides before he stops, as if he's just seen me. 'You all right?'

'Where's Stella?' I blurt.

'Out putting up posters for the play. Shop windows.'

I am utterly silenced by this. Because she didn't invite me to go. I want to know when she'll return, but cannot bring myself to ask because I will not have Ross know how I feel.

'Then she's got radio and newspaper interviews, and a rehearsal at the Town Hall. She's gone all day.'

He vanishes down the hallway and I hear him somewhere, a filing drawer opening, closing. Back again, he hurries past me with the MLA vendor book and an envelope.

'Tuckers are picking up some steers. I'll be back soon, Mum. To get us lunch.' He strides to the porch – a pause while he pulls on his boots – and he's gone.

It is a very small word, 'Mum', nothing really, but he said it so naturally. I take a small breath against the tension that is always holding me in, as though I'm wearing an elastic corset.

In the kitchen I wash up the breakfast dishes, and make two sandwiches.

*

We eat cheese and ham toasties and drink hot milky tea. Ross seems relaxed, although he's not talkative, not like he was last night when Chester was here. He's staring into his iPad and I wouldn't mind having a look at it myself. Jemima has found some excellent information on this thing she calls an 'ap'. There are hundreds of birder sightings up here in the north-east with recorded bird calls that she says are uploads. But I think it's only on her iPad and not Ross's. These things confuse me, but

I'd like to see other sightings of white-eared honeyeaters so I can compare them with what I saw this morning.

I try to think of things to talk to Ross about, but he's only interested in the weather and cows. And then I'm talking anyway – my voice is soft, as though I'm afraid of being heard.

'That letter, Ross – the revelations about Chester . . .'

He looks up and glances around, and I think he'd rather remain quiet, but I'm staring at him. That he and Stella know about my private business is intolerable; it makes the air feel thick and me feel very small.

I take a sip of tea.

'I don't know.' He shrugs. 'It was all a bit of a mess back then.'

'Yes,' I say.

He turns back to the iPad, dismissing me, or perhaps he's just reading something he's interested in. I think again how he looks very like his father.

I reach for the local paper and read the front page. Something about the council elections that doesn't interest me. The room is warm. I hear a strong breeze outside and for a moment think it's rain and look to the window. The Japanese maple gusts in the wind, a blaze of orange and red; some leaves fly away.

I turn the page, and there's a story about the North East Hospital, a fundraising venture for a disease I've never heard of. It's about wasting muscles, I discover, and there's no cure for it. I had my babies in that hospital; Mark was born in the old wing. And I was there after Norman hit and kicked me and made my kidneys bleed.

Further into the paper is a story about a young woman who's just returned from the war in Afghanistan. Private Natalie Scales. She must be Ray and Dulcie Scales' granddaughter. Imagine that. Ray was the head of the CFA up here for forty years, was awarded an AOM for his services to the community.

Dot and I went to the dinner in his honour. Last I heard, Dulcie was in high care with dementia. I think to mention all of this to Ross, but I don't speak up because he probably won't be interested.

Here we are, Ross and I, sitting quietly together, both absorbed in our thoughts.

He pushes his mug forward and glances at me. 'Another cup, Mum?'

'No, thanks,' I say. 'This one will do me.'

And he returns to whatever he's reading.

Stella

ON Sunday afternoon I give Margie the option of staying at home with Ross and the kids or coming to the rehearsal at the Town Hall with me. It's like she's been waiting for the chance to gather herself up and walk to the car. She's in the passenger seat before I've even found the car keys.

Down Maryhill Road, a left turn into Marion Road, and after several kilometres we're on Black Wattle Road and approaching Chester's stone house. The thick hedge of lilly pillies coming up on the left is flushed with pink berries. I suppose Margie and I are both thinking about Chester.

To make it safe, I don't look at her but stare straight ahead. 'I don't blame you,' I say. 'You had a horrible time with Norman. Chester showed you kindness. You were vulnerable. It's understandable.'

Her eyes tear up – or is it just an old lady's watery eyes? She clasps her hands on her lap and looks at the entry to a grassed laneway: old pine posts, a rusted gate.

'You want to talk about it?' I ask.

She shakes her head. But speaks anyway, a whisper. 'It was wrong. But I loved him.'

'How do you feel about him now?'

'I can't really say.'

I want to tell her that Chester is a nice-looking old man who I've been slow to call a sleaze. The way he puts his arms around me; the hand low on my back; the unnecessary hello and goodbye kisses, sometimes on the lips. But I've been a bit naive too, thinking he was harmless – wanting my sets built, needing his cooperation – and not paying too much attention to the foolish overtures of a poet in his late seventies.

Margie's shoulders have a proud line, the way she's sitting back, chin up. I can see she's used the velcro rollers I bought her – her white hair has more body, a slight curl. Clipped to her lobes are those lovely sapphire earrings. Her pink lips are tightly closed. Clothes seem very special to her; today she's wearing the grey blouse and black pants with her knees primly pressed together.

I'm with Ross: it's hard to imagine Margie inflamed with lust, pulling at a man's belt buckle. But she would've been very attractive once. Perhaps it was a challenge for Chester, the seduction of Mrs Ballantine – her aloofness, beauty, poise. A conquest. But, then, that wounded aura of hers calls for a saviour. Maybe he really cared. I feel a deep need to reach out to Margie, and I wonder if she's come with me today because she expects he'll be at the rehearsal. Except Chester now sees Margie as an old woman, sexless and no longer important to him. Surely she understands this.

'Did Chester help Ross with the sets?' she asks.

'Yes, on Wednesday. Chester only needs to paint them. I have to use a full kettle instead of having a sink with running water, which still works. They've done bookshelves and they look better than I thought.' I explain they've designed the shelves to allow a three-metre-wide space in the centre so photos can be projected between the books and framed family pictures, a tall vase of flowers and a 1980s-style television.

We drift to silence, yet I feel there's something else she wants to ask me.

'Chester isn't coming today,' I say.

She rubs her finger where her wedding ring once was.

'What happened to your wedding ring?' I ask.

'Never mind.'

'Are you all right?'

She shakes her head while staring out the window at a giant cairn of stacked stones, a lichen-covered granite outcrop. Whatever is bottled up inside Margie, I know to shut up now. So I leave her be. Perhaps the outing is enough for her, the change in routine.

*

As our footfall claps along the black and white diamond-patterned tiles, I sense the thousands of souls who've walked here before us. The memory of them is etched in the oak-panelled walls, brass window frames, door fittings and intricate pink-and-green fretwork. The timber-framed commemorative plaques display the names of former councillors in faded typeset letters; the Town Hall was built in 1883 and was also once the shire office. It's easy to imagine the hurried movement of important business, the dipping of nibs in black ink, the neat lines of bookkeeping, the clicking of a typewriter.

We enter the theatre; the crimson-curtained stage is in front. This is my perfect venue. I exhale. Sometimes when I'm shopping in town, I come here just to stare and wonder. Long swirling skirts would've swept across the shiny blue gum floor. The leather soles of men's boots. The tapping rubber stop on a walking cane.

I should be nervous, but that will come Thursday week on opening night.

Margie stands to the side and looks around for a seat. There are none. 'Wait,' I tell her and hurry down the back, returning with a stacked group of three chairs. I space them ten metres away from the stage. Margie sits.

Felicity has arrived before us and is standing in the corner, talking silently to herself, going through her lines, her arms and body moving expressively.

Up the narrow stage stairs, I open the heavy weave crimson curtain. I walk centre stage and wave to Margie. She lifts her hand from her lap and signals back: not a wave, but acknowledgement.

'The acoustics are awesome,' I call out to her.

As we were arriving, Margie told me that sixty-four years ago her parents watched her graduate from school in this theatre. That she stood on this stage, uniformed, with big hopes for her life. I was too distracted while reverse-parking, then too busy gathering up scripts, the basket with tea and coffee, to properly listen. She said something about her friend moving to Melbourne and that she would've liked to go with her, but her parents weren't keen. Margie's timing to chat was off. On the pavement I asked her what she did then, in those years before marrying Norman. But her answer got lost as we stepped into the portico and discovered the glossy black front door was already unlocked.

Now I call out, 'Come onto the stage, Margie. Show me where you stood.'

She's about to stand when Owen walks in. Holly isn't far behind, holding an iced cake on a plate in her upheld palm. She puts it on the spare chair beside Margie. They huddle around her and start talking to her – or each other, I can't tell. Either way, Margie is involved, or perhaps she's trapped.

Felicity joins them, and from where I'm standing on the stage all I can see of Margie is her ankles and her flat tan shoes.

I check my phone for the time. Noah and Amber are late. That's not on; they should've let me know. I look to the door as if searching for them. So we wait. I join the others and we update on gossip about what people are saying about the play; the story on page five of the *Benalla Ensign* about Noah, the violin-playing actor whose day job is a tractor mechanic. I'd missed it, but Owen shows me his copy. I quickly read that it's reporting the correct details on the play dates, then hand it down to Margie so she can read it too. Holly tells us that we've only sold seventy-one tickets for the opening night, but Friday and Saturday nights are much better. I'm not worried. More will come.

Noah and Amber still haven't arrived. Felicity tries their phones and they don't answer. We decide to start on the warm-up. Margie stares at us suspiciously as we sing 'I Think I Love You' – Owen leads with his lovely tenor voice. Holly takes the chorus. It's fun. We dance and clap our hands. We keep it up while we slowly get into the zone and are ready to rehearse. But Grace's children are still missing. It's my turn to phone. Amber asks for a message. Noah wants a message, too.

It seems pointless rehearsing without them so we eat slices of Holly's cake, mandarin with cream-cheese icing. We drink not-quite-hot tea from the kitchen urn, and we're all frustrated now. Felicity puts on her schoolteacher no-nonsense voice and phones Amber's mother and Noah's friend's friend, who for some reason she thinks might help track him down.

Holly is chatting to Margie, and I can't tell whether Margie is happy about it or not. Owen is staring into his phone. Last rehearsal he faltered over his lines; he should be in a quiet corner practising and going through his moves.

Just after four, Noah and Amber saunter in – a violin case is under his right arm, Amber under the other; they're looped like the couple they must be, both unabashed, saying they arrived at the right time. 'Really, we're late?' Amber says, and I'm unconvinced by her bad acting that it's a mix-up. New lovers, they were probably shagging and forgot the time. Next rehearsal I'll individually text them about the arrangements.

So the run-through can finally begin, although we're unsettled with each other; the community mood is disrupted, like we're now two groups: us adults, and Grace's kids.

Because of the late time we don't sing and go through our breathing and stretching exercises. It's a mistake. I should've got the spirit back into our hearts and minds before anyone stepped up onto the stage.

I sit in between Margie and Owen, who isn't up until Act Two. I look expectantly at the cast members onstage.

'Let's start at the top,' I say. 'Act One, Scene One.'

The actors are stiff, the lines don't flow, movements seem forced. Felicity is focused, but because the others don't have the timing right, she appears too forceful and loud. I can tell she's furious with Noah and Amber – not a bad emotion when playing Grace. Method acting at its best, but they won't cope if she vents at them through her lines. I stand, clap my hands and say we're going to start again. I'm acting myself, being falsely cheerful as I try to settle things down. Owen calls up from his chair, saying he must leave at five.

This isn't going well, and I say so.

'Everyone,' I say, 'we've got off to a bad start. We need to move on. Can we?'

It's all so precious, the individual egos – but that's what makes the magic, when strangers come together and surrender to something bigger than themselves.

They glance at each other, and away.

'Let's take a two-minute break,' I say. 'We need to breathe and focus.'

I hate the way I sound, preachy, with my voice resounding around the theatre. But I am in charge. Erik taught me that: to own my role.

They take me seriously and circle around the stage, heads down, staring at the floor. I let them get impatient, waiting to begin – wanting to begin.

'Now,' I say, moving towards the stage, arms out, imploring them. 'We've got only one more rehearsal before opening night. Please focus. Are you ready?'

No one speaks.

'Scene One, Act One,' I say. 'Begin.'

I take my seat between Margie and Owen. My script is on my lap, but I don't read it. I watch their moves, hear their words. The rhythm comes and there's joy between them in the banter, the gruff tones; Noah's violin is shaky but all right. He smiles and winks out to the audience, and I know it'll get a laugh. I see that they all like doing this, separating from reality for a short while to become something else. It's fun and hard.

I interrupt a few times. Lines have been forgotten; moves haven't been made. But at the end of Act One, I stand up and clap, telling them I'm proud.

'Thank you,' I say.

Margie is contained, sitting upright, taking it all in, and I can't read her. Only that she remains seated. I figure she's coping, that I needn't worry about her.

Owen has forgotten his need to leave at five. We work through Act Two. It's difficult keeping the energy up; we've done this so many times. 'Throw yourself in,' I say. 'There's only three nights.'

We all know we're babies. If we were in professional theatre, we'd be pushing ourselves for up to seven shows a week for a whole season, up to twelve weeks. But then we wouldn't have day jobs, either.

By 7 pm we're done, exhausted but ready. I embrace each one of them: Felicity, Noah, Amber, Holly and Owen. They're my team, my beating heart. The old theatre feels like it also needs to rest, have its solitude again, until we return.

*

I find Margie in the entry hall, sitting in a studded green leather chair, staring at the front door. She's been impatient to leave for more than an hour. I apologise, explaining we started more than an hour late, that it was the most important rehearsal in the lead-up to opening night. She fidgets with the hem of the blouse, then settles her hands around her handbag.

We are the last to step outside into the night. Squally rain makes us hesitate before leaving the portico's shelter. I lock the heavy black door and twist the knob to be certain it's properly secure. There's nothing for it; I grip the handle of the basket in one hand and Margie's arm in the other, and we step down to the footpath and hurry to the car as fast as she can go. We get a little wet. I think of Ross, see him staring out a window, arms crossed, satisfied.

Slowly as if burdened, and silently sighing, Margie straps the seatbelt around herself. I hear the clip. I buckle myself in. 'I'm tired,' I say, 'but really happy. How'd you find it?'

'I'm quite hungry and need a rest.'

I start the car, put the wipers on, check the mirrors and make a U-turn. Driving across the bridge, I call Ross. He answers and I say we're headed home. 'What's been happening?' I ask.

'Isobel had another driving lesson. Got to fourth gear.'

'Not bad for a fourteen-year-old,' I say.

He tells me that another set of twin calves was born, one abandoned; he's got it in the yards but doesn't know how it'll go. He's fed the girls and himself – lentil and veggie soup waits on the stove for Margie and me when we get home.

'Love you, darling,' he says.

'See you in forty minutes.'

'Road's wet. Be careful.'

'Okay.' I press end call.

So it's late and I'm a drone, flying dumb down the Hume on 110 k's. It's a dual carriageway and I'm in the left lane. A B-double passes on the right and buffers the car; water splashes on the windscreen and I put the wipers on high.

Then a Kenworth appears on my bum. Through the rear-view mirror all I can see is the shining slats of the truck's grille – forty tonnes coming towards me at full force. I gently slow to 100 in order to force the driver to pass on the right, but the truck stays behind. Kilometres pass and I can't ignore the threat behind me. I speed up. So does the Kenworth. One hundred and fifteen. One hundred and twenty. In front are the red tail-lights of a car-carrying transport truck, its tyres spraying water onto the windscreen. The wipers are in a frenzy.

I'm anxious. Margie is staring at my hands gripping the wheel. I tell her the problem.

'Just ignore him,' she says.

So I do. I return to the speed limit. But in the mirror is the truck's silver snub nose. I'm scared. We pass Baddaginnie Road and there's no reason why the truck doesn't move to the right lane.

'You bastard,' I yell.

On impulse, I decide to take the short cut up into the pine plantation. It'll rid us of the Kenworth, take time off the trip; we're both tired, Margie is hungry and wants to go to bed. I indicate, slow to ninety and veer into the exit lane. The driver in the mighty Kenworth continues on, thundering south towards Melbourne.

'I don't like this way,' Margie says in a quiet voice. She sounds afraid.

'It's okay. We'll be home sooner.'

A half-moon tattoos the dark sky. A wallaby prances alongside the car, then disappears into the black verge. The skeletons of eucalypts race past, shadows, imaginings; I'm watching for kangaroos, a deer.

Margie appears more concerned now than when we were being chased down the freeway. She's clutching the armrest; her jaw is tight. I wonder why she always protests when I take this short cut.

Margie

SOMETIMES Norman drove through the pine plantations from Benalla to home. And when Stella comes this way, one particular time returns from its hidden place in my memory.

It was Sunday, the fourth of March, 1968. I know the exact date because we were returning home from my parents' fortieth wedding anniversary celebration – we'd had a two-course set lunch in the McKelvie Room at the Rose Hotel.

Norman didn't like associating with my parents, or my sisters and their husbands. He used to say, 'They ask too many questions.' I always tried to explain that they were just being friendly, taking an interest. I flattered him by saying they liked him, although I'm not sure that was true. He reluctantly came to the lunch and kept to himself most of the time. I was about five months pregnant with Caroline and dressed in a maternity outfit my mother had made me: a watermelon-pink rayon skirt and matching smock with a white round collar. I felt very attractive wearing it and was proud showing off my expanding waistline because it proved something; I suppose it gave everyone the impression we were a happy family.

We were in the green Holden Premier sedan and Mark would've been two years old, sitting between us in the front seat. Norman was unusually cranky that day and easily provoked. So I should've known better than to tell him to go slower, even though he was pressing the accelerator far down as if he had a death wish for us all.

The engine revs were high. A storm of dust trailed the car. The road was badly rutted. I gripped the armrest, terrified. 'Slow down, you fool of a man,' I shouted.

He had some cruel things to say back to me. So I joined in, hissing some home truths. Little Mark taking it all in. I should've held my tongue.

About five or six miles from home, he did slow down. And stopped the car just past the wooden bridge and got out. He came around to my door and opened it, grabbed my arm and pulled me out. He didn't say a word, but left me there on the side of the dirt track. Mark was a witness to his mother being abandoned in the middle of the bush. I watched the car grow smaller as it trailed along the road beside the creek and disappeared out of sight.

I started walking – my white slingback sandals were unsuitable for such an excursion, but I was quite strong in those days and knew the way. Even so, I expected my husband to return and pick me up.

When I was resting, sitting on a granite outcrop, holding my belly and quietly comforting my baby, 'it's all right, don't worry,' a sambar doe silently stepped out from the undergrowth. I believe she deliberately showed herself as a way of uplifting my spirits, letting me know I wasn't alone. We gazed at each other until she turned and walked deeper into the unknown wild bush. I thought of my parents' happy marriage, *my-Lily*, and how they would feel if they knew where I was. I felt ashamed.

I set off again along the isolated track. The sun was lowering; shadows lengthened. The air cooled. My sandals caused blisters and for a short while I walked barefoot, but I worried about stepping on something unknown and dangerous. I strode through the pain on my blistered toes, reaching deep into myself as I considered this moment in my life, how trapped I was, that my marriage wasn't what I wanted. The world seemed so big, and me so small. By the time I reached the corner of Maryhill Road and Marion Road, I was once again resigned. This is how it was for me, that in some way I deserved it. I needed to be strong.

A car approached and stopped. Keith Sanders unwound his window. 'You all right?'

My face twisted in shame before I put on a bright smile. 'Taking a walk. It's a lovely time of day.'

'Want a lift?'

'No, thanks.'

He seemed unsure about leaving me. But I waved him on and set back on my way, forcing even steps to hide that for the past hour I'd been limping through the agony of bleeding blisters. Who knows what Keith thought I was doing out on the road at dusk.

*

And here I am once more. Stella has again taken this terrifying drive back to the house. I grit my teeth and hardly dare to breathe. The speed she's driving seems fast, especially in this rain; I see she's doing about fifty. I want to call out that she must slow down, that 'you are a fool of a woman'.

The wipers push the rain off the windscreen. The headlights on high beam show us the gradual winding climb into the tableland, past a couple of timber houses, long kilometres of pastoral fences. We travel along the narrow stretch that follows the creek. The bridge is ahead. Stella slowly crosses; we feel the heavy planks absorb the car's weight. The track veers right and leads into the isolation of the pine planation where the sambar deer are. Stella turns and this is about where Norman abruptly stopped the car. Two-year-old Mark staring with wide eyes, wondering. I patted his knee and smiled so he wouldn't worry.

Stella suddenly stops the car.

I gasp.

'Shit,' she says. She opens the door, gets out and walks ahead into the rain.

The headlights show a mass out in front. I lean forward and stare. Through the thrashing wipers, I make out a fallen eucalypt with a girth as thick as a bull's neck. Its branches are splayed wide. Our path home is blocked.

Stella hurries back to the car, gets in behind the wheel. Rain glistens silver on her face. Her hair and clothes are wet, and she needs to dry herself, but I can't work out how she'll be able to do that.

Something on the dash worries her. 'Black spot. No signal.' She exhales, saying the four-letter word. Then she pulls her big handbag from behind the back seat and searches for her phone.

'Does that mean you can't call Ross?' I ask.

'You got it.'

'We'll have to turn back to the freeway,' I say.

I appreciate it that she apologises to me, saying, 'It was a bloody dumb idea coming this way in the rain.'

Stella puts the car into reverse. The space for turning is tight. I think to suggest she should get out and have a good look to see exactly where to back and angle the car. But I don't want to distract her so remain quiet. She takes her time staring through the back windscreen. The big wiper is doing its job, but it's dark; nothing can be seen.

Looking over her shoulder, she carefully presses the accelerator and the car creeps backwards. Then a little further – it feels like centimetres – edging back, back, back, until she stops. She turns the steering wheel to the right and moves forward. We're still a good way off being in line with the bridge. I hold my breath.

Stella's neck is craned; she's looking in every direction – front, back, out the side window. Everything is dark; the rain is pelting down. She must be cold and ignoring it while she sorts this out. She taps the accelerator a little more, and she must think that she's in drive, that we will go forward.

We reverse. It happens so fast. The car slips and slightly tilts. Then a metal scraping thud. We've smashed into something.

Stella hits the brake, but I think the car stopped moving before then. She says the four-letter word three times, turns the motor off and then gets out of the car. 'Don't move,' she says to me, as if I might be going somewhere.

The door slams. I twist around to see her walk behind the car. She bends down and I don't see her for a minute. Back behind the wheel she starts the car, puts it in drive and tries to move forward. The motor roars.

Nothing, not even a budge.

She shakes her head and turns the motor off. 'We're stuffed,' she says.

'What's happened?'

She tells me that she is the four-letter word and an idiot. Then explains that the back left wheel has rolled into a thirty-centimetre ditch. She opens her arms to show me, about a foot. 'It's stable,' she says. 'I'm so clever, a pine tree trunk is wedged in there too.'

I would like to relieve myself, but decide not to mention it.

Stella takes a deep breath and closes her eyes. 'Ross will be wondering where the hell we are, and he won't think to look here.'

'You need to dry off,' I say.

She talks with her eyes still shut. 'We'll have to sit here and wait for someone to find us.'

'It's all right. We're unharmed and safe.'

'Thank you, Margie.' She's taking deep breaths and I'm not sure what's going on with her.

'Perhaps you should put the motor back on and turn up the heater so you can get warm.'

'I'm too angry to get dry. I deserve to get fucking pneumonia.'

'It'd be better if you didn't swear so much.'

'Thanks for that.'

The pressure in my bladder has been building for some time. I should've used the facilities before we left the Town Hall, but I thought I'd wait until we got home.

'I'd like to go to the toilet,' I say.

She looks across at me. It's so dark I can only see the halo of her blonde hair, the shadowy mask of her face. 'Can you wait? It's still raining. I don't want you to get wet, too.'

'I'll try.'

She presses her fists against her forehead. 'Ross will be out of his mind. We should be home by now.'

'We can't be worried about that. Everything will be all right. We need to relax.'

She turns to me again and I hold her stare. I know she's got lovely hazel eyes, but right now her eye sockets are large black pools. 'So you're good in a crisis, Margie?'

'This is only one night and it will pass.'

She turns the motor on and twists knobs to make the temperature rise to twenty-four degrees. Shifting in her seat, she presses her jeans straight, pulls the sleeves and collar of her shirt, and tousles her hair – motions to be rid of creases and make herself tidy.

Rain pats on the roof and drips on the windscreen. The

wipers are off. Ross might be worried about where we are, but he'll be thrilled with this weather.

An hour passes and I feel the rain has eased enough for me to raise the issue of my bladder. Actually, it has become an emergency.

'Toilet,' I say as I open the car door. My tan shoes sink into the fine wet gravel. I step behind the car so I have privacy. Balancing with one hand on a pine tree, I pull my trousers, then my underpants, down to my knees. It's not enough, so I tug more. It's not raining anymore, but the air is damp and cold. Squatting is impossible; I cannot get down that low, and I now have a terrible dilemma. I try to hold on so I can work out what to do.

Stella's door closes. 'Margie,' she calls.

Then the full force of warm release. It is a joyful letting go and a disaster.

I turn to her.

'You all right?' she asks.

'I've wet myself.'

She snorts a single laugh. 'Need help?'

I tell her I'm quite capable of pulling up my own pants.

'I've heard that before,' she says, and I don't know what she means.

When we're back in the car, Stella searches around to see what we have and concludes there's nothing except what's in the basket. Leftover pieces of Holly's cake that were supposed to be for the children. Half a bottle of water.

It's almost ten and we were due back at Maryhill about two hours ago. Stella thinks Ross might imagine we've dropped in to do some supermarket shopping or made a last-minute decision to have a drink with the group. Yet when she spoke to him, it was clear to me we were headed home.

Inside the car is the smell of my urine. I apologise to Stella, but she says she doesn't notice, although I see that her window is down a couple of inches. The motor is still running, the temperature displayed on the dash is twenty-four degrees, and I feel we're about to germinate: with the heat and the yeasty scent, it's like being in a smelly hothouse.

'Turn the heater off,' I say.

She must agree. Her hand touches a button and we instantly cut to silence. There is no knife to slice the cake so Stella breaks it apart, a rough half each. It's more delicious than ever because it's all we have. I eat slowly, trying to make it last. We lick our fingers to clean up the messy icing. Two mouthfuls of water each; I'd say another three each to go before the bottle is empty.

Stella puts her seat back, an unseen lever on the side. She tells me how to do it. I'm thankful for it. I can stretch my legs out and, in a wishful way, pretend I'm fully lying down.

Sometimes rain lashes the windscreen; a leaf sticks. The wind lightly buffets my side of the car.

Time passes. I cannot sleep. And I know Stella is watching and waiting for Ross to find us. I can't say I'm cold, but I wish for the comfort of a blanket, something to snuggle into. Huddling into a blanket has always provided relief; it's where I can close my eyes and know I'm safe and secure.

Stella speaks; her voice is soft but louder than a whisper. She's almost sighing. I turn and see the circles of her eyes and realise they are closed.

'What were you telling me this afternoon about wanting to go to Melbourne?'

I take a breath and consider if I'll answer. Part of me wishes to remain silent because I am tired. And yet, it was a peculiar thing today, being back in the old Town Hall where I graduated from high school. Mum and Dad were sitting in the middle of the hall, about twenty feet from where I was sitting today.

I can no longer bring their faces to mind or hear the pitch of their voices. Or, if I do, I don't trust it; there are too many fragments to make sense of, like a complicated puzzle that no longer feels worth the effort. Their memory is more in my heart, more of a feeling than an image or sound. I'm clear about my mother's large, steady hands; she had arthritis in the end knuckle of her left pointer. And the shape of Dad's small, wire-framed glasses, his brown bushy eyebrows sprouting above them. Over the years, photographs have fused with my recollections: the posed, serious expressions on their wedding day; Mum holding me in a white crocheted blanket that draped almost to the floor; black-suited Dad looking important in the bank manager portrait. These reflections can lead me to feelings of regret and, if I'm not careful, to melancholy – a burden of sadness I sometimes find difficult to shake off.

And so I tell Stella it's foolish to regret things, then immediately contradict myself by telling her I always wanted to live in Melbourne and even travel overseas. 'I didn't have the courage. My parents weren't willing to let me go. I was their youngest, the baby. So I stayed.'

Stella doesn't have anything to say. And it's not like me to share private things, but here we are in the dark, in the middle of nowhere, and over the past few weeks I've developed a fondness for her. She's not my type of person, but she is always kind to me. And there's no one else. Caroline hasn't called me in at least a fortnight, and the last time all she did was complain about her job at the art gallery, how tired she was. Before she hung up, a pause, an afterthought – she said she was seeing someone. I assume that means a man, a boyfriend. Caroline has always had form in that area, so I didn't ask; I wasn't sure what to say. She said his name, but I can't remember it: something unpronounceable and foreign. An ethnic man, which troubles me. Although those dark-skinned workers at the hospital were very pleasant. But I can't be worried about her life. It's hard enough living my own.

'Do you have any regrets?' I ask Stella.

Between the limbs of trees is the trace of the half-moon, a sprinkle of stars. Deer will be moving about, navigating in this terrible dark. Something scratches the side of the car, perhaps a fallen twig. We both turn as if trying to see it.

Stella exhales and looks into the distance, probably hoping to see that Ross is approaching.

'I wasn't very nice to my mother,' she says. 'I was angry with her for a long time, even for years after she died.' She releases a single burst of laughter. 'I could even blame her for us being here.'

'How on earth is your mother responsible for this?'

Stella shifts in her seat, hugs herself. 'Grace is my mother.'

I've no idea what she's saying.

'I wrote the play as a way of trying to get to know Mum. She died from a brain tumour when I was seventeen. But in the end, I don't think a child can fully relate to a mother as a regular person.' Stella rubs her arms, as if to get warm. 'It got boring analysing all that old stuff. She did her best, like all of us try and do. Anyway, here we are. Thanks to her.'

It takes a moment for me to piece together what this means. The play is about her mother and is going to be performed in public – the private confidences of a broken family. The implications come in waves. Ruby is Stella. I feel vaguely astonished to know so little about her past, but then I'd never been interested enough to ask anything.

Ross and Stella married in a funny old building in Melbourne, an abandoned bakery that had been converted into a theatre. The guests were a strange mix, from bedraggled types to the very glamorously attired. I spent the afternoon and evening in shoes that pinched, nursing a head cold, anxiously waiting for the whole affair to be over. Stella's mother wasn't present, and it was Caroline who whispered to me that she'd died: 'Cancer.' I studied the man she pointed out as Stella's father. Red curly hair, pale face and green eyes that I couldn't bring myself to look into. He moved his body too freely as he played the piano, and I said back to Caroline that he was 'full of himself'. But he was good enough to take requests all afternoon while people danced and drank – and did the alcohol flow; I've never seen anything like it.

And now, for the first time, I've made the connection to Isobel's talent. And Jemima's red hair and green eyes.

'So Ruby is you?' I ask.

'Yep. Two years before Mum died, she kicked Dad out. And within a fortnight of her funeral he returned to the family home with his girlfriend. That's when I moved out.'

'You should be proud,' I say.

Her voice is loud, demanding. 'Why?'

'Because, in spite of all that, you've made a good life. You've got a good marriage.'

'You think?'

'It's what I see.'

'That's a big thing for you to say, Margie.'

Her tone seems accusing, or perhaps I'm too sensitive. Either way, enough has been said between us. I press my arms across my chest and feel my inhalations. This talk of regret and marriage returns me to the day Norman died.

*

The roses were late that year. Perhaps the cooler winter was the cause, but it wasn't until early December that I needed to sharpen the secateurs and deadhead the finished blooms. I'd woken early with the desire to go to the garden. The paths needed sweeping too, some weeding and mulching, always little jobs. The whole morning was ahead of me.

I tidied my front porch refuge and closed the door. Passed the red-and-green panelled front door, down the long hall to the family room. Norman's bedroom door was closed, and since our estrangement I had no concerns about knocking on the door to check on him.

Ross was already up and dressed in his school uniform. We ate breakfast in silence, and before I drove him to the bus stop I made his lunch and put it in his bag. I also filled Norman's thermos, cling-wrapped a slice of pineapple fruitcake and put it in his canvas workbag.

So, it was about 8.30 when I pulled the small green wheelbarrow around to the east side of the house and started snipping the dead roses off their stems. I vaguely expected to hear the back door slap as Norman left the house.

It was as though the birds were whispering that morning; their quiet songs seemed hymn-like and took me to a place of peace. It was warm, and even at that hour I felt heat on my back. I breathed in the sweet fragrance of Louise Odier, probably the oldest rosebush in the garden.

At ten I returned to the house to make a cup of tea. Norman's canvas bag was still on the bench. I put my hand to my mouth, wondering.

I stood outside his closed bedroom door. It was a room I'd shared with him for twenty-four years. A fast movie of humiliations came and went. Sometimes I can pretend I'm not the woman who slept in there. Other moments I can only swallow and clench my jaw so I don't weep.

I didn't knock, but twisted the knob and entered. The curtains were closed; the room was dark, only the edges of yellow light framed the window. I smelled urine. I pulled the curtains back and opened a window. Norman was lying deep in the old mattress. He was on his side; a cream woollen blanket was pulled up to his chin.

'Norman,' I said.

He didn't reply.

I peered down and at first thought, *He's asleep*. His eyelids flickered. A dribble of saliva had wet the pillow.

'You should be out of bed,' I said.

He didn't move. Or he couldn't.

'What's wrong?' I asked.

He made long rolling sounds, trying to say words, but it was as though he had no control over his tongue.

I pulled back the blanket. His knees were bent up, foetus-like; one arm was ramrod straight against his hip, fingers strangely curled. Through his blue and white striped pyjamas, I could see his body was rigid as if all his muscles had seized. His groin and the bottom sheet were wet.

I covered him up. And stood watching.

His eyelids opened and closed, and he repeated the mumbling sentence.

He knew I was standing there.

I didn't say anything else to him, but walked away and closed the bedroom door behind me.

I went straight outside, without my tea, and resharpened the secateurs. Then I pulled my wheelbarrow along the lawn to the hedge of pink scabrosa – their petals were as pretty and delicate as fairies' skirts – and started cutting away the dying blooms.

The morning passed. I drank water from the garden hose and didn't eat lunch. And when all the roses were beautifully groomed and looked their best, I still didn't enter the house. I went for a walk down the lane and sat for a good while beside the old stone ruin, the first Ballantine house that William built a century ago. Belonging to this family was all I had to be proud of. I considered I'd done my best as Norman's wife. Nothing else could be asked of me. A feeling, and I looked across to the layered granite near the peppercorn tree. A brown snake was uncoiling, moving deeper into the stones.

It was hunger that led me back to the house. And knowing that the school bus was due in an hour.

I was afraid to enter Norman's bedroom again. He might've been standing in the centre of the room waiting for me, a knowing shift in his eyes, ready to punish me for leaving him earlier.

He was dead. I stared for long enough to see that he didn't move. His eyes were open and didn't blink. My breath was shallow and I felt cold.

I sat on the dressing-table stool and watched his still body. I wanted to feel pity for him. Something. We'd had three children. I had been his wife. Nothing. Not even relief.

I'd not eaten since breakfast, so I went to the kitchen and ate a large slice of the pineapple fruitcake and drank a cup of tea. Then I phoned the ambulance.

Poor young Ross, I see now that I failed him. I sent him off to Keith Sanders and his wife for a few days, and didn't see him until the funeral. I didn't want him to witness me reordering the house. Caroline stayed in Melbourne, so she wasn't around.

I packed up all of Norman's things in the car and dumped them at the tip. In the bull paddock, I burned his clothes, and all our towels and bedding. Then I redecorated our bedroom, bought a new bed and had an oil heater installed. I claimed something back for myself, a sort of healing.

Yet when Ross returned home, I can't say the two of us were happy companions. His interest in flying aeroplanes was a problem. We often fought.

*

Stella uncaps the water bottle and passes it to me. I wipe the opening and take two sips. She finishes the bottle. I wonder if we should put it outside to capture any coming rain, but I don't speak up. I lie back on my reclined seat.

'Another regret I have, Margie, is that we haven't always got along. Before we met I had this hope that Ross's family would love me. But we all got off to a bad start.'

We are now on very shaky ground. I will not revisit those early days when she nearly took Ross away from his responsibilities at Maryhill. Her, with her piercings and tarty, cheap clothes. How inappropriate she was, and sometimes still is. Suddenly this familiarity is distasteful and I'm irritated with her. I look out the window and see the faint outlines of trees; they will be wattles, pines, eucalypts. I've seen she-oaks around here, too.

'If Ross were here, he might admit to a regret,' Stella says. 'He'd just accepted an offer to join Cathay's pilot program. We were in Phuket on a holiday when I told him I was pregnant with Isobel. I said I wanted to raise our kids in the country, and if he became a pilot, we'd be apart all the time. Neither of us wanted that. I love it here. Ross now seems content.'

And so. Stella is claiming credit as Maryhill's saviour. It might be right that she does. I'm trying to consider this when she informs me she and Ross had a son.

I press the lever and sit up.

'That's another thing I regret, that our baby boy didn't live.'

'A boy?' I say. 'What are you telling me?'

'He is our third baby. Harry.' Stella sits up, too. 'We never found out why, but he was born early, at twenty-one weeks.'

Quiet envelopes us. Harry is the name on her breast, the lost baby. I still can't fathom the notion of tattooing your body. Mark is indelibly written on my heart; I don't need his name on my skin to help me remember.

'I'm sorry you lost a baby,' I say.

'Thank you,' she says. 'We've both lost sons.'

I will not compare our grief and think it's unfortunate she's made the connection.

'Perhaps we should try for some sleep,' I say.

I lie back on my reclined seat. It's cold now and I hug into myself. It's as if the inner core of me is on fire and the outside is freezing, and I consider these might be the early symptoms of a chill and in a few short days I might be dead, like Dot was. I notice this thought. The idea of dying disheartens me. There are things I'm looking forward to. Isobel's piano exam is in three months, and I like listening to how she works, one by one, through the movements, perfecting and getting faster. And Jemima wants me to bird spot in the garden with her and reference them on the 'ap' on her iPad. I will enjoy that. And I'm intrigued to see Stella's play properly performed – the household has been in an uproar because of it ever since I moved in, so it will be interesting to see how it goes.

And there's the possibility of seeing Chester again – although I am chastened by our last meeting when he came to dinner. He spoke unkindly to me, but I'm loath to dwell on it; the implications are devastating when I think that Chester doesn't cherish our past like I do. It has raised several questions about what our years together meant to him. But there. After all this time, I can still picture his delighted gaze on me in that cosy narrow bed in the nook behind his work shed. Yes, he loved me then, but doesn't now. I'm old and no longer worthy of his attentions. It seems we can't even be friends, and that's a disappointment to me. But, then, we never were friends, not in the traditional sense of two people who share confidences and experiences in the normal course of daily living. We were intermittent lovers. Laura was his friend.

As best I can, I shuffle onto my side and close my eyes. There's a weight on my chest, and I pay attention to it. Yes, that's it: Ross had a son. I bring the image of a baby before me; strangely, it's Mark's newborn face that I see as my little unknown grandson, Harry. I frown at the dreadful misfortune of his death because he would've been Maryhill's next heir.

Stella

I try to see things how Ross will. At seven I phoned him to say we were on our way home. At about seven-forty-five he'd have been expecting us. He'll think we've had an accident: anything from a flat tyre, to hitting a kangaroo, to a fallen tree blocking our way. But I've not called to explain a problem and there's a strong mobile signal all the way along Black Wattle Road to the freeway. At first he'll be alert, waiting to hear me speed down the drive. After an hour or so he'll lift his head from whatever he's doing and pay attention. That's when he'll start to worry. He'll try my mobile and hear a message saying my phone is switched off or I'm out of range – you'd think that would be a hint. Yet it would never occur to him that I'd take the high-road short cut. The couple of times I've recently come home this way, it didn't cross my mind to mention it; I don't even know the name of the track we're on – it's just a dirt line cut through the pine plantation.

He might phone Felicity or Holly to see if he's missing out on a spur-of-the-moment party. At some point he'll decide to go for a drive, but he won't want to leave the girls on their own.

So he'll probably call Eddie and tell him what's going on. He and Dianne will take the girls; they'll say that won't be a problem.

Then Ross will travel our regular route down along Black Wattle Road. He'll drive slowly, expecting to see us stranded around every corner. And when he arrives at the freeway and there's no sign of us, he'll be confused. That's when things will ramp up. He'll think we've run off the road somewhere along that winding stretch with the sheer drop that goes all the way down to the flats where the golden poplars line Little Clemet Creek. Even though he's told me never to swerve to avoid hitting an animal, he'll be working through the scenarios and coming up with only one answer.

He'll call the police. Perhaps triple-O, or direct to the station in Benalla. They'll tell him there are no reported incidents on the freeway. So he'll drive back along that familiar road looking for tyre marks that leave the bitumen, and by the time he reaches Maryhill Road he'll phone Eddie again. They'll discuss the mystery.

Margie softly moans in her sleep as she searches for a way to get comfortable in the curved, narrow seat. It's the right thing, staying in the car when it's dark and wet. The heels on my boots aren't suited for distance, but when it's light I'll go looking for a mobile signal.

I'm wired and can't sleep. I want Ross. For my own sake, and because I hate it that he'll be so worried. If it were the other way around, by now I'd be in a panic, thinking the worst. It happens. Death comes without warning.

Last year, Nadine Richards from the farm opposite the walnut orchard ran off the road on the way to Violet Town. She was found dead at the base of a manna gum. She'd kept to herself and I hadn't known her all that well, but I'd admired her – growing commercial garlic and pressing her own Leccino olives to sell oil at the local farmers' markets. Mauve, her four-year-old daughter, is now living somewhere in Melbourne with her father, and I still worry about that little girl, what's become of her. I'm getting carried away now, thinking of all the local tragedies. Those weekenders that let their two kids ride a quad bike and next thing one is dead in a dumb, avoidable rollover. That mare at Grey Willow Stud that kicked their property manager's two-year-old son in the head. Stop.

If it wouldn't wake Margie, I'd put music on: the radio, or *19*, an old Adele CD I have in the glovebox. Anything to clear my mind and distract myself. What a bloody idiot I am, letting that dickhead driver in the Kenworth intimidate me into coming this way at night and in the rain.

I start doing this strange thing, sending mental messages to Ross to let him know we're okay. I wonder what he's thinking, feeling. Maybe the SES are out by now. Half the goddamn tableland will be; word spreads fast. Spotlights on the back of utes will be turned downwards, searching deep into the treed gullies for our bronze Prado. Because I'm impulsive, I've created an emergency.

My phone tells me it's 2.06. It's cold and I'm done with hugging myself for warmth and subduing that internal urge to shiver.

Margie must be cold too, but thankfully she's still lulled in sleep. It surprises me she's not anxious about our situation, that somehow she's relinquished all the worry and problem-solving to me. That's a good thing.

I press for the engine to start – it responds as it should, yet I feel surprised and relieved. I put the heater back on. And it's about now I'm getting angry with Ross for not having found us. You'd think, weighing up all the options, this track would be considered, that he would've asked someone to check it out. My mind starts playing tricks. And I see Ross sound asleep in bed, slumped on his side, oblivious that I'm not spooned into his back. He might've gone to bed before we got home; after all, he'd been up since six to check on the pregnant heifers.

I drift to sleep, but my senses are acute – the feeling of sounds, or dreams – and I'm still cold. I blink awake at the irrational notion it's not safe to be stationary and have the motor running for so long, that if Ross were here he'd tell me I shouldn't be doing it. You'd think the rising panic in me is because a hose is coming in from the exhaust through the window.

I turn the motor off. Then, soundlessly, I open my door, take a few steps away and piss onto the wet ground. Back in the driver's seat, I pull the door shut. Margie sleeps.

Someone will knock on my window and I'll jolt awake with the shock. I close my eyes and wait for it to happen.

At 5.11 it's still dark, perhaps with the first aperture shift in the light. I stare through the side window looking for movement, but the terrain is the same small scope I've been staring into during the night: a skein of blackberries, scrubby wattles and unknown shrubs that fill the space to the heavy planked bridge. The creek will be running, but I can't hear it from inside the car.

Margie stirs and opens her eyes. She takes me in, sitting across from her, then folds back into herself and returns to sleep. This worries me. She didn't take her evening slow-release tablet to correct her arrhythmia, it's cold and she's wearing damp clothes. I reach across and feel her forehead. She doesn't stir at my touch and I wonder if there's something I need to pay attention to. She's clammy, not hot or cold, but that damp in-between feeling. I study her carefully: her hunched body in the passenger seat, the slow rise of her chest, the quiver under her eyelids. I think about waking her to check how she's feeling. I'm unsure what to do.

I leave her be and stare into the outside gloom, watching the slow dawn. I expect to see wildlife, but nothing passes my line of vision. It's irrational, but I keep checking to see if a phone signal has kicked in. I tell myself these things can be intermittent; some weird tower radio waves that I don't understand might flicker on and somehow reach me.

At 5.59 I put the local FM news on, half-expecting to hear we're the lead story. Margie blinks awake and sits confused, arms tightly gripped around her chest.

'How're you feeling?' I ask.

'Why haven't we been found yet?'

'Don't know. But how are you?'

'Fine.' She sniffs and turns, still trying to find a comfortable position in the reclined seat. So Margie is herself and I'm relieved.

The newsreader tells me a television celebrity I've never heard of has died from complications relating to dementia. A weather event in the west of the state has saturated wheat crops. The local council elections have attracted more would-be councillors than ever before.

And so. We sit. Dawn breaks in lighter shades of grey until it's possible to tell a red box eucalypt from a black wattle. Still there's no wildlife – perhaps we are being watched from secret hideouts.

Margie tells me she's desperate to pee again, but it's a fraught exercise and I can't think how to sort this out. She can't crouch into position and I know she won't let me help her.

She leaves the car and moves towards the back. I open my door and stand away so I can't see her, but I'm close if she falls. 'Should I hold your arm, Margie?'

No answer, but a great deal of deep sighing and little steps as if she's trying to find the right way to go about it. I hear the gush. And wait.

'It'd be much easier to be a man,' she calls, shuffling back to the car.

She's wet again. And it's this that makes me decide I can't

wait any longer and need to get going to locate a mobile signal or find someone. Should I go ahead? Or backtrack? Ahead could be twelve or so kilometres. Not so bad, and I could make the whole distance in under three hours if it wasn't for these useless, but gorgeous, high-heeled boots. It's more than thirty kilometres back to the freeway. I can't decide which way to go because I don't know where the closest signal is.

'You can wear my shoes,' Margie says. 'What size are you?'

'Eight.'

'No good. I'm a seven.'

I tell Margie I'm going ahead, further into the pine forest. 'It's Monday morning. Maybe there are loggers working who've come in from the other side.'

There's a moment of waiting, a hesitation, and Margie reaches across and clumsily grasps my hand and gives it a little shake. Her skin is dry, leathery. With her ancient brown eyes, she holds my gaze while nodding her head. This is her way of communicating because she's unable to say what she feels.

But it's easy for me. 'Love you, Margie. If I don't see anyone in an hour, I'll turn around and come back. So you'll see me in a couple of hours.'

'I'm not sure you should leave the car,' she says.

'Me either.'

'Then stay.'

'I can't keep sitting here. Bloody Ross, where is he? Sometimes he uses this track. Why hasn't he thought to come here?'

'Someone will come.'

'But when? We've got no food or water.'

'There's the creek,' she says.

'Cows shit in there. I'll just go and take a look ahead. It'll be okay.'

*

My ankle boots are Italian, two-toned tan and black, and cost the price of a fully grown steer in a high-value market. Last year Ross bought them for my combined birthday and Christmas present, a luxury gift that makes me very spoilt. It was either them or getting every flywire screen in the house replaced, involving bespoke workmanship and lots of detailed painting. The decision was easy. I said we'd buy a can of flyspray, then we went shopping on Collins Street. My boots are crafted to be adored and to make the wearer feel very classy – not for long-distance walking. The heels are about the height and thickness of a lipstick case, not too narrow, but slender enough to depress centimetres into this wet, rough, bark-covered earth.

I step through the branches of the fallen peppermint gum and stride on. Rivulets run along the track from rain hitting dry, hard ground. Above is a choir of unseen birds. The creek gushes with new water. I walk fast for maybe two kilometres. The track is now a road, wide and strong enough to carry logging trucks. No one is working up here. I keep going, the stubby wasteland of harvested pines is on both sides. I feel the isolation, the deep quiet. I don't like it. Another few hundred metres and I stop.

I've always had this niggling disappointment with my beloved boots – the slight rub on my left toe that is so easily ignored when I'm standing still, taking short walks to the car, striding thirty or so steps from a front door to a seat at a dining table. There's a raw blister on my little toe and I know I won't make any distance, especially if I have to turn back.

I'm uncertain what to do. I sit on a flat granite stone so perfectly moulded to my bum it could be a bar stool. No signal on my phone, the bloody useless thing. I'd like a drink of water and here I am stuck in this remote nowhere: stillness, silence, the absence of birdsong. I feel and see the beauty of this remote place and elevation – perhaps eight hundred metres above sea level – yet I feel afraid, vulnerable. I'm so unbelievably dumb to have put myself here. I should've walked back towards the freeway.

I stand up and turn back towards Margie.

Beside me in the wet dirt is the twin-hoof imprint of a sambar deer. It's unmistakable, not a kangaroo or anything else. I keep walking; we're both headed in the same direction.

'Stella.'

A man's voice. Fast and urgent. Then he's jogging towards me from the direction of the car. Blue fleece, jeans, the giveaway cap he always wears, even in bitter winter and now so early in the morning. It's Eddie. I'm stupid. His approach is confirmation of my bad decision. He's found the car and had to come all this way to find me.

I hurry to him.

I'm held.

'Jesus,' he gasps. I feel the rise of his chest as he takes fast, full breaths. But he's grinning, laughing to himself.

'I'm sorry,' I say.

He shakes his head, bends down to keep taking in air.

'You made a grown man cry,' he says.

I whisper my husband's name.

'Poor bastard,' he says. 'He's going to be one happy boy now.'

'Where is he?'

'Out looking. Let's go.'

We walk and I don't care that my left little toe is being mangled with each step. I hear how the police were short on crews and suggested that maybe I'd decided to nick off somewhere else rather than go home and I'd probably turn up this morning. The SES couldn't be mobilised until the police said so. By 10 pm Ross had everyone he knew out searching.

'The girls?'

'Our place. Dianne's got them.'

I tell him what happened, the truck, blurting out my several excuses, confessing to being reckless.

He pats my shoulder. 'It's all good now. Bit of excitement never hurt anybody.'

Eddie's black 4WD is backed onto the bridge. He's already pulled the Prado out of the ditch and has it facing in the right direction – back the way we came, towards the freeway. Margie is still sitting in the passenger seat, and as I get closer I see she's asleep again, an open bottle of water loosely grasped in her hand.

I take my boots off. Nothing to do except get in the car and drive home. Eddie is already in his driver's seat; I've said I'll follow him and phone Ross as soon as there's a signal.

It's a strange anticlimax: driving normally, Eddie's car in front. He takes the corners on our descent without hesitation. I'm sure he's pleased with himself, the hero, and fair enough. 'About five this morning Ross told everyone to go home, that he'd keep looking on his own,' he told me. 'But I stayed on and drove into Benalla and took a good look around. It was only on a whim coming back down the freeway I thought to veer off to the short cut.'

Two bars appear on my dash. We're down on the flats; a white weatherboard house is to the right. Red, blue and white horse-jumps are in a dirt paddock. I think to pull over, but I keep following Eddie's ute. His tail-lights flash red as he arrives at the freeway; a pause before he accelerates, turns left and heads south.

I press Ross's number.

Only two rings.

'Stell?'

My face breaks into crying, and he hears my pathetic wailing in the open space of the car. I can't speak. Margie touches my arm. 'Pull over,' she says.

'Where are you?' Ross asks.

I press the brakes and stop under a yellow gum, white leathery skin with tongues of falling bark. The freeway is fifty metres ahead; a B-Double booms past, then a small van.

I sniff.

'Darling?' he says. I'm still gathering up words when Ross says, 'Mum?'

Margie looks around and speaks too loudly, unsure she's doing the right thing by talking into the air that she breathes. 'We decided to take a short cut. I said I was tired and hungry, so it seemed like a good idea at the time.' Margie is smiling. 'But we got into a bit of bother.'

'What short cut? Stell?'

And so I tell him the story and, feeling calmer, I start driving. Onto the freeway, I pick up speed and take my place at 110.

I keep telling Ross I'm sorry. He's silent, too quiet.

'You all right?' I ask.

'I couldn't make sense of it. You know what I was thinking.'

'Yes,' I say.

Margie joins in, telling him it wasn't too bad; that she slept all right. 'But it got a bit chilly around three. I'm looking forward to a shower and getting into a proper bed.'

I tell Ross I'll see him soon.

'You okay to drive?' he asks.

'Yes. I promise.'

Eddie is long gone along Black Wattle Road, up into the tableland, the road they've been searching all night. The wild fig tree on the left has fruit. Rosellas are feeding. Approaching is a lycra-clad cyclist, head down. He whips past. We travel through the long, winding eucalypt tunnel. The car smoothly moves through the auto-gears as I slow at the approaching corners and accelerate out of them.

We pass Chester's place. A silver Audi nudges from his driveway, waiting to turn. Margie stares. Chester has visitors.

Maryhill Road, our paddocks on the left, one kilometre, two, three. The letterbox is ahead. I indicate and turn into the driveway.

Ross is leaning against his ute, arms folded, waiting.

He's at my door as I open it and holds my arm as if to help me out. I stand up and am embraced. We exhale. He's warm and smells of a long night.

Margie is out of the car. Her door shuts. She comes towards us, her sad brown eyes, hands balancing on the bonnet and shuffling steps. She says, 'It's all right, we're all safe now.'

Ross opens his arm and pulls her in.

I see our feet in a tiny circle: Ross's worn workboots, Margie's tan flats, my black socks. Nothing is said; I just feel the strength of Ross's hold on me. And his right arm is around Margie, clasping her the same way.

Margie

THERE'S a hush across the theatre. The lights are off. We wait. I take a deep breath and grip my hands between my knees. I'm nervous for Stella. People are still moving into their seats, yet it's past the starting time.

Jemima is sitting on my left; her feet don't touch the floor. Isobel is on my right. We are in the centre, three rows back from the stage – an expectant trio, staring forward. Isobel pulls her ponytail undone, smooths her curly hair and twists the band back on. I can't tell what difference that made. A young couple shuffle past us to their seats; I remain seated, which doesn't make it easy for them. A man sits in front of Jemima and blocks her view. She glares at me, mouth open. I'm standing, swapping places with her, when the stage lights come on.

Felicity is alone on the stage, sitting at the kitchen table. She's staring to the side, flat-faced, pretending to be Grace. She's behaving as if no one is watching her and I think that must be a strange thing to do. She's wearing a bright-orange suit jacket with thick padding across the shoulders – business clothes. The impression is it's a work day. It's pin-drop silent; the audience is paused, expectant. Felicity brushes something invisible off the sleeve of her jacket. We stare and wait.

Ignoring the staring faces out in front, Felicity stands and slowly walks to the fridge: an Electrolux very like the one Norman and I bought soon after Ross was born. She opens it and pulls out a Tupperware container and puts it on the bench. Then picks up a wine bottle and glass. She seems in no hurry as she saunters back to the table, twists off the cap and pours. It's as if she's lost in thought as she stares out into the audience, above our heads. She sits and casually sips from the glass. I want something to happen – and just as I think that, Noah rushes onto the stage.

'It's your turn,' he yells to someone behind him. Amber follows. They stop dead in their tracks when they see their mother, Grace.

Stella is backstage. Ross is upstairs in the lighting booth. He's sitting with Kyle, someone Stella asked to come up from Melbourne to help with the lighting, music, and the photos that are to be projected onto the stage. I imagine the timing is very important; that he'll have to concentrate all the way through. He's staying at Maryhill with us for the duration of the season, sleeping in the storeroom cum bedroom off the family room. I'm not that keen on him, although he has good table manners. He's movie-star handsome – oval face, square jaw, blue eyes, athletic body – yet he has the demeanour of someone who's had lots of bad luck, is worn down by life and has had no benefit whatsoever from his appearance. He smokes cigarettes in the pergola and I've wondered what he does with the butts.

Chester isn't here. Stella said she'd phoned and he answered from Julie and Ian's place in Cottesloe. He'd flown there Tuesday. When Stella told me, she must've seen my disappointment because she clicked her fingers in front of my face and told me to snap out of it. 'He's not a very nice person,' she said. 'He's not worthy of you.' I'm flattered she thinks so well of me. And, to be truthful, in my deepest private thoughts, I knew Chester was self-interested: it's just that my need was so much greater. Perhaps I should've come to terms with that notion a long time ago. Never mind now, it's done with.

Noah plays the violin. Then stops. Seconds pass as he stretches his arm as though he's got a cramp. He begins again and I don't know if that was deliberate. Felicity is drinking red wine with Holly and I know it's coloured water. They're saying their lines. The audience laughs. Then the mood changes and it doesn't sit well with me – all the anger, the accusations. There's too much going on around me to trace the origins of my discomfort. Felicity puts her hands across her face and I think she is supposed to be crying. At the rehearsal she was pretending to have a good old howl, but right now I can't tell what is going on.

Amber and Noah sit at the table and demand takeaway pizza for dinner. Felicity makes the call from an old-fashioned phone like we had on the dresser outside the kitchen. It was in a good position because we could reach it from several locations.

Felicity is angry and leaves the stage, saying she's fed up. I look around to see what the audience is doing. It's a good turnout: some empty seats to the side, a few at the far back. Everyone is still, alert, staring ahead.

It's between Act One and Act Two when the family photos are projected onto the back wall of the stage. Photos of Stella's mother, father, brother and her as a girl. It could be Jemima up there. I don't feel like moving and mixing with all the people milling out in the foyer. I reach down to my bag, find my purse and give Isobel ten dollars, saying they can go and buy ice-creams, but they must return straight away.

'Can we have a drink, too?' Jemima asks.

I give them every gold coin in my purse and say they can keep the change.

The theatre empties and only a few of us are left seated. And here I am. An old woman. I've been in this hall many times. Not just for my graduation, but also for Mark's and Caroline's school concerts. I can't say I attended Ross's, as I have no recollection of it. And this is where I connect with Grace, her struggle to manage her own life while her children nipped like pests, demanding attention.

Anyway. I'm here now and quite happy. Ross and Stella have bought me an iPad. It arrived in the post, so I'm not sure how or when that was organised. And somehow the bird app Jemima has been showing me is on it. It's not very difficult to use: I just press the button with the tiny white bird and the screen changes all by itself – sort of like changing the station on a television. I'm cautiously experimenting with it. The other morning, around eleven, the moon was west but still high in the pale-blue sky. The sun was to the east. For years this has been a mystery to me, how it's possible for both the sun and moon to be in the sky at the same time. In my room I pressed the blue square called Safari and typed in the letters for astronomy. Many options appeared and none helped me with what I wanted. Jemima told me I need to narrow my search and I don't know what she meant. But we'll get to it in good time.

And on Monday night, before Kyle arrived, when we were all seated around the dinner table eating a rice dish called *paella*, Stella tapped her wineglass with her knife. She looked quite lovely with her hair sitting on her shoulders, wearing a blue jumper with a cowl neck. Ross put his fork down. We all turned to her. I wondered what the sense of occasion was – it was no one's birthday.

Stella looked across the table to Ross and said, 'You say.'

So we looked to my son.

'What?' said Isobel.

He took a breath. 'You got them?' he said, back to Stella.

She put folded white papers on the table. 'Yep.'

He wiped the side of his mouth, a thinking gesture, finding the words. 'Well, there's a gap between Isobel's exam and calving in July, and Eddie said he can look after the place for us.' Ross looked at me; Norman's eyes, the brown curly hair. 'We've booked five flights to London, Mum. We thought you'd like to go.'

Stella reached out and touched my hand.

Well, then. I had no say in it and, of course, I'm very upset about it. The idea that I'm going to London on one of those big aeroplanes. My stomach doesn't agree with the idea. I think I'm very excited.

We'll be in London together for ten days, then Stella and I are going on a cruise. It'll take us around all the British Isles and other places – Spain, I think. The ship docks back in London and we'll fly home from there.

Stella showed me the tickets they've booked on the internet and printed off. The London accommodation hasn't been organised yet, but they say they're going to find an apartment so we're not all squashed in together, which I think is a very good idea.

And by the time we're due to fly all the way to England, I will most likely have relocated to the retirement village behind the hospital. Last Thursday, before rehearsal, Stella took me for a drive, saying there was no pressure, but she didn't think Bishop Street suited me anymore. 'It's too big and you're so alone there. The mess those bloody trees make. You're not up to all that raking.' There's no argument from me on that score. She's right.

The unit we looked at is quite nice: two bedrooms with a reasonable-sized kitchen. The idea of cooking proper meals appeals to me – porridge and fruit for breakfast, a simple sandwich for lunch, and meat, chicken or fish and veg for dinner – none of this quick and easy stuff I've endured in the past few weeks. And doing my own laundry will make me feel more myself. I'm accustomed to my own company and I'm quite looking forward to it. I've got a quiet routine that is more enjoyable with no one watching on, making their judgements. There are things to be worked out, like shopping and appointments, but Stella seems confident she can manage to take me. There's a community hall at this village, and a group that plays bridge interests me; I used to partner with my mother before I married Norman, so I know the game.

Jemima says I can send her regular messages on my iPad, using something she calls Messenger – a different blue button. She's told me about Instagram and Facebook, but I feel confused. The sweet child, she patted my arm and told me not to worry, 'You'll catch on.' Isobel's music teacher is only ten minutes' walk away, so me being close could be helpful.

I'm not forgotten. Stella, Ross and the girls want to include me, and I don't have the words to properly express how I feel.

The photos keep changing on the stage wall. Grace in a hospital bed, oxygen tubes in her nose, Grace looking young and strong wearing a swimsuit, Grace holding a baby; perhaps it's Stella. Loud music plays from the speakers, something I remember from when I was in my twenties. The girls trail back between the seats to me. They've got choc-tops and cans of fizzy drink. I look around and see other people carrying in food and drinks, so I suppose they're allowed to have them in here. I would've quite liked an ice-cream myself, but it's too late now.

All at once the theatre darkens, the music stops.

The audience is suspended, waiting.

Seconds pass.

I know from the script and rehearsals that the bad language is coming up. I glance at my granddaughters and wonder if I should do something. Then the stage lights up brightly, and Felicity is standing in its centre. She's wearing different clothes: a pair of bright-pink pants and a yellow blousy shirt. There's a knock on an invisible door. She shouts angrily, 'Who is it now?'

Jemima taps me on the arm. I lean down to her. 'I can't eat this,' she says, holding out her ice-cream.

I don't know what she expects me to do with it, but I take it from her. She's eaten all the chocolate from the top, which I suspect was the attraction. So there's nothing for it. I take a lick and decide it's mint. It tastes quite nice so I keep going.

The play continues on as it should. Everyone laughs at something and I've missed the joke. Jemima leans on me; poor pet, it's past her bedtime, yet there will be an afterparty. Stella says it's a standard thing, but it won't go on for long because the production will be on tomorrow night, too. 'But we'll all need to come down, so we're going to have a couple of drinks,' she said. I offered to mind the girls for the next two nights, and Stella happily accepted; it means she and Ross can stay out later if they want.

Felicity is swearing now and I shrink into myself. It's so unnecessary and a poor example. I look at my granddaughters and I hardly think they've noticed. I can't tell for certain, but they don't seem very shocked.

I'm tired now and close my eyes. The violin is playing again; it's a Beatles song that Mark used to play in his room, 'Let It Be'. I think of my lost boy and, as I've always done when something distresses me, I think of those two kissing black cockatoos perched in the silver wattle, the branches hardly carrying their weight. They fly off together, and more than once I wished that I could do that, just fly away and land somewhere else.

I think I've arrived.

Isobel leans across and hands me her finished can of fizzy drink, and I'm about to tell her to put it on the floor at her feet, when I take it from her.

Jemima slips her hand into mine and whispers up to me, 'When are we going home?'

'Not long, pet,' I say.

Acknowledgements

THANKS to my wonderful first readers, Meg Webster, Chris Power and Jill Bartlett for their thoughtful feedback and encouragement. Also, Carol Crowe for her dedicated final read of the manuscript.

My appreciation to Manfred Ruff from Box-Ironbark Birding, who sat with me one morning in our garden and identified thirty-five different birds and their song. I gave all of them to Margie. I also gave her some other birds I've seen in the years we've lived here in north-east Victoria. The powerful owl appeared twice, high up in an ancient conifer, but hasn't been seen again. The black swan appeared last year, and now as I write it's returned and sitting in the dam. Its mate is probably nesting nearby. We often see wedge-tail eagles gliding in thermals. I've seen magpies chase a wedge-tail eagle from their territory.

Special thanks to Lance Williams for checking I've got the trees and birds accurately recorded. However, any errors are entirely my own.

I'm indebted to Lorraine Monshing, OAM, for helping me understand the passion, culture and activities in community theatre. Also, Let Us Entertain You, LUEY, in Benalla, and the Wangaratta Players, for allowing me to observe them in action at meetings and rehearsals.

I'm honoured to have HT Thomas write a beautiful poem for Chester, *Purple Clematis*.

I appreciate the efforts of the Benalla Historical Society for the information about Queen Elizabeth's visit to Benalla in 1954.

I'm grateful to be part of a supportive writing community at the Wheeler Centre. Thanks to Antoni Jach and the members of Masterclass 5+. Also Toni Jordan and Kathryn Ledson.

Years ago, when I worked in overseas aid, Ita Buttrose was a patron for women's projects. We travelled to Asia and Africa together and shared many unique experiences. It's very special to have her endorse this book.

Thanks to my literary agent, Sheila Drummond, for her advice, support and commitment to my work.

To my publisher Bev Cousins, editor Lex Hirst, and everyone at Penguin Random House for their enthusiasm and great skill in getting *Stella and Margie* out there – thank you.

Finally, to my friends and family, especially Alistair, thanks for the love and unwavering support.

Glenna Thomson lives in north-east Victoria on a cattle property. She portrays her experiences on the farm, and in her extensive garden, vividly in her writing. For several years, Glenna and her husband also managed a commercial blueberry orchard, which inspired her first novel, *Blueberry*. Glenna grew up on an apple orchard, married, had children, and before moving to the country she developed a career in overseas aid and business. *Stella and Margie* is her second novel.

Stella and Margie book club questions

1. If you were in Margie's marriage, would you have done anything differently? If so, what and how?

2. Do you consider Margie a weak person because she didn't leave her marriage?

3. From the perspective of deceiving another woman, how do you judge Margie for having an affair?

4. What is the significance of the birds? What do they represent?

5. How do you feel about the phrase, 'I did my best', in the context of motherhood, and the judgements we make of our mothers, and ourselves as mothers?

6. Do you relate to Stella's determination for self-expression and independence beyond being a wife and mother?

7. What is good about Stella and Ross's marriage?

8. Was Stella right to bring Margie back to Maryhill against Ross's wishes?

9. Do you think Margie might have succumbed to Chester's charms had she been in a different relationship?

10. Is the relationship between daughters-in-law and mothers-in-law with differing personalities always bound to be fraught?